HIDDEN NATURE

ELIZABETH KNIGHT

Knight, Elizabeth

Hidden Nature

Editing: Swish Editing Services

Cover artist: Ruxandra Tudorica | Methyss Art

www.methyss-art.com

Formatting: Creative Wonder Publishing

ISBN: 979-8-88958-047-8 (print)

Don't hide from how you feel, emotions are powerful.

They can bring about destruction as easily as they can fulfill dreams.

CONTENTS

AUTHORS NOTE

Dear Readers,

Hidden Nature is a book that contains quite a bit of darkness, that could be triggering to some people.

If you feel like this could be a problem for you, please protect yourself.

No work of fiction is worth your mental health.

Elizabeth Knight

The full list of content warnings is available on my website.

Link found here: https://www.elizabethknightbooks.com/omega-assassin

CHAPTER ONE

ZANDER

It's been two days since Finley went missing and we were no closer to finding her. I looked over at the woman sagging in the metal chair she'd been strapped to for the last two days in one of the cells Colt and Lane built for unruly wolves. Peggy was our only connection to this whole situation and I didn't believe a word that came out of her mouth.

"Please let me go. I've told you everything," she begged, snot dripping from her nose with all the crying she'd been doing.

As I circled, my alpha energy flowed over her. She flinched, baring her neck in submission. "The thing is, Peggy, I don't believe you've told me everything I want to know. How did they get into contact with you? Why didn't you tell any of us that people from the Senate were looking for her? Was the vampire with them, or is there another party that is looking for my mate as well? The more you talk, the more questions I have."

"I was given a note with a location to meet them out in the woods off our land. They told me they needed to get Finley out of the pack and then asked me how to do it. I knew you wouldn't let her do something risky, but they said she was an assassin before she became an omega. So she could take care of herself... right?" Peggy explained, giving me the same line she had for the past forty-eight hours.

Sighing, I sat on the stool that we had placed in front of her chair. "If they are from the Senate or even the same place that Finley came from, they would have picked you for a reason. I know you didn't like Finley. You made it clear that she wasn't welcome that day in the greenhouse. Just so you know, she never brought up a complaint about you. She just took your judgment and moved on. You kept saying that it wasn't safe for Finley to be here... care to tell me why?"

This caught Peggy's attention, her chocolate-colored eyes glaring at me with her blonde hair in shambles around her face. "Just look at the trouble she brought with her! I knew she was going to be in trouble the moment she started to pull our alphas away from us. The pack needed them. We are growing and thriving now as the largest pack in Tennessee and it's all because of their leadership. The moment they brought *her* here, they started to ignore us."

"The pack or you?" I asked, feeling like she was finally showing her true colors.

Milly, her older sister, warned me she had a major crush on Lane and hoped to one day catch his eye. Now with Finley in the picture, Lane would never see another woman. Jealousy could be a large part of this, but I had a feeling that there was more to it than that. Why would she risk sending Finley away when it would only piss Lane off, hurting her more than helping if she had hoped to get him back?

"The pack, of course. Why would you think this had anything to do with me, personally?" Peggy snapped.

My brows shot up at her vehemence. "It's no secret that you've had feelings for Lane."

"Have you been talking to my sister?"

I didn't acknowledge her question, only sat there waiting for her to talk to me. Colt and Lane had asked me to do all I could before resorting to physical violence, not wanting to be that type of pack. Having grown up in a pack that didn't allow for anything other than complete loyalty and submission to the alphas, I knew exactly what they were talking about. The reason why my first reaction to Finley not following my orders was to use discipline because that's how I was raised. It was all I knew and the biggest reason I was living here and not with my mother's pack. She was a fearsome alpha and her fellow alpha's supported her demand for absolute control and order.

I could easily break Peggy if I wanted to, but I promised I would hold off on taking that course. However, we were quickly approaching the point where something needed to change. Elias had been taking turns with me not letting her sleep, hitting her with question after question, hoping the sleep deprivation would loosen her tongue. Seeing how she was handling the assault without breaking in the slightest had me considering she could be more than just the grumpy gamma that ran the greenhouse for the pack.

"How long have you been a part of this pack?" I inquired, changing topics completely.

This seemed to surprise her and she frowned at me. "Five years. What does that have to do with anything?"

"Did you come with your sisters, or did you discover the pack first and then bring them with you?" I pressed, and an idea developed in my head.

"When our parents died, we didn't want to stay in Michigan where it was so cold. We contacted the Senate, knowing they have a roster of packs that are actively seeking members for their packs, and this was one of them. There were a few we were interested in checking out, so we divided them up and eventually decided on this pack," she answered, still not sure what I was looking for.

Nodding, I got up from the stool and paced the room, scratching my jaw as I put the pieces together. "So, how long have you been a spy for the Senate?"

The room went silent and I could feel the tension in the air at my question. "What? Why would you think that I'm a spy?"

I glanced at her with a withering look. "Don't play games with me, Peggy. You won't win. I've been living in the world of politics for longer than you've been out of diapers. The Senate never does something out of the goodness of their heart. If they gave you a list of names, then it was packs they wanted to keep an eye on. Have you ever noticed that some packs get left alone to live their lives while others are constantly fending off attacks from other packs or the Senate's involvement?"

She looked at me wide-eyed, shaking her head slowly. "It happens to every species of super, so don't think it's just us poor wolves. This is how the senators stay senators for so long. They wipe out their competition before they can get big enough to gain recognition."

"You're saying this about your own mother?" Peggy asked, confusion clear in her words.

"My mother is a smart woman who knows how to play the game, but no, she isn't the one who goes after the other packs. She is the figurehead that keeps her hands clean while the other four alphas of her pack do the dirty work. Granted, she doesn't prevent it from happening but putting a spy into the pack under the guise of just wanting to keep an eye on an up-and-coming pack is a load of bullshit. If they told you it was for the pack's sake, you were here reporting back to them. It means we are on their radar of packs that are growing too fast. Not to mention, it's also the same time I moved here, and Father would love nothing better than to make sure I keep out of trouble. They don't really approve of what I do or how much I tell the world about us supernaturals."

I could tell that she'd tuned out after I said the pack was in danger because of her meddling, I was close to breaking through to her.

"How much have you told them? Now that we have an omega, this pack will become even more sought after. So why would you want to get rid of Finley if all you want is the betterment of the pack?" I questioned, taking a seat on the stool again, resting my elbows on my knees as I looked her over.

I could see the light bulb turning on in her brain as I talked. Now she realized that she was being manipulated and what she told them could actually hurt this pack in the long run.

"I didn't know," she pleaded. "How do I fix this now that they took her? Lane and Colt are going to hate me. They might even kick me out of the pack, which would be rather cold and selfish of them. What would I do then? I'd have nowhere to go."

Sitting back, I knew I'd finally broken her to the point she would really tell me what was going on and hopefully what happened with Finley. "Start from the beginning."

"You were right. It started out they wanted me to be their eyes and ears with you here. They didn't know why you picked this pack when it was so new and small, so they figured you must be up to something else. Then as I spent time here and saw the way that Colt worked with the pack and how Lane complimented him, it made sense. You didn't have anything to do with the pack as a whole, and Lane detests you, so it was Colt's goodwill that you were even able to stay," Peggy shared, making me want to roll my eyes at how quickly Lane figured out he wasn't getting rid of me now that we shared a mate.

"My contact started to ask more about the pack and how things were going than about you. Soon it was like you were an afterthought and all they wanted to know was what Colt and Lane were up to. Especially when Mason, Noah, and Elias started to take on more responsibility. If Mason ever became an alpha, they wanted to know right away, something about them wanting to nurture the new alpha."

That sounded about right for the others from my mother's pack. They were so good at faking good intentions, but it's how they got where they were today—letting people walk into the trap themselves, none the wiser. "What happened last night?"

"Those were different people, but they said they were told to find me, and I would help them," Peggy explained. "There were three of them, two women and one man. They refused to tell me their names. When I was leaving the other night, I caught a name, Tabitha. She was the leader of the group and seemed to know Finley personally by the way she talked about her. They told me she was an assassin and got bit on a job, turning her into a werewolf. I didn't think that could happen with omegas..."

I waved off her implied question. "We aren't going to talk about that. What did Tabitha want from her?"

"They said she had a job to finish and wanted my help to get her out of the pack lands unnoticed. I was made to promise that I wouldn't say anything to anyone, not even my sisters or they would kill them. Being an omega must have really changed Finley because that woman was void of emotion. She said that to me like it was no big deal to just end their lives because I told them something. I didn't even know what the job was or anything important!"

The fear written on her face told me it was the fact she thought her sisters were going to die that kept her quiet this whole time. So Peggy wasn't some super spy like I thought at the beginning. She was just scared and didn't want to lose the last part of her family.

"Let that be a lesson to you, Peggy. Finley was trained just like Tabitha," I warned, wanting to instill a sense of respect for my mate. "Elias told us he found you out in the woods past the pack lands. What were you doing there?"

"They were holding me there to ensure everything went according to plan. If I'd managed to tip anyone off or lied to them about what would happen when the pack was attacked, they would have killed me. Once Finley showed up, my life was safe," she answered, hanging her head low. "I hated the fact Finley got everything I wanted the second she showed up in this pack. Everyone fawns over her and the look you all have when you see her is what every woman hopes for. I thought if I could just send her back to wherever she came from, life could get back to normal for us here."

"Do you know if the vampire was part of their plan?" I asked.

Peggy shook her head, shoulders slumped. "I don't know. They never told me what was going to happen. I was the one who gave them the evacuation plans and that they would send all the women and children to the tunnels. They seemed to think Finley would be able to figure out the rest because, after that, they went silent."

"They said the job was for the Senate? I need you to be absolutely certain about this." I growled, adding my alpha energy to the question.

Depending on how this was answered, we would at least have a guess as to what was going on.

"Yes, they said they were sent by the Senate and told to find me. That the Senate needed her to finish a job, one she started before coming to our pack. I did ask them why they couldn't just come in and ask you guys to let her come with them. The only kind of answer I got back was that the rules were different with an omega," Peggy answered.

My hands clenched into fists hearing this. Of course, those selfish bastards would send my mate after the Dark Ring regardless of her being an omega or not. They knew the Dark Ring's threat to the whole supernatural community and wanted it to be taken care of silently so no one knew humans could enslave supers. It would throw the entire world into chaos, and that's something the United Senate couldn't allow to happen because an assassin missed her target. The trouble was, now I had this information, there wasn't a whole lot I could do about it. None of this told me where she was or had been taken to. She could be on another job on the other side of the world for all I knew and that pissed my wolf and me off to no end.

Part of me wanted to call my mother and demand answers, but she wouldn't give them to me even if she knew. The Senate always came first and the fact Finley was my mate would have no influence on the choice of the full Senate. Of course, if my mother had told them she was also a Light Elf, it might have changed matters, but she promised me to keep that secret from the rest of the Senate. That was the trouble out of the seven members—my mother was only one vote. Yes, she had ruled over all domestic shifters, and the dragons had mythological shifters, but Modeos and Mother hated each other, so they never agreed on anything.

Knowing that I'd gotten everything I could from Peggy, I stood and started out of the cell.

"Wait! Aren't you going to let me out? I told you everything I know!" Peggy yelled after me.

Spinning on my heel, I looked at her with the fury I'd been holding back during this whole situation. "Let you go? Why the fuck would I do that when you led my mate into a trap! I don't give a damn about your reasoning. You don't turn on your pack like that. You put everyone at risk and not just in this one event. The whole time you've been giving the Senate the information they wanted. So no, I'm not going to let you out. Maybe you'll have better luck with Lane or Colt, although it's their mate that is missing now too."

Done talking to the rat, I left the shed where the cells were located and stormed up the steps to the pack house. Tossing open the door, it slammed into the wall, causing a dent, but I didn't give a shit. I got the information we'd been trying to get and it does nothing for us.

"Fuck, man, who pissed in your cereal?" Mason asked from his spot at the kitchen island, nursing a cup of coffee.

None of us had been sleeping or functioning well in our efforts to find our mate. We'd promised her that nothing would happen and that we would protect her, but then when it came time to do that, she slipped through our fingers. Granted, from what Peggy said, Finley left us, but she'd warned us from day one that she would finish the job she fucked up.

Finley didn't know the meaning of failure. I could see it in the way she took the whole situation of being an omega and an elf head-on. Finley wanted knowledge to understand every facet of who she was and what it meant. Now that I knew she was most likely on her way to kill someone from the Dark Ring, I wasn't sure if that was better or worse than knowing she was simply missing. Missing meant she might be in less danger. Going after a Dark Ring member, she was absolutely in danger.

"Peggy finally talked," I answered through gritted teeth.

Mason shot to his feet, knocking the chair he was sitting on to the floor. "What the hell are we doing standing around? Let's go!"

"Go where?" Noah asked, coming out of the walk-in pantry.

"Zander got the bitch to talk," Mason said, pacing as I saw his wolf flickering in his eyes.

Noah all but chucked whatever he grabbed from the pantry into the sink and ran upstairs to grab Lane and Colt. They would all be pissed when they found out that I didn't have good news for them. How do you find an assassin who was trained to go unnoticed as their job? I saw Mason heading down the hall where the betas' room was located.

"Mason, wait," I called. "If Elias is sleeping, let him sleep. He hasn't gotten more than a few hours over the last two days."

The beta frowned at me, clearly not agreeing with my order. "Why the fuck should I do that? If I were him, I'd want to know what the hell is going on."

"If I had anything helpful to share, I would make sure that he was here for it, but as it stands, I've got less than nothing. We spent two days wasting time on a woman who knows practically nothing," I grumbled.

"Practically nothing is still something," Mason argued. "Besides, you're not my alpha."

When it came to interactions between Mason and me, that was his favorite thing to point out. Something told me that wasn't going to be the case for very long if they all moved in with me as Finley wanted. There was no way I could still be on the fringes of this pack when I shared a mate with the two founding alphas.

Walking over to the coffee maker, I pulled out a mug and filled it to the brim, praying it would give me the energy and sanity to deal with what I was about to encounter with all these stubborn males. As I turned around, leaning on the counter, I found them all staring at me, tense and ready to move the second I told them what they hoped I would tell them—where our mate was.

"Take a deep breath, guys. I don't have a location and we aren't going anywhere fast," I explained, then took a sip of coffee. "Peggy has been a spy for the Senate for the past five years she's been in the pack. Originally, it was to keep an eye on me, but then it changed to keeping an eye on you two," I shared, pointing at the two alphas. "They like to make sure no up-and-coming alphas are going to be gunning for their spots on the Senate."

"The fuck!" Mason snarled. "We've had a traitor in our midst for that long?" Mason turned on Elias, getting up in the man's face. "How did you not know about this?"

Elias let out a low warning growl as he shoved Mason back a step. "There are how many people in our pack? Do you know what they are doing *all* the time?"

"No, because it's not my job! How are you going to keep Finley safe, Sentinel, if you can't keep tabs on the dangers here in our own pack?" Mason challenged.

"Enough!" Colt bellowed, lashing out with his alpha energy. "Let Zander speak and we will deal with the rest of this mess later. I want to know where my mate is, so shut the fuck up."

That got through to Mason. Colt hardly ever used his energy on his betas, so the fact he did it now proved just how pissed off he was with them.

"Peggy doesn't know where they took Finley because she is finishing her job for the Senate," I answered, getting it all out there in one go. "She's going after the Dark Ring."

Lane and Colt knew what I was talking about, but we hadn't gone into great detail with the betas about it other than that's how she got bit.

"Call your mother," Lane demanded. "She can do something about this. I mean, she's an omega, for Christ's sake."

Letting out a heavy sigh, I shook my head. "My mother can't do jack shit. Maybe if we told them she was a Light Elf, but that would put her in more danger, if that's possible, than she is now. In the Senate, there is a vote, and if they sent a team to get her, it means Mother lost that vote. They want the Dark Ring issue settled and done with as soon as possible. They have leverage on Finley. She is no longer with the Organization and she failed the last job. Peggy said it was a team of three and one knew Finley personally."

Noah slumped into a chair. "This is so much worse, isn't it?"

"That depends," I offered.

"On what?" Elias asked, glaring at me.

"How good she is at her job."

CHAPTER TWO

FINLEY

"Y ou did it, heart of my heart, you healed me," he whispered.

Then he pulled me down into a kiss that took the air right out of my lungs, but I would gladly give it to him if it meant he didn't leave me. Breaking the kiss, I looked down at him, running my hands over his chest to see a strange mark that had bloomed in a mass of swirling lines that made the shape of a heart. I knew what he was saying was important, but I just couldn't seem to wrap my head around the fact that I'd just healed him. Me. The assassin turned omega, now coming into my elven powers. Then my hearing seemed to come back as he cupped the side of my face, lifting it so I met his seafoam green eyes that looked into my soul.

"Seems you claimed me, mate of mine," he murmured, a smile tugging at his lips. "My heart now beats for you. My soul is tied to yours forever, and my life after a hundred years is just beginning as your Guide."

I balked at his words. "You're a hundred years old!"

"Out of all of that..." He chuckled. "I am a hundred and fifteen if you really want to be specific, but many of us stop counting after a certain point. Keeping track is tedious past the three hundred."

As he spoke, it was like my brain got a kickstart back to reality, and I looked around the room with the dead bodies bleeding out all over the floor. "We need to go."

"Yes, I believe that would be best," Rathal agreed. "I must say, I'm surprised your mates would let you do this kind of work. Werewolves are awfully protective of their mates, let alone one that is an omega as well," he commented as he got to his feet, ripping off the rest of his blood-soaked shirt.

His skin was so fair it almost glowed in the moonlight and had faint hints of a green shimmer that matched his eyes. Rathal was mesmerizing to look at and it was taking everything in me not to rub up against him like a cat.

Shaking my head, I looked around the room, trying to think of the best approach to getting us both out of here. If what Blakley said was true about them not expecting me to get out of this, then Vicky could be in on the plan. Tabitha worked for the Organization and would never turn her back on them, so she was most likely being used the same way I was.

"Finley," Rathal called, causing me to snap my head up to face him. He was so incredibly tall now that he was standing here in front of me. "*Nin mel,* what has you so troubled your mind is turbulent with worry."

"You can feel how I'm feeling?" I asked, frowning, not sure how comfortable I was with that.

"Yes, now that we are mated, I am able to access all your emotions and thoughts, but you have a remarkable barrier in your mind that is keeping me out. At the moment, I'm only getting flashes of your emotions, and none of them seem to be good ones," Rathal explained, his face matching the concern I heard in his voice.

Now it was my turn to frown at him, not at all pleased he could read my mind, but that would be a discussion for another time. "My mates don't know I'm here, but I'll worry about that once I know we are safe. First step is to get out of this house and off the island without getting caught and the person keeping tabs on the security might be trying to kill me."

"Ah, the emotions are making more sense now. Now that I am out of that cell and the iron shackles they used to keep my powers locked away are gone, I will help any way that I can."

I cocked my head to the side as I took in my newest mate. The words he was speaking were English, even if he had a slight accent to them, but I can't say I understood half of what he was talking about. There was no time to deal with all of this and our time for getting out of this place undetected was getting shorter the longer we stood here. Grabbing his hand, I pulled him after me as we made our way back downstairs and out the back door I'd come in.

Blackley had to have parked the boat somewhere around here. He wouldn't have let it drift out into the ocean.

"The man who shot you brought me here on a black inflatable boat. If we can find it, then we have a better chance of getting out of this without drawing attention," I said over my shoulder as I let go of him to search.

The coast was pretty clean since so many of the people here had landscapers to maintain the area, so Blackley would have to find some place to stash it out of sight. I spotted a dock where a few boats were moored for one of the houses. If I were going to hide a boat, I would put it in plain sight, where it wouldn't be odd for it to exist.

The ramp to the dock had a motion sensor light, so it looked like I was going for another swim since it was the only way to get around the thing. Even though my wet suit helped fight the frigid water, I still hissed as it hit my stomach. Deciding it was better to simply get it over with, I dove into the water and swam for the dock.

Sure enough, the inflated boat was tied in the back, going unnoticed in the darkness as the other boats were docked. Grabbing onto one of the handles on the side, I heaved myself into the boat and cut the rope tethering it to the dock. I let it drift a little further out before I started the engine, bringing it to the shore before cutting it, so it shot right up onto the beach where Rathal stood. He didn't look pleased with me, but I was more worried about getting us out alive right now. "Can you shove us off and hop in at the same time?" I asked.

"I can do one better," he answered, stepping into the boat and taking a seat at its bow, letting his hand drift into the water.

Unsure of what he was trying to do, I waited in silence and watched, curious about elf magic. His hand in the water started to glow, and the water around us seemed to swirl, drawing the boat from the shore and pushing us further out into the ocean. When we got a safe distance away from the beach, he pulled his hand out of the water and dried it off on his pants.

"Water isn't my strongest element to work with, but I can manage simple feats such as that," Rathal shared as I gaped at him.

"Can I do that?" I asked, feeling like being an elf might be the best thing that's ever happened to me if I could do tricks like that. Being able to control elements would make my job so much easier getting in and out of places.

"It will take us time to figure out what your talents might be, but clearly, healing is one of them. Not many could heal me as fast and perfectly as you did. Even some of my old injuries are gone," Rathal shared. "As your Guide, it is my duty to train you in your magic and help you to discover these talents. In due time, we will find what your magic is drawn to."

"Guide, you mentioned that before. Is that part of the *Nos* thing like my other mates being a Sentinel, Hunter, and Companion?" I inquired, curious as to why they hadn't mentioned the title when we talked about it before.

"For a *Nos* to have a guide isn't common. Only a powerful female will draw one to her so that ensures she is trained properly," Rathal instructed. "Some knowledge we didn't share with others, feeling it was wise to keep them to ourselves in an effort to protect our mates from being sought after for their powers."

That made sense, so I merely nodded as I pulled the cord to start the engine. "My plan is to get us to Miami. It will be easier for us to find a place to hide out there and the airport is close as well. If I can get ahold of my mates, Zander can send the plane for us so there won't be a trace of either of us in the flight system for them to track. It's gonna take us about an hour, so get some rest if you need to. This is the safest we are going to be for the night."

"No, *nin mel*, I will stay awake with you. Two pairs of eyes looking out for danger is better than one," he yelled over the sound of the engine as I gunned it.

The sooner we got farther away from the scene of the crime, the better. Nothing about this job went according to plan but what haunted me more as I left that house behind was what Blakley said before he killed himself. There was more going on in this situation than any of us realized. Would it be worth reaching out to Miranda and seeing what she knew? When I told her what went down at Delilah's, she seemed displeased with how much we didn't know about the situation. The Senate had given us everything, even providing a way in, so it didn't make sense for them to set a trap like this for me. Could it be that not all the Senate knew about the mole they had in their midst?

There were way too many questions and not enough answers. What made it worse was that I didn't have the same connections as I did with the Organization... Or did I? No one knew what happened within the Organization and I'd cultivated my own contacts over the years. It might be worth reaching out to see what I could gather. The only trouble was both the Senate and the Dark Ring might be groups people didn't want to go against. Well, there was one I knew of who would gladly give me information on the Senate, but I didn't trust him enough not to slip it to the Dark Ring. Even so, for the right price, anyone would talk.

Since I was in need of bribe money, it seemed it was time I started to shift some of my assets around that I'd been saving for the past twenty-some years. When almost everything was provided to me by the Organization, I didn't really spend all that much of it. I had a hefty nest egg sitting in a few offshore banks, but I had a feeling I was going to need to pay a pretty penny for this information.

I'd started to bring up the fact I had money when Zander made us go shopping, but he was hearing none of it, always telling me it was his place as my mate to take care of me. My omega side had been incredibly excited about them wanting to take care of me, I decided not to argue about it.

A shifting in the boat had me snapping my attention back to my surroundings, but it was only Rathal moving to sit next to me. He pulled my hand off the tiller and grabbed the handle, holding it steady while his other arm wrapped around my waist. Yanking me into his lap, I suddenly realized how cold I was with the added body heat from him penetrating through my wetsuit.

"How can you not notice that you're cold enough to be shivering?" Rathal asked, speaking right into my ear so I could hear him clearly.

Taking stock of my body, I noted I was indeed shivering. Training had taught us discomfort was simply an issue of mind over matter. We could drown out anything with the power of our mind freeing us from limitations due to discomfort or pain. Unconsciously, I'd shoved that worry out of my head to deal with the need to get us out of danger.

"I'm an assassin. We do what's needed to get the job done. My job isn't done until we are both safe and back with my other mates," I answered. Only with that answer came a revelation—if I went back to my mates, I would be putting the whole pack in danger.

If the Senate and the Dark Ring were after me, they wouldn't bat an eye at the thought of wiping out our entire pack.

Could I go back there?

I knew my mates would never let me walk away from them, and that's not what I wanted either, but could I knowingly walk back into their lives with the possibility of destroying everything they worked for?

"*Nin mel*, whatever you are thinking, stop it right now. You are tearing yourself apart over something, and I can tell you, if it has anything to do with your mates, the only option is to go back to them. Light Elves, once marked and mated, can't survive without being around them. Clearly, you can have some separation, but if you were to leave all of us, it would kill you. The fact that I was in the house kept you from having any side effects, but there is no way you can cut us out of your life once having claimed us," he snapped, making me flinch at his icy tone. Even my wolf wanted to hide and beg him to forgive us for even thinking of leaving our mates.

I deserved the scolding. Deep in my heart, I knew it was the coward's way out of this to leave them, but I was still learning how to share my life with them. I've been on my own my whole life and it terrified me to the depths of my soul that I could lose them. Then from deep inside me, where my power had laid dormant for so long, it came rushing to the forefront, furious with me for being so weak. It was as if the part of me that was the assassin had been my elf nature all along but somehow muted. Now that my magic had been released, it counteracted some of the omegas' urges.

Was I an omega, yes, but I was also a fighter, a survivor, one who'd made it in this world on my own two feet. If the Senate and the Dark Ring wanted to take from me, it would be over my dead body.

CHAPTER THREE

FINLEY

We made it to Miami with no issues, and thankfully, it was a big city which meant there were places open twenty-four hours a day. The biggest problem was I didn't know if the codes I still had for safe houses would work or not. If Miranda had done everything she was supposed to, she would have wiped them all from the system, but I was willing to try. There was one safe house here that was on the wrong side of town and in a dilapidated apartment building. It wouldn't be hard to break into. I remember overhearing they were going to relocate it to a different building since this one was becoming too unstable.

If the house was still intact, it would give us a place to rest a little until I could contact my mates. Once the sun was up, I could go to the bank and get money from my account, freeing us to do whatever we needed. Using my skills, I stole an 'I love Miami' T-shirt for Rathal since wandering around without a shirt on would draw more attention than I wanted. Even with the shirt on, my newest mate drew attention with his long white-blond hair and fair skin and the muscles rippled under his skin. If it was distracting to me, I could only imagine what other people must think when they saw him.

The stench of vampires filled the air as we approached the apartment building. *Could this be what they meant about it becoming unstable?*

Vampire covens were unpredictable. If they were hiding out in an area like this, it meant they were blood junkies. They drank from the vein, getting high when they killed their living blood donors. It became addictive, which was why it's illegal to do since it led to too many massacres in the past, especially if it was a newly created vampire without a strong mentor. People always thought shifters were the dangerous ones with their animal nature, but vampires no longer had souls to guide them.

"I think you're in the wrong place, little wolf," a voice whispered out of the darkness, followed by a hollow chuckle.

"Don't chase them off. It's been ages since we had *that* kind of meal," another voice slithered across my skin from somewhere above me.

Rathal stepped up behind me, reminding me he was there watching my back. It was thoughtful of him but not needed. I'd been caught off guard with how strong the scent was to my werewolf senses. Now that I'd adjusted, I knew just where the four vampires were as they slinked closer in the cover of the night.

"There's going to be no meal for you from either of us," I announced. "If you try, it will be your life that ends, not mine or my mate's."

"Mate," a voice hissed, stretching out the word as if it was strange for them to hear. "He doesn't smell like a wolf. No, he smells like power."

"What a glorious moment we have found ourselves in tonight. The power he's putting off will give us the high these putrid humans can't." This final voice was far closer, but I was tracking him out of the corner of my eye as he flitted nearer with his supernatural speed.

Vampires might be faster than a werewolf, but my money was on the fact they didn't know how to deal with prey who knew how to fight back. Taking slow, steady breaths, I let myself fall into my cool, calculating assassin nature as I let my feet slide apart to keep me balanced.

"*Nin mel,*" Rathal started, but in the next moment, two vampires attacked.

Using all my force, I shoved Rathal back, knocking him to the ground so one of the vampires flew over him and the other hit me right in the gut. I used the vampire's momentum to my advantage, and as we flew back, I twisted so I was looking down at the vampire's blood-red eyes and bared teeth. Sweeping a hand behind me, I grabbed my knife made of pure silver, and when we crashed into the ground, the vampire loosened its hold on me. Shifting back, I plunged the knife into the vampire's heart, making it scream in pain as the blade sliced through its heart, the silver burning its way through the flesh. The lovely thing about vampires was when you killed them, they shriveled up into a husk of dry skin, turning into a small pile of sand.

"*No!*" one of the vampires screeched.

I had enough time to roll out of the way, but it still managed to catch my ankle. Unfortunately, my water shoes didn't provide me with a solid enough base to get the impact I wanted as I slammed my other heel into his face. The pain shot up through my foot as I'm pretty sure I broke my heel. I thrashed, twisting like an alligator while the vampire was disorientated. Once free, I surged to my feet, hissing at the pain, but I shut it out, there were two more vampires to deal with, and I had to protect Rathal. Not waiting for the vampire to recover, I dove at it, using all my strength to slam him to the ground. In my anger at the situation, I felt my newly awakened power rise in me, and my hands started to glow. Unsure of what it would do, I shoved it into his chest, causing the vampire to writhe and scream.

Then before my eyes, something appeared to change. His blood-red eyes seemed to fade and a warm brown color replaced them. The deathly pallor of his skin started to pink up as if he'd freshly fed, and the sunken tissue from going without blood for so long seemed to fill out, making him almost appear... human. An odd sensation thumped under my hand as if his heart was beating once again.

But that couldn't be.

He was dead.

"What have you done to me?" the vampire rasped, snapping at me in an effort to remove me. His teeth were normal. The longer incisors were gone, leaving him harmless.

Finally, my power trickled to a stop, and I was able to scramble off of him. Taking the vampire in from head to toe, I realized that I'd *healed* him from being a vampire and returned him to human form.

"How is that possible?" I gasped, looking around wildly for Rathal to explain this phenomenon.

When I spotted him, the bodies of the other two vampires were at his feet headless. This would have been a more impressive feat to me if I hadn't just used magic on a vampire, turning him back into a living, breathing human.

"Rath..." I rasped, drawing his attention. He stalked over to me and looked at the man still cowering on the ground. "I made him human."

Rathal looked from me to the man a moment before he took the knife from my hand and slit the man's throat. Bright red blood spilled from him as he slumped, twitching as the life I'd just given to him slipped away.

"No one can know, *nin mel*," Rathal explained. "That kind of power is one that will send every supernatural being after you until your dying day."

Lifting my gaze to him, I blinked a few times, trying to process what he was saying. "Why?"

"Finley, with that kind of healing power, you could strip any supernatural of its power if they were once human, rendering them helpless. That kind of threat in the wrong hands would be chaos," he explained, cupping my cheek with one of his large hands, stroking my skin with his thumb. "We need to get moving before someone comes to investigate the noise."

"Trust me, no one will come looking for trouble in this part of the neighborhood," I commented, unable to process what he'd just said about what I might be able to do. "But I agree, we need to get moving. Now that we've cleared the building of vampires, we should be able to see if the apartment is still functional."

Rathal watched me with a worried gaze as I walked away from the dead human that was once very much a vampire. Heading up to the second floor of the building, I led the way to the end of the row of rooms until we reached the last one. The number thirteen hung askew on the door and the normal handle was replaced with a keyless entry number pad. I punched in the six-digit code and held my breath, hoping it would work. The keypad flashed, then clicked open, allowing me to push the handle down and enter the apartment. The room was dusty and hadn't been used in quite some time, but it was, for the most part, safe, and we would have a place to crash until morning. Looking at the watch on my wrist, I grimaced that we only had three hours before the sun would be up, but the banks wouldn't open until eight.

When I went to flip on the light switch, nothing happened, making me think they had cut the power to the place. The keypad must have a battery backup for it to be still working. Heading to the sink in the small galley kitchen, I lifted the handle, and it thankfully produced water. It must be this way for the whole building, even if it was only vampires living here. The building had codes to live up to, if whoever owned the complex was still alive. With the power out, I didn't dare open the refrigerator, afraid of what I might find in there. Instead, I looked through the cabinets and found some canned soup and instant ramen noodle cups left in the back of one. The stove was electric, so heating any of this was out, but it wasn't the first time I'd eaten cold soup out of a can on the job.

"Do you want me to heat those up?" Rathal asked, holding out his hands for the soup cans.

My brows shot up as I handed them over. "You can do that?"

"There are many tricks I can do. Using magic to manipulate molecules in soup is child's play," Rathal answered with a smirk.

Holding the cans, he closed his eyes, and I watched as his hands began to glow with a soft light. My own magic had lit up where I made contact as I healed the vampire. I was beginning to understand it signaled the use of magic. So I shook the thought out of my head, not wanting to deal with that issue until I was someplace safe to dissect all this with Rathal.

Within moments, Rathal set the can on the counter to pop the tabs and pull the metal lid back, revealing steam. Quickly, I searched the drawers for spoons and found there were some plastic ones left in the wrapper from some sort of takeout. Taking my piping hot can of beef and lentil soup, I headed for the couch, my stomach growling at the scent of food. Being a werewolf, I found that I had to eat a lot more and a lot more often. It was still something I needed to work on remembering, but the past two days had been anything but normal. Mason was the one who always reminded me or handed me snacks before I realized I was even hungry.

Thinking of them made all the emotions I've been trying to hold back flood to the forefront. My omega side wanted nothing more than to break down and cry at the fact we were alone, in danger, and with a man we didn't really know, even if our elf nature trusted him. I wanted to give into that, but I knew it wouldn't help either of us at this point. I simply needed to get through this, and once we were home, then I could have the meltdown my omega wanted in the arms of our mates. My wolf seemed to accept this compromise and settled into the background, letting me do what I needed to ensure we would get that outcome.

"*Nin mel,* talk to me," Rathal coaxed, wrapping an arm around my shoulders to pull me into him. "I can't ignore the emotions I'm getting off you any longer. They are slowly ripping you to shreds internally and that isn't good for your mental or physical well-being. Please let me help you."

I looked up at this new mate of mine that I'd claimed in the heat of panic and danger. How could I innately trust someone whom I knew nothing about, other than his name and that he was an elf? Yet, in my soul, I knew he was here to look after me and that I could trust him with my worries. He felt safe and everything I could sense from him confirmed exactly that.

"What if going back puts my mates and the pack in danger? The Dark Ring and now the Senate is after me just for knowing what I know and being an omega. What will happen when word gets out that elves aren't dead and I can do what I did to that vampire? Wouldn't it be best to just leave and hide away until I can kill the threat to my new family before returning?" I shared, searching Rathal's eyes for answers.

He took a deep breath and pulled me into his lap, taking my soup from me and setting it on the coffee table before wrapping me up in his strong arms. Seconds later, he was wrapping a fleece blanket around me, cocooning and sheltering me with his body. Instantly, I knew this was exactly what I needed to help my spiraling nature. My wolf let out a sigh of contentment as we finally felt secure since I left the bed with all of my mates two almost three days ago. Apparently, even with my full elf nature released, I still needed to be aware of what my omega nature needed to feel safe and secure. Rathal must have sensed I was slowly unraveling and knew just how to fix it for the moment.

"Oh, my sweet mate, you have such a big heart. I can see why fate decided you should also be an omega. You might not believe me, but the fates knew what they were doing when they sent you so many mates right away when you needed them. Trust that they will be exactly what you need and will care and protect you no matter what comes your way. Is the Dark Ring a group you shouldn't underestimate? Absolutely, but they are just humans and can be stopped. The Senate, on the other hand, might be slightly trickier, but as we learn more about that matter things will become clearer." Rathal nuzzled into my hair, pressing a kiss to my head, just letting me soak in his reassurance. "Now get some rest. I will watch over you and keep the nightmares away."

"Only for a little while. We need to get out of the state as fast as we can. It's not safe to be here with them hunting me," I argued.

Rathal lifted one of his elegant fingers and placed it over my lips. "Shh, rest. We will not linger here longer than we need to, but you need rest, or you will risk making a mistake somewhere along the way."

As his soothing voice spoke, I felt my eyelids drooping, and my body became heavy with exhaustion. "Okay, I'll rest... just for a little bit..."

CHAPTER FOUR

FINLEY

When I woke up with the morning sun streaming in from the front windows, I felt more rested than I had in ages. It was as if I'd been rejuvenated through sleeping so deep my body couldn't do anything but rest. My mind was in such a relaxed state I didn't realize I was rubbing my cheek along the bare skin of someone's chest. He smelled like spring, fresh flowers and clean air after being trapped in the house all winter long. If freedom had a scent, this would be it, and it was glorious.

Fingers combed through my hair, making me purr with delight at the loving touch that my body craved from our mates. With that simple thought, I shoved up from the body I was sprawled over and came face to face with Rathal. His seafoam green eyes sparkled with happiness and mirth as he waited to see what my reaction would be.

"Good morning, *nin mel,*" he murmured before lifting to give me a peck on the lips. "Did you sleep well?"

"What does that mean?" I asked, having heard him use that phrase often.

He smiled, brushing his hands down my arms. "It means my love, but not just a simple love, the all-consuming love you have only with your mate."

"Oh," I answered, blinking at him in surprise.

I didn't really know how to respond to that since the whole idea of mates and fated love was new to me. Clearly, this was normal for elves and even werewolves, but for us humans, it was a thing for movies and books.

"It is now nine, and I was just going to wake you, knowing you wanted to get moving," Rathal commented, pulling me out of my internal thoughts.

Sliding off him, I stood and found I was only in a sports bra and my underwear. He'd removed my wetsuit and water shoes at some point, which I was grateful for, if not slightly impressed with since I didn't wake up during the process.

"Your magic is quite strong, my mate," Rathal shared as he stood and pulled on his clothes. "I put you into a healing sleep, and normally, you have to be brought out of it, but you were able to wake yourself once you had gained all you could from the sleep."

This made me freeze as I started to wiggle back into the wetsuit. Slowly, I turned to face the elf, who I'm hoping didn't just tell me he magically drugged me so I would sleep. "You. Did. What?"

Rathal paused as he started to pull his shirt on to look at me. "By your emotions and the look on your face, I feel like I might have done something to make you upset with me."

"Why would I be upset about the fact that we are in danger, on the run, and squatting in a building that was taken by vampires? There could have been others that we didn't see or returned when the sun was coming up. Would I have woken in time if something happened, or would I be left vulnerable to anyone's attack?" I asked, keeping my voice calm and cool.

He seemed to ponder my point before answering as he finished getting dressed. "While I understand your point and can see why this would be upsetting to you, I'm also slightly offended that you think I would put you in danger. You are my mate. We are connected on a soul level, meaning that if one of us dies, so does the other. If you were in true danger, you are more than strong enough to easily break out of that enchantment, but I want to also make it clear that I am a trained warrior and don't need you to protect me."

I so badly wanted to argue this more because I felt it had been a clear violation of my safety. I didn't know him, and I'd never been good about trusting others to have my back. It's why I always worked solo. Now that he pointed out his life and mine were tied together, it freaked me out more than it helped. Not only did I have to trust he would take care of himself if something happened, but if he didn't, it would take me down with him.

"Don't you think that is something you should have explained to me earlier? You already can read my emotions and possibly my mind if I was more open to you. My life is in your hands, and I can't be apart from you or my other mates for more than a day. What else do I need to know about being mated as an elf?" I demanded, feeling my irritation turning into anger the more I thought about his words.

Rathal studied me like I was a puzzle he couldn't figure out. "What have they done to you to make you so distrusting and fearful of any kind of connection? Both elves and werewolves thrive and seek out community, but you run the other way at the thought of it."

"Since I was five years old, I've been trained to be an assassin, someone who lives and works in the shadows. My purpose is to be the best soldier I can be, accomplishing my mission with none the wiser, leaving death in my wake. I'm extremely good at my job, that is until I failed the last one and got bit by an omega, changing my life forever. I've had a week to adjust to being a werewolf, finding out I've never been human, and now having mates on top of everything else. So yeah, I'm not used to relying on others or trusting people when I know every corner of the darkness our world holds," I answered, my anger bubbling over as I spoke. All at once, it was as if my magic was building, seeking some kind of release. The vibration running under my skin made me feel as though I might burst.

Rathal stepped up to me, resting his hands on my shoulders before bending his head, so our foreheads touched. "I'm so sorry, *nin mel*. This is not the life I would have chosen for you, but it's the life you've lived. While I have to accept that and learn how to best support you as my mate, it will take me time to do that well. I'm sure I will make more mistakes along the way. All I ask is that you have patience with me as I learn. You are my whole world now, so whatever you need from me, I will strive to give you."

Hearing the truth and feeling behind his words allowed me to calm my anger enough that my magic settled to a low simmer. There had been so much changing in my life and I didn't think I could handle another thing at this point. When he pulled me into a hug, I let my ear rest over his heart and listened to it as it beat in time with my own, showing me another sign we were bound together.

"I need you to treat me like I don't know anything, that I'm human and never even knew there were elves in the world. Hell, even what I thought I knew about werewolves was all wrong. It goes against my training and nature to be going about this blind, so I'm trying as hard as I can to catch up, but more issues keep coming that I have to deal with first. What I need most is truth, honesty, and information about everything to do with elves," I murmured into his chest.

"I can do that," he answered, squeezing me tight as he pressed a kiss to my temple. "Finish putting that weird bodysuit on and I will change it into something more fitting to be out in public."

Doing as he requested, I watched as he ran a hand over his own shirt, and it transformed into a forest green T-shirt that fit snugly across his chest, showing off his muscles while his tan linen pants changed into jeans.

"Elves can manipulate natural fibers into anything they need, such as clothing," Rathal explained as he reached out to my wetsuit. "Now, there isn't much natural about this, but this kind of manipulation is what I am strongest with. Do you have any requests?"

"Ah, a shirt and jeans like you would be best, I think. Maybe boots instead of these water shoes?" I answered in more of a question, unsure how much he could do.

He smiled before closing his eyes, appearing to be concentrating on what he was doing, and soon, I had on a black pair of jeans and a simple T-shirt with black combat boots. Stepping back, he looked at his work before giving it a nod. "I couldn't do anything with the color since there was no other pigment to pull from, but something tells me you are comfortable in black."

"Your assumption would be correct. Zander, one of my other mates, got me a whole new wardrobe, and he didn't include much black, so I'm learning to embrace more colors," I shared with a smile. "Fashion is far more important to him, but I suppose that comes with being a rock star."

Rathal's brows shot up. "Wait, the famous werewolf singer... that *Zander* is your mate?"

"The one and only. He lives on the edge of pack lands my other two mates, Colt and Lane, own in Knoxville, Tennessee. The other three are betas, Mason and Noah are twins, and then there's Elias rounding out the group."

"You only have marks from your alphas, though, correct? I didn't see any others while you were sleeping," Rathal stated.

"Yes, the other three are tied more to my elf nature, so we assumed that wouldn't happen until I came into my power," I explained as I headed for the door. "We should head out. The sooner I can find a phone to call from, the better. It will take them a few hours to fly here, at which point I can get my hands on some of my funds to get us a decent meal."

Rathal followed after me without comment as he took in our surroundings as if he was expecting something to come jumping out at him. Without hesitation, I took his hand and interlaced our fingers, needing to soothe my mate's emotions as I felt them hidden just under the surface. Once I had contact with him, I was slapped with his protectiveness over me and his admiration for how attractive I was to him. The emotions were so intense I gasped and came to a stop trying to figure out how to turn off his feelings at this moment.

"*Nin mel*, what's wrong?" he questioned, reaching out to touch me with his other hand, but I held a hand up to stop him when he wouldn't let go of my other hand.

"I need you to put up a shield or something to tone down your emotions if you're going to touch me. My omega side is a strong empath and touching you makes it like a direct line to your feelings, and they are oppressive at this moment," I explained. Seconds later, they were gone as if they'd never existed at all. I took a deep breath, finally feeling like I could hear my own thoughts. "Thank you. Normally I can handle it, but it was almost as if they were screaming at me."

Rathal took my hand and kissed the back of it. "I apologize. That is my fault. Your mental barrier is so strong that I didn't bother to shield it from you in the hope it would help me read you better. I should have known that contact would create a link and been prepared."

"Does it bother you that you can't hear my thoughts or feel my emotions well?" I inquired, curious. Being able to feel people's emotions all the time, I couldn't imagine adding in their thoughts as well.

"If you were anyone else, it wouldn't be an issue, but since you are my mate, and it's such an intimate part of being bonded together, I feel a little lost," he answered honestly. "We have been taught at such a young age the wonders of finding your mate and the bond we have with them, mind, body, and soul, that we long for those moments. I acknowledge that our bond is different between us, not having gone through the courting process or building a relationship like most would. Our bonding was instinctive and rushed, so now I must adjust, which I will gladly do for you. You'll just need to give me a little time to do so."

Not really having much I could say to all that, I decided maybe words weren't the right move. Pulling my hand out of Rathal's hold, I instead wrapped them around his waist and hugged him tightly, willing my mind to share with him how much that meant to me. His arms curled around my shoulders, holding me to him as he pressed a kiss to my head.

My wolf started to purr at the physical contact, and happy emotions flowed through us, making my chest vibrate and Rathal chuckle. "I envy your ability to purr. It shows the others exactly how you're feeling. Come. We have much to do this morning, and if I were in my *gwanur's* position, I would be out of my mind with worry."

"*Gwanur?*" I asked as we started back down the street.

"It means brother, but not the same as a sibling by blood but by sharing a mate."

"Seems I'm going to need to learn another language to truly understand you," I teased, grinning up at him.

Rathal flashed me a smile. "I have a feeling you'll pick it up in no time. It is your native tongue. I feel like your mother would have spoken it to you growing up."

"Sadly, I don't remember anything much before Miranda and the Organization took me in. My life changed so much going right into training. I didn't have time to realize what I'd lost since the others were the same as me," I shared.

The conversation fell off and we continued in a comfortable silence until we reached the nicer part of downtown Miami. I entered a small bookstore that sold rare and antique books heading right for the desk where I rang the small bell on the counter.

"Coming!" was heard deeper in the store, but with my supernatural hearing, I knew he was walking up from the back storage room.

It took Oscar a few minutes to reach the counter, but when he did and spotted me, he came to a halt. "Finley." His voice squeaked in surprise.

Oscar was exactly the type of person you would picture working at a bookstore like this. Thick round glasses, polo shirt with khakis, and penny loafers that were perfectly worn in from daily use. He'd been one of my contacts that the Organization didn't know about. He kept backup supplies for me and I sent him enough money to keep his store running even if he never made another sale.

"It's been so long since I've seen you, I figured you'd forgotten about me," he explained, adjusting his glasses nervously.

I gave him a smile and shook my head. "Do you think I would be sending you that much money if I'd forgotten about you?" I waved off the question without really needing him to answer it. "I need to get to my stash. Can you let me into the vault?"

"Of course, you both can follow me." He turned and started to walk, then paused, looking back at Rathal. "Um, unless you'd rather leave him up here? You don't usually have people with you."

"It's fine, but thank you for not assuming. That might come in handy one of these days," I said, giving Oscar a full smile in appreciation.

Oscar seemed stunned by the smile and a blush started to creep up his neck and onto his cheeks. "Ah, yes... well, I know our arrangement is less than standard, so I didn't want you to be acting against your will or anything."

Rathal stepped up behind me and settled his hands on my hips in a move that clearly stated his claim on me. "I would never force my mate to do something against her will. *Nin mel,* who is this man and what arrangement is he talking about?"

"Business, nothing more, right Oscar?" I asked, cocking a brow.

He gaped at me and Rathal like a fish before turning on his heel and scurrying to the book vault in the corner of the store. I couldn't help but snicker to myself at how the two men were acting around me as if I needed either of them to stand up for my honor. When we reached the vault, which was really a secure environment for the rare books to be housed, the door was cracked open, and Oscar was nowhere to be found.

"I think you scared the poor man, Rath," I quipped, looking at him out of the corner of my eye.

"Then he shouldn't have been looking at my mate like he wanted to sleep with you. It's rude to make advances when you have clear marks on your skin marking you as taken," Rathal justified.

Shaking my head, I grinned. "Come on, we best close the door. The ocean air isn't good for the books."

The room wasn't large, every inch of it covered in bookshelves, but the door. I walked over to the table used to repair or restore any damaged books and took a pair of cloth gloves. Heading over to a bookshelf, I removed a section of books to reveal a safe behind them and typed in the code, using my pointer fingerprint to unlock it with a *snick.* Once opened, it revealed a set of knives, a gun, passport, driver's license, a stack of cash, and a burner phone. I grabbed the license and the phone but left everything else there in case I would ever need it later.

I turned the phone on and dialed Colt's number, knowing he would answer any unknown number on that specific cell phone just like he had the first time.

CHAPTER FIVE

COLT

It was hard to focus on anything when my wolf wanted nothing more than to hunt down our mate, no matter how long it took. How I wanted to give in to that need, but I was responsible for more than just Finley. Plus, we had one of our own wolves leak our evacuation plans to the Senate, and who the hell knows who else.

Lane and I still had to decide what to do about Peggy. Neither of us was ready to make the call that had to be made with what she'd done. With her actions, she endangered our whole pack, no matter her intention.

Elias still felt like the vampire might be part of some other party looking for Finley. Maybe even the Dark Ring themselves, if the rumors of how they turn supers against their own kind to survive are true.

I sat at my desk staring at my phone, willing it to ring and it be Finley on the other side. If I knew she was alive, it would take such a weight off my shoulders, but the not knowing part was torture. It was as if I was reliving losing my brother all over again. Cory had been my responsibility to keep safe just as Finley was. Now, I'd failed them both when it mattered. When we got her back, I didn't care what I had to do. Even if it meant chaining her to my side, I wouldn't lose her again.

Just then, my phone started to vibrate and ring loudly, scaring the shit out of me until I realized that the number calling was blocked. Diving for the phone, I snatched it up as it almost skittered off the desk, hitting the answer button. "Hello? Finley?"

There wasn't an immediate response on the other end, making my heart beat wildly in my chest. "Finley, if that's you, I expect you to answer me this minute," I snarled using my alpha voice, knowing she couldn't refuse my command.

"Yes, alpha, it's me," she answered with a whimper in her voice at the forced response. "I'm sorry, I'm so sorry, please don't be upset with me," she begged.

"Hand me the phone," a male voice insisted. "I will speak with him if he can't handle his temper."

A growl leaked from my lips as rage built in my chest.

Who is this man?

Did he have Finley captive?

Was he hurting her?

Could she get away?

"Who the fuck are you?" I demanded.

The sound of whispers and a soft whine made me wish I could crawl through the phone to throttle whoever was making my omega and mate upset.

"Tell me he isn't one of your mates? This is why people always say shifters are more like their animals with all the growling and power trips," the male said as he brought the phone closer so I could hear him better.

His words had an accent I couldn't place, and the way he talked was unusual, far too elegant for the average person.

The man cleared his voice a moment before speaking directly to me, "I am Rathal Zintris, Finley's elven mate and Guide. I presume you are one of her Alpha Mates that's claimed her?"

My mind and body froze at his words... *elven mate*? What the fuck is going on?

I rushed out of my office and barged into Lane's. Seeing him on the phone, I ran over and snatched the phone out of his hand, ending the call.

"What the hell, Colt?" Lane snapped. "That was an important phone call with a lead that might tell us where Finley is."

Hitting the speaker button on my phone, I set it down on his desk. "Repeat what you just said."

"My, how polite you ask," Rat-Zin-elven-fuck-all drawled. "I hope whoever has joined in on this phone call will be more reasonable to deal with. I'm Rathal Zintris, Light Elf, mate to Finley, as well as the Guide in our *Nos*. Whom am I speaking with?"

"Did he just say Light Elf?" Lane asked, eyes wide in shock as he looked at me, then back down to the phone. "Wait, are you with Finley right now? Is she okay? Where the hell are you and what the fuck happened?"

Rathal let out a heavy sigh as if he was dealing with a pair of idiots. "I can see you are more reasonable to talk to but still just as demanding, full of that alpha need to control everything."

"If you told us what we wanted to know, we wouldn't have to demand it," I shot back, my wolf feeling the need to establish our dominance over this man.

"Finley is fine. She completed her mission and, in the process, freed me. I was shot, but she saved my life and in doing so, completed our mate bond. So remove any delusions you will be able to get rid of me. We are in Miami, Florida and would appreciate a ride home. Finley shared that there was a plane that could come get us?"

Lane grabbed his phone and shot a text to Zander, who was still at the pack house with the betas working on finding our girl. "Yeah, that won't be a problem. We'll be heading that way the moment we can get the plane in the air. Now let us talk to Finley. I need to hear it from her that she is okay and confirm who you are."

Rathal scoffed. "Elves cannot lie, wolf."

"How the hell am I supposed to know you're really an elf when we are talking over the phone?" I challenged. "Also, it's Colt or alpha to you, not *wolf.*"

"There will never be a moment in our extremely long lives together that I will ever call you alpha, so Colt will have to do," Rathal stated. "I will give the phone back to her if you promise not to bully her. Your effect on her even over the phone is overwhelming and we haven't had the easiest few days."

As much as I hated to admit it, I knew he was right. Finley needed to be strong while she didn't have us to watch her back. This douche might be claiming to be all these things, but who knew if it was true—I didn't know the elf.

"You both still there?" Finley asked, sounding more like herself.

"Yeah, little one, we are here. You okay?" I asked, keeping my voice light even as my wolf and I *needed* to hear it from her lips.

"I'm fine. We both are," she added.

Lane leaned forward, elbows on his desk, and he got closer to the phone. "Zander is calling to get the plane ready. Then we will head out there."

"He needs to do whatever he can to ensure that no one knows it's his plane that's coming here. It's not safe, the Dark Ring is after me, and they have people in the Senate giving them information. I need you to know that it's dangerous for me to come back to the pack. The job was a setup. They tried to kill me when I completed the job. They planned on me getting caught so they could use me to make more omegas," Finley said, speaking swiftly.

Even though her voice was calm, I could feel there was a hint of fear mixed in. If there was one thing an omega would hate more than upsetting an alpha, it would be putting the pack in danger.

"Sweetheart, we will deal with whatever comes, but we need to be together for anything to work. I'll make sure Zander knows about the danger. He's a rock star. If anyone knows how to get around unnoticed, it will be him," Lane answered, trying to soothe Finley's fears. "Do you have someplace safe to be while you wait for us?"

"Yes, I have contacts here in Miami from working with the Organiza- tion. I'll be able to keep a low profile until you get here. I'm using a burner phone. Let me send you the number so you guys can call me when you get here," she offered.

"Please be safe, little one, we just started our lives together, and I don't know that I could survive losing you so soon after Cory," I pleaded, needing her to know how much she really meant to me.

At my words, I heard a sharp intake of breath at Cory's name. I knew it had been hard on her not being able to save him. It unsettled my wolf and me that she would hesitate to return to the pack, thinking we couldn't keep her safe. Now it was going to be my mission in life for her never to doubt us again.

"I promise I'm not going anywhere. I'm done running and hiding secrets from you. I thought I owed it to the Senate, the Organization, and myself to finish this job, but as it turns out, the Senate doesn't deserve my loyalty." Finley growled, surprising me at her anger about the situation. "Once I'm on the plane out of here, I'll fill you in on everything, including what happened with Rath."

"We'll see you soon, sweetheart," Lane called out before she hung up, leaving us to stare at each other.

Lane and I have gone through hell and back the last ten years looking for Cory, starting this pack, and now being mated to the same woman. It seems the universe decided that we needed to journey through life together, and I couldn't think of a better man to have my back. Zander's name flashed on my phone, and I realized I'd seen a whole new side of him over the past week, and even Lane was warming to the guy. Answering his call, I once again put it on speaker.

"The plane takes off in twenty minutes. I'm coming to get you guys," he informed us, not bothering with a greeting. "What the hell is going on that we need to go in stealth mode? Did you talk to her? Is she okay?"

"Yes, we talked to her, and she's fine for now, but we got a lot to discuss. Are the others with you?" I asked, knowing they wouldn't want to be left behind.

"Did you really think you could make us stay home?" Mason yelled from somewhere in the car. "If you try, I'll fight you right here, right now, because that's not happening."

I could hear Noah groan in the background. "Twin, you need to calm down. He hasn't said one way or the other on the matter."

"Yeah, well, he doesn't need to because I'm going," Mason bit out.

"Enough!" Zander snapped. "Shut the fuck up and let the adults talk." The line went silent and I almost questioned if he'd hung up or not until he spoke, "Why do we need to sneak into Miami to get our mate?"

"She didn't tell us much, only that the Dark Ring set her up, and they have people in the Senate. Seems they tried to trap her, and when that didn't work, they resorted to killing her. Thank God she's good at her job and made it out of there along with a new *friend*," I muttered at the end, still not at all sure how I felt about an elf we didn't know already bonded to our mate.

Zander and the others let out a snarl, picking up on my energy about the matter. "What friend?" Elias demanded, an icy edge to his voice.

"Like I said, we didn't get a whole lot of information. She said she would explain it all to us in person once she got on the plane. Right now, she is laying low and has contacts in the city. We just need to be there to pick her up," Lane cut in before I said something that would make the situation worse.

Being stuck with six pissed-off werewolves in a plane for two hours wasn't an experience anyone should have. The sound of an engine roaring up to the building we had our offices in told me they were here.

"We'll be out in a moment. Just have to grab a few items first," I said before hanging up and walking over to the wall safe in Lane's office. Opening the door, I pulled out two guns, checked to make sure they were loaded and handed the second to Lane. "There is no fucking way I'm taking any chances or letting anyone take her from us. I will use whatever means necessary to ensure her safety."

Most supers felt it was beneath them to need to use a gun since we were enhanced predators as it is. But I wasn't fooling around when you were dealing with the Senate and possibly a company that trained the best assassins in the U.S.

Lane took the gun and nodded in agreement, tucking the holster into his pants as we headed out to meet up with the others. Time to get our omega back in our arms safe and sound, even if it meant we needed to burn the city down. Nothing would stop us, that's for damn sure.

CHAPTER SIX

FINLEY

After talking with Colt and Lane, I felt like I could breathe a little easier, even if the conversation didn't start out the best. I knew telling them about Rath was going to cause some upset, but I hadn't pictured it going down the way it did. My guilt and Colt's concern created the perfect storm that made my wolf become a puddle of anxiety and I couldn't manage to say anything I wanted to. When Rath took over the call, I stepped out of the vault separating myself from the conversation until I could come to terms with my choices.

Now I had come into my elf nature, it was much easier to balance my emotions. I could reason with my wolf instead of only having my omega nature ruling my life. Yes, I still wanted to please my alphas and look after my newfound pack, but I was able to look at situations more objectively and still feel like my true self—the Finley before getting bitten. Obviously, there would be a learning curve. My elf nature seemed to be fueled by my emotions, good or bad, and my omega side felt every emotion around me. This was the area that was going to take the most work and no one knew exactly how to help me since it's never happened before.

Tucking the phone into my back pocket, Rath and I headed out of the bookstore after letting Oscar know we were leaving. Apparently still uncomfortable with Rath being around, he just gave me a wave and disappeared into this maze of bookshelves.

"This question might sound beyond ignorant, but is there any special concern with what you can eat being an elf?" I asked Rath as we headed down the sidewalk.

His seafoam green eyes danced with laughter at my question, but he didn't tease me about it. "While we prefer to eat a more clean diet of items we've grown ourselves, I can eat anything without complication."

"Just wanted to check before we ended up someplace you couldn't eat. My bank is right up here. After I get my money moved around, we can have breakfast unless there is something you need to do?" I questioned, stopping before walking into the building.

"No, there is nothing pressing that I must do. I really don't even know if there is anyone left. I've been with the Dark Ring for so long I'm sure they've moved the commune," Rath answered, his shoulders sagging slightly as he talked.

My brow scrunched up at the way he made it sound like he's been held captive for years. I suppose it never crossed my mind that he might have people to get back to since I'd been so focused on staying alive.

"How long were you down there?" I asked, my voice barely above a whisper.

"Twenty-five years," he answered as he reached out a hand, cupping my cheek, allowing me to feel the sadness and loneliness he must have felt. "I wasn't in that location long, they were planning on moving us to the auction, and I would be sent to my new master. Being bound with iron cuffs kept me from my magic and weak as a human so I could be controlled. The Dark Ring knows that there are some of us left, not many, mind you, but that just makes those they catch all the more valuable."

Covering his hand with my own, I couldn't help but imagine what it must have been like to be held captive for so long. From his appearance and attitude, you'd never guess he had been a prisoner for a quarter of a century. This proud, strong man had to bend to the will of others, never knowing how long he would remain somewhere or who he would be transferred to next. I felt my wolf brush up against his magic, adding her support, trying to banish the emotions I was feeling at this moment coming off him. Never again would this man be alone. He would always have me at his side, and I will keep that from ever happening to him again.

Rath chuckled as he looked down at me. "What a fierce mate I've found myself. You look as if you will destroy anything that gets in your way right now." Bending down, he kissed me softly on the lips. "It is an honor to see you so protective of me, *nin mel*. I feel very much the same about you. Now enough of this depressing talk. Let us get what you need sorted out so we can eat. Our cans of soup last night left much to be desired and I am rather famished."

Shaking myself out of my emotions, I squared my shoulders and headed into the bank, walking right up to the counter.

"Good morning, how may I help you?" the woman behind the thick bulletproof glass asked through the speaker.

"Morning, I need to speak with someone about transferring some funds from offshore accounts and adjusting some preferences and access to my current accounts," I shared, knowing this would have to be done with a specially qualified employee.

She flashed me a smile and nodded, picking up the phone and speaking quickly. Pausing to listen, she nodded her head along with whatever was being said to her before she hung up and addressed me. "One of our personal bankers will be up to escort you to their office momentarily. If you head over to that small seating area off to the left, they will meet you there."

Offering her a smile, I headed to the seating she gestured to. Before I could even sit, a man in a pressed black suit with a soft blue tie and shiny shoes approached. He paused when he saw me probably not being what he expected or the people he was used to dealing with. Most who would require offshore accounts didn't dress in jeans and a T-shirt their mate created from a wetsuit.

The man quickly caught himself and reached out a hand to greet me. "Good morning, I'm Brian, and I'll be helping you out today."

When I gripped his hand, I discovered that he was attracted to me and not at all a fan of Rath, who was looming protectively over me. This elf was as bad as the wolves when it came to defending what they claimed as theirs. "Thank you. I appreciate the help," I answered, trying to keep the two men from causing a scene.

"Right this way to my office. Can I get you a coffee? Hot tea?" Brian asked, leading the way into his cushy office.

"We're fine, thank you," Rath answered, his voice gruff.

It took everything in me not to roll my eyes and remain professional, but I've discovered some cracks in my cool, calm, and collected exterior with all the new emotions.

"Thank you for the offer," I added, smoothing over Brian's ruffled feathers as he glared at Rath. "Now, I have a few different accounts, but I would like to withdraw from one of the offshore Swiss accounts and pull enough over to the stateside, main account. I would also like to add on names of people who can access it as well."

"Certainly. Do you have account numbers, or will I need to look those up for you?" Brian asked, rolling his chair up to his computer.

"If you hand me a piece of paper, I will write them all down for you," I said as I slipped my ID over to him. "I assume you are going to need that as well to verify along with my signature and pin code?"

Brian blinked at me a few times before he got moving on what I'd asked him for. I quickly wrote out the account numbers and all the other information he needed to find them as he slid over a number keypad for me to input my code. Now that I had proven who I was, things moved quickly.

"How much did you want to take from the Swiss account?" Brian asked.

"Two million, please. I believe that should leave another eight in the account?" I questioned, wanting to make sure I'd kept track correctly.

"Actually, you have almost twelve in the account before we move anything. Does that change your numbers?"

I shook my head. No need to have more where I could get taxed or have someone trace it when I didn't need to. "Two should be fine, and is it possible to get three hundred pulled out in cash for me to use now?"

"Absolutely, we can do that, not a problem," Brian assured me as he typed away on the keyboard. Then something made him pause. "I'm sorry, but you want me to add Zander Vaughan to your account, the superstar?"

"Is that a problem?" I pinched my eyebrows together, forming a crease.

Brian shook his head, looking extremely confused. "It's none of my concern, just seems strange when I'm sure he has more than enough money he wouldn't need yours. I just want to make sure he isn't running some kind of scam on you."

Hearing him bad mouth my mate made my hackles rise and my magic spark under my skin. "You're absolutely right. It is *none* of your concern. The only reason I am giving you justification is because, the last thing he needs is some rumor going around saying he's tricking women into giving him money. He is my mate, and in the supernatural world, that is the same as being husband and wife. I'm sure you have plenty of people who add their significant other to their account, do you not?" My voice was hard as steel as I spoke, even as I kept my body relaxed and face blank, hiding the fact I wanted to rip out his throat.

"I'm so extremely sorry, ma'am. I never should have made assumptions," Brian stuttered, panic was written all over his face.

Rath reached over and took my hand in his, pulling it up to his lips and flooding me with calm, soothing emotions to stabilize my own. "My love, forgive the ignorant human. He didn't know any better," he cooed before turning his gaze to Brian. "Is there anything else you need from her, or can you complete the rest on your own?"

While I never was the type to make others doing their job feel bad, Brian had no right to say what he did. What I did with my money or my personal life was none of his concern. "I agree. If I can get the cash I requested, I believe you have all the information needed." I stood, settling my hands on Brian's desk, and gave him the death stare of an assassin as I spoke the last part, "If I hear anything about Zander using women for money or the fact that we are mated, I will know where it came from and personally deal with the problem."

Brian gulped audibly at my words as he stood, trying to put the office chair between us, letting me know he was taking me seriously. "Of course, ma'am, I apologize for speaking out of turn and butting in where I had no right. Give me a moment to get the cash and you can be on your way."

Rath chuckled as he stood, wrapping an arm around my waist and pulling me tight against him, showing me just how much he enjoyed my possessiveness. "*Nin mel*, do your other mates know how lucky they are to have you? Not many women would think to ensure Zander's reputation stays intact. It's not widely known he's tied to the Senate, but we elves find it best to know who the dangers are as we stay hidden. That and I'm around the same age as him, I believe."

Gasping, I turned in his hold and looked up at him. "Zander is a hundred years old? How did we not know that? The Organization also likes to ensure we have all the best information on big players in the supernatural and human world."

"As I said, they like to keep his information close to the chest with who his mother is," Rath pointed out.

I was unable to ask more about that since Brian returned with an envelope of money and a paper for me to sign. As soon as we were finished, he escorted us to the front door. "Can I call you a cab to take you to where you're going?"

"Thank you, but that won't be needed," I said before Rath could share his feelings on the matter. With a quick wave, I pulled my mate out of the bank and onto the streets. "Remind me that I should run errands like this alone. You all seem to make situations so much worse."

Rath huffed as if I'd offended him by saying that. "*Nin mel*, there is no way that you will be going anywhere without one of us. The

Dark Ring might not know yet that they failed to capture you, but they will be after you soon enough, and we don't know the extent of the connection to the Senate. Personally, I wouldn't discount your previous employers being a part of this as well."

"The Organization doesn't pick sides. They stay neutral until someone pays them to be otherwise. Even then, it's only for a job, and they go back to not caring about what happens in the world unless they can make a profit off it," I countered, not willing to believe that Miranda would go so far to allow them to play me like that.

Now that he'd introduced that idea, it made me think the risk of contacting Miranda would be worth it. She might be the face of the Organization, but she wasn't at the top of the ladder. There was a mystery figure at the top that only stepped in when needed. Could this person be working without telling Miranda what they were doing? Out of the situations I could think of, that seemed to make more sense to me than for them to turn on me so fast. If that was what was happening, then I needed to talk to her. She might be in as much danger as I am if they bring down the Senate on them.

"Whatever has you worried, know that we will figure it out together. Seven brains are better than one, don't you think?" Rath asked as he took my hand in his, giving it a squeeze. "So, where shall we eat?"

Stepping out to the road, I waved my hand at a cab that drove by and it pulled over to pick us up. "I know just the spot. It's near the airport they will be using to fly, so we will be close." Turning to the driver, I gave him the address, and we were off.

One step closer to us all finally being back together.

CHAPTER SEVEN

RATHAL

My mate took us to a restaurant that, at first glance, I wasn't sure was safe for us to even enter. The parking lot had major potholes and the building itself needed some maintenance. The sun-bleached sign read 'The Corner Spot,' but it wasn't even in the corner of the building. Taking in the restaurant, I knew being gone from the world for twenty-five years, things would change, but it was nice to see not too much had passed me by.

"Take a seat where you like and someone will be over to help you," an older woman called out from where she stood, filling a man's coffee mug.

Finley led us to the far corner, the perfect spot for her to see everything going on in the room. The space was clean and open, filled with tables and booths set for whoever might use them next. While the outside left much to be desired, the inside looked far more professional and like I wouldn't get sick of eating whatever I ordered as I feared.

Peeking at Finley's watch, I guessed we had about another hour before her men would land, allowing us to take our time with the meal. There was so much more that I wanted to learn about my mate. Her story was full of mystery and the part of me that grew up among our people felt saddened she didn't get to experience that. Lucky for me, we had nothing but time to talk as we ate our meal and waited.

"What do you suggest?" I asked, a little overwhelmed with the choices. Anything and everything I could possibly want to eat in the breakfast and lunch area of the menu made choosing difficult.

"Anything breakfast is going to be amazing. If you venture outside of that, it becomes a little more questionable," Finley shared, looking at me over the large plastic menu.

Her cobalt eyes seemed to see right into my soul, but they liked to keep their secrets to themselves. I knew she didn't realize that keeping her mind from me was leaving me with a half fulfilled connection with her, but my hope was that when she grew to trust me more, that would change. She didn't know how to trust what her instincts were telling her, that elves don't lie, and neither can their magic. The fates deemed that we would be a fitting pair, and I could see why, but both of us had emotional wounds to contend with as well. While I craved connection, the need to belong and feel safe in my community, she was the opposite. Connection to people scared her, having spent a life where they convinced her she was better off on her own. Then to be made into an omega, I can only imagine the whiplash she must be going through.

Earlier she had commented that her empathic ability was strong. I had a feeling it was her omega side but also a natural giftedness to being a Light Elf and female on top of it. Elven females always had stronger magic abilities, so it didn't come as a surprise when I felt them earlier when she was upset with me about putting her to sleep. It was clear she needed a Guide to make sure she could handle her magic, or she was going to hurt herself or someone else accidentally. Much like when shifters go through their first shift and become more aggressive, having a hard time controlling their wolf, it's the same with magic.

"What can I get for you two?" the waitress asked when she wandered over to us.

Finley gave her request, and I'd been so lost in thought, that I hadn't really looked over the options. "I'll have the same thing, please."

"Alright, I'll be back with the coffee, cream, or sugar for those?" she asked, jotting down on her pad.

"Both please, for me," Finley answered.

"I'll take mine black," I added.

With a nod, our waitress bustled off, leaving us alone once again. There was so much I wanted to ask and talk about, but I could feel Finley start to retreat into herself, full of worry and frustration.

Reaching out, I took her hand, lacing our fingers together, craving contact with her any chance I could get. The physical touch seemed to offset the need to know what she was thinking at all times. At least I could feel her giving me some clue as to what I was dealing with since most of the time her expressions were guarded. I couldn't help but wonder if it was because of me or if that's how she was with her other mates as well. Soon enough, I'd figure that out, but what worried me was if they would accept me. Werewolves were not known for their ability to share, being extremely territorial and possessive on every level.

"Why the frown?" Finley asked, tugging on my hand.

My gaze snapped up to meet hers at the question. "I'll admit I'm a little nervous to meet your other mates. There has never been a *nos* created in such a way, so I don't have any clue how they will take having me added into the mix."

The affectionate smile she gave me as she wrapped my hand in both of hers melted my heart. "I won't lie to you. Well, I guess I can't now that I think of it, but they are alphas and tend to be more reactive, but they are good men. Once you all have a chance to get to know each other, I think emotions will work themselves out. None of us expected to have someone added into the mix, but they knew there was a chance there could be more. We've only been together for a week, so there's a lot we are still working on ourselves. Since I've come into maturity with my elf side, I have no idea how I will respond to situations. My omega nature was running the show, and let me tell you, that was a hard adjustment compared to what I was used to. Although, if I'm being honest, there are traits of it that I'm learning to really enjoy."

Hearing her reassure me, the soft lilt to her voice soothing my nerves was the kind of support only a mate could supply.

"Alright, two orders of chocolate chip pancakes with extra chocolate and whip cream with a side of bacon," the waitress announced as she set the food down along with our coffee. "Here is the syrup for the pancakes, anything else I can get you?"

Finley's face beamed as she looked down at the meal before her. "No, I think we have all we need," I answered, seeing as my mate's attention was fixated on her meal.

With a grunt, our waitress left, and I chuckled, looking down at the giant chocolate-filled pancakes sitting before me. Personally, I wasn't someone who had a large sweet tooth, but it would seem that Finley absolutely did. Taking the syrup, she drowned her plate and hummed as she popped the first bite in her mouth, doing a little dance in her seat. It was the most carefree moment I'd seen from her yet. Joy shined in her eyes as she smiled at me.

Forgoing the added sugar, I cut into my first pancake and took a bite. It was light and fluffy with a hint of vanilla that balanced well with the chocolate helping me understand her obvious delight. "These are excellent."

"They are some of my favorite pancakes in the world, so any time I end up in Florida, I make an excuse to come here to get them," she shared as she snacked on a piece of bacon. "I have to say I was surprised you went for them. You strike me as more of a savory over sweet person."

"You would be correct on that, but I couldn't decide on what to order and figured I would trust what you chose. Next time, I'll have to listen more closely when you order." I laughed.

For the rest of the meal, we talked about our likes and dislikes, information you would ask anyone when you were getting to know them. It was refreshing to feel like I was courting her, even if we were already bonded. We would be spending the rest of our lives together and knowing that she liked the color blue and hated to have cold feet was important to providing her happiness.

We'd just finished our meal when her phone started to ring. Instantly her whole demeanor changed as she looked down at it, then relaxed seeing the number.

"Hello," she answered. With my keen hearing, I was able to pick up the conversation easily enough to know it was her mates.

"Little dove, it's good to hear your voice," a man with a deep voice said. "While I'm glad to hear you're safe and soon to be back in my arms, I feel it's only fair to warn you that there will be a discussion about you running off like you did."

Knowing that I talked to Colt and Lane before, my guess was this must be Zander. Finley's face flushed at his words, telling me that this man wasn't truly upset with her, otherwise there would have been a fight on our hands. Mates do not raise a hand toward their female, no matter what's happened, they are to be cherished in all ways.

"Understood, alpha," Finley answered, her wolf flashing in her eyes and her arousal notable to my senses. "Have you landed?"

"Yes, they are working on refueling and getting the plane ready to return when you get here."

"Perfect, we just finished eating breakfast, but we are in the area, so we should be there in ten minutes or so," Finley said as she caught the waitress's attention.

There was a growl at the mention of her not being alone, but he didn't comment, so I guess the other two had caught him up to speed.

"Be safe, little dove. We will see you soon," Zander purred before hanging up.

Just hearing the way he talked to Finley warned me that he might be the one I needed to watch out for. Colt was quick to anger, but Zander's dominance oozed out of him even over the phone. Watching Finley pay irked me, knowing I didn't have any money to contribute. The commune of elves that I grew up in pooled all the money we had together to keep us hidden and safe. Our chosen queen would be in charge of the money and provide what we needed when we needed it. Our people didn't venture out into the world often, hiding behind our illusions and barriers to ensure that what happened to me didn't happen to everyone.

Since I looked more 'human' than most, I was sent out to gather supplies or information when we needed it. Unfortunately, it was on one of these trips when I'd been caught.

"Ready?" Finley asked, joining me by the main entrance.

Shaking myself out of my thoughts, I flashed her a smile and tucked her arm through mine. "Yes, let's get you home and safe. Then we can plot how we are going to destroy the Dark Ring."

"I like the way you think," she said, nudging me with her shoulder. "It's not too far for us to walk if you're okay with that?"

"A little more time with you to myself, I'll never turn that down," I answered, pressing a kiss to her temple.

CHAPTER EIGHT

FINLEY

Waring emotions of excitement and worry battled inside me as I headed into the lobby of the airport. When I last saw them, the pack was being attacked as a diversion to get me out of there, and I left them. If they did that to me, I would be furious, so I had no right to expect anything different from them.

Zander had already made it known I wasn't going to get out of this without some sort of punishment, but the one person I really didn't know how they would react was Elias. Deep down, I just knew he would be blaming himself for ever leaving my side and sending me alone into the tunnels. He was the type of man to shoulder all the responsibility even if it wasn't his to carry. I still didn't know his story but the feelings I got from him told me it was full of pain and shame. In time, when he was ready, I would be there to listen, but I wasn't going to press the matter.

The moment their scent hit my nose, my wolf rushed to the front of my mind pushing to take over, but I held her back. It took me a second to reason with her that it was best to stay human so we could greet them better, and thankfully, she let me keep control. Dealing with another entity in my own brain was still taking some getting used to, but now that I'd come into my elf nature, my whole body felt more balanced. I spotted them at the back of the lobby area by the bar, some of them sitting while others stood leaning against the bar. All six of them had made the trip this time. I'd wondered if they needed to leave someone behind, clearly, I had my answer on that.

Mason was the first one to notice me and a huge smile graced his beautiful face. His green eyes shone with excitement as he stood and hurried his way over to me, scooping me up in a bear hug and spinning me around. "Snuggles, fuck, it's good to have you back in my arms," he murmured, shoving his face into the crook of my neck and taking a deep breath. "You smell like home and spice."

"Stop hogging her, twin. The rest of us want to get a chance to hold her," Noah grumbled, pulling me from his brother's arms.

The moment Noah pulled me into a hug, all the stress and worry that had been running through my head settled. His chocolate scents seemed to soothe me in a way only he could as he ran a hand down my back, whispering into my ear, "You have no idea how much we missed you. Please don't ever do that to us again. I don't think any of us could survive if anything happened to you."

I should have known my tender-hearted companion would feel the loss more than the others. "I'm sorry, I never should have left."

"All that matters is you are back now, but you better go to Elias before he combusts," Noah directed, pulling back and turning me, so I was facing the man in question.

Looking at my Sentinel, you never would have guessed I'd only been gone for two and a half days. He had shadows under his hazel eyes, his shaggy brown hair looked like he'd been constantly running his hands through it, and his shoulders were rigid as if he had been expecting the worst. "Elias..."

I didn't get more out before his hand darted out and pulled me to him in a bone-crushing hug. He tucked my head under his chin, and his body started to shake like he was crying but being able to sense his emotions, I knew it wasn't tears he was holding back but anger. "Why, why would you leave me? I told you to stay in the tunnels, then you vanished. My heart, you can't do that to me. I can't lose you like I lost all the others. I'm not strong enough to stay human if that were to happen. The world would burn if it took you from me and I would burn with it."

Gently I pushed back from him and lifted my hands to grip his face, pulling it down so he could look me in the eye. "Elias, I'm so sorry. You didn't deserve that from me. It will never happen again. I won't ever run from you or the others, I swear on my life. If I did, then I deserve to be burned with the world who betrayed you." Pressing up onto my toes, I sealed my lips to his in a promise knowing my words held power in them backed by my magic.

My chaste kiss wasn't enough for him as he grabbed my ass and hauled me up, so my legs wrapped around him. He kissed me like I was the one thing who could give him life, nipping at my lower lip before sucking it into his mouth and cleaning the blood off it. He growled and thrust up against me and my body hummed with need for him in a much less intense version of my heat. My body knew he was ours, and we wanted to claim him in all ways, not just with a kiss or words but in every way I could. Elias hissed, causing me to pull back, looking at him questioningly as he set me down. Slowly he lifted his shirt to show the same mark of swirling lines that looked like a heart Rath had. It seems I'd permanently claimed Elias as my own and he had the mark to prove it.

"You came into your magic. We're mated now," Elias whispered in awe as he looked from the mark to me, pride glowing in them. "I can feel you in my mind and heart. The connection, it's tethering me to you forever."

I couldn't help but grin at the excitement he had in his voice as he spoke. Rathal took that moment to step up and introduce himself holding out his hand to Elias. "Welcome to the *nos* officially, *gwanur*. I'm Rathal Zintris, Finley's Guide and another of her mates, but please feel free to call me Rath like *nin mel* has chosen to."

Holding my breath, I waited to see what Elias's reaction would be, but he surprised me by taking Rath's hand and pulling him into a back-slapping bro hug. Out of all the reactions that could have happened, that was not one I was expecting *at all*. I felt my jaw drop at the sight. Elias released Rath and looked over at me, giving me a wink. My surly, brooding beta was winking at me and giving bro hugs—this had to be a dream.

"It's crazy. I can feel him in our pack connection, like I know he's family," Elias explained, turning to the others who looked at him with equal shock and amazement.

Lane frowned at Elias's words and rubbed his chest almost as if he was checking for himself if he was right. "Now that you say that, I can feel him on the edge, only attached to my mate bond with Finley, not the pack, though."

"As you get to know me, that might change," Rath commented, brushing a hand down my back, unconsciously drawn to touch me.

I glanced at him over my shoulder, trying to tell him I was going to my other mates, and I didn't know how things would go after that point. Colt and Zander were not ones to share. Well, neither was Elias, even before we were mated. Maybe there was hope for us all to work this out and live together without anyone trying to kill each other.

Rath nodded at me, pressing a kiss to my temple before stepping back, letting me know he understood.

Zander stood there large and imposing, his arms crossed over his muscular chest. His silver eyes watched me approach with warring emotions in them. Even without touching him, I could tell he was mad but also relieved to have me back. Lane looked stressed and tired, his ever-present hands shoved in his jeans pockets, baseball cap off-center like he kept taking it off to run his hands through his hair. Warm brown eyes shone with love and need, but his emotions told me it wasn't sexual need. It was the comfort of knowing I was in his arms. Colt, on the other hand, was a blaze of emotional extremes, making me need to shield myself from him as I came to a stop right in front of them.

Colt took a step forward, his curly blond hair wild like the wolf that he was, but his body hummed with alpha energy that wouldn't allow you to forget who was in charge. His full beard hid his expression, but I sensed he wasn't smiling. It was only a guess since I couldn't look into his amber eyes with the power he was giving off. My wolf was prone and begging for us to do something to show we were sorry, but my magic flared, pushing back at his energy. I might not be able to meet his gaze because I was an omega, but no longer was I helpless to resist him as I once was. I didn't want to fight him, he was my mate and one of the alphas who loved and cared about me, but I wasn't going to back down.

"Get on the plane, Finley," Zander ordered, stepping up and putting a hand on Colt's shoulder. "We can't deal with this here. They won't understand."

Taking in my surroundings, I noticed that every single person in the lobby was watching what was going on. So much for keeping a low profile, people would recognize Zander, and it would get out that he was here. I should have made them promise that they would send the plane empty so we could have avoided this. Lane stepped around both alphas and wrapped an arm around my shoulders, leading me away from the others.

"You have to understand he feels like he failed again, letting you get taken from him," Lane murmured. "He was right back in the same place when he first lost Cory and his pack all those years ago. Colt's never been one to deal with his emotions well, but he loves you, sweetheart, we all do."

My eyes flicked up to him, wondering if he realized that he had just told me he loved me for the first time.

Did he really mean it?

We've only been together for a week, how can you know something like that?

I decided not to touch on it. If he said it to me again, then I would address it. He was likely running on instinct, having had his mate in danger and now back safe with him. I've learned that wolf nature can be an incredibly powerful thing to contend with and you don't always notice when it's pushing you to do or say things.

Lane led the way from the airport building to the open area where all the planes were parked, waiting for their passengers. The last time I was on this plane, I was headed to Tennessee, starting a new life. Much changed in such a short amount of time. Now, I had four mates and three more that I knew would follow when the time was right. This time, I wasn't overwhelmed by my omega nature, needing to hide in a pile of blankets.

Taking a seat where I could look out the window, I enjoyed how much space I had while curling up in the chair as I watched the others board the plane. The twins gave Colt a cautious look as they sat on the couch, where Elias joined them. Zander headed to the front of the plane to talk to the pilot and other staff, leaving Colt to stare me down as he sat across from me. Before Lane could take the seat, Rath swooped in, stealing the spot next to me, acting almost protectively as if he was worried Colt would get out of hand and I would need him to protect me. If I had to be honest, the one I'd been concerned about was Zander, though he seemed to be holding himself in check better.

"Do you have anything to say for yourself?" Colt asked through clenched teeth. His hands were gripping the armrests as if forcing himself to stay seated.

I took a deep breath, pulling his scent into my lungs, the rich aroma of evergreen and fresh air you only found in the mountains. I didn't pick up any genuine anger that I needed to worry about. Instead, I caught a bite of pain. Reaching out with my magic and omega senses, I sorted through his emotions in more detail after what Lane had told me. The pain I was picking up was twisted up in a knot of self-loathing and failure. Colt had taken this as hard as Elias had, even though they both knew I'd walked away from them. They hadn't done anything wrong.

Slipping out of the chair, I walked over to Colt and dropped to my knees, placing my head in his lap. Right now, words wouldn't mean anything to him with the pain clouding his mind. I could, however, show him how sorry I was. Turning my head, I bared my neck, showing him the spot he'd marked me as his mate, offering up my life to him to do with it as he chose. The tension in the plane was thick enough to cut with a knife as we all waited to see what response Colt would give to my offering. I could feel Lane shifting in his seat like he was going to reach for me, but Colt snarled at him, making Lane freeze.

"Colt," Zander warned.

If there was going to be a problem, Zander was the only one who could do something about it being a stronger alpha than Colt was. I knew deep in my heart that he wouldn't hurt me no matter how upset he was about the situation, so I calmly lay there waiting for Colt to make his move. Colt was my mate, our bond strong between us, humming with the contact as I rested in his lap. Fingers brushed along my skin, moving stray hairs out of his way before leaning down and kissing my neck on his mark. My body shuddered with pleasure at the touch, but when he ran over it with his tongue, I let out a whimper, my body clenching with need. Hearing it, Colt began to purr, nuzzling into the space behind my ear, then buried his nose in my hair.

"*Mine,*" he growled as his hands clamped around my waist and pulled me onto his lap.

I was locked in place by his arms, but I wasn't trying to get away from him. He needed to know that I was okay and back in his arms. I felt a tug as he pulled my hair out of its bun and let it fall free, showing how long it was now. Seeing it, his purr grew louder as he shoved his face into the thick mass, rubbing his cheek along skin, marking me with his scent as he took a deep lungful of mine. I didn't even notice the plane was moving until the captain came over the loudspeaker telling us we'd reached the proper height and were free to move about the cabin.

In a flash, Colt had me cradled in his arms as he got to his feet and headed to the back of the plane, where I discovered a bed. The king-size bed was covered in blankets laced in their scent like they were telling me they'd done this for me, knowing it would settle me. Even though my mates were upset with me, they were still looking out for my needs, and it warmed my heart.

How had I ever thought about not coming back to them?

There was no way I could've known how much they would mean to me in such a short amount of time. Colt settled us both on the bed, then curled around me. I nuzzled my face in his neck as he shielded me from the world, purring and stroking my hair, soothing us both at the same time. The others must have sensed that Colt needed this time alone with me, so they let us be, talking amongst themselves.

Part of me was concerned about Rath. Through our bond, I reached out, and he instantly answered, telling me he was fine and all was well. Finally able to relax, I let out a sigh and snuggled into Colt's warm body.

"As your mate and your alpha, I say these words... you are *never* allowed to leave me like that again. I forbid you to leave pack lands without our approval," Colt ordered, putting his alpha energy into it, making it a command.

I shivered under the power of his words and nodded my head. Something told me that if push came to shove, I could break his order, only I didn't want to. I was willing to accept that command was my punishment for leaving. If giving me that order made him feel better, more secure in my loyalty, then I was fine with it...

... for now.

FINLEY

C olt began to nuzzle into my neck where my mate mark was, running his nose along my skin. When his lips touched my skin, sparks of electricity hummed through my body. He ran his tongue over the length of my neck, causing me to moan as my core clenched with need. Colt knew exactly what he was doing as he teased my mark while I wriggled in his hold, needing to touch him. I slid my hands under his shirt, letting my fingers roam over his skin, enjoying the feel of his warmth. His purr turned into a growl as I flicked one of his nipples playfully.

Seconds later, I was on my back with him looming over me, his eyes burning with the heat of his need. "Are you sure that's the game you want to play, little one?"

"Who's playing games, alpha?" I asked, trying to keep my voice even as I fought back a grin.

Colt darted in and nipped my lower lip. "I thought you were going to be a good girl and beg for my forgiveness?"

"Is that what you want me to do?" I questioned, raising a brow.

"Take off your clothes and get on your knees, mate," Colt ordered, a hint of a growl coating his words as he moved to stand at the end of the bed.

It wasn't a serious order. If I wanted to refuse him, I could, but that was the furthest thought in my mind. Slowly I sat up, holding his gaze as I pulled off my shirt, followed by my sports bra. Getting up on my knees, I unbuttoned my jeans and slowly slid the zipper down, pausing when I hooked my thumbs in the waistband. In a tantalizing sway of my hips, I worked the material off my body, watching as Colt started to breathe heavier and his pupils dilated, watching me hungrily. When I worked my pants down to my knees, I sat back on my heels and kicked out one leg, then the other. Colt surged forward, grabbing them and ripped them off my body, sending the fabric flying across the room.

Colt pounced on me, grabbing my throat while he kissed the fuck out of me, his other hand latching on to one of my breasts. As if seeking payback for flicking his nipple, he found mine and pinched it between his fingers, causing my breath to hitch.

His possessive need was all-consuming, and my wolf purred in plea-sure, wanting more. I wrapped my arms and legs around him, needing him closer as our kiss deepened. Holding him firmly to me, I lifted my hips, grinding into him, his hard cock begging to be set free.

After I slightly relaxed my hips, I reached down, yanking his pants open to wrap my hand around his hard, silky length.

He groaned into my mouth before pulling back. "Fuck, little one, your touch feels so good, but I need more. I need to see your lips wrapped around my dick as I claim that pretty mouth of yours."

Scooping me up, he laid down and flipped me around so my ass was in his face and his cock was ready for me. I attempted to shove his pants down further, allowing me more room, but he kicked them off.

His hands massaged my ass, his fingers ghosting past where I wanted his attention desperately, making me buck my hips, begging him to do what I wanted.

"Oh no, little one. It's not going to be that easy. You need to atone for leaving me. You'll get what you need when I feel you deserve it," Colt taunted as he ran a finger through the valley of my ass down to my clit, giving it a little flick at the end. I cried out at the simple touch and knew I was drenched, my omega anatomy helping me out, making sure I was ready to be knotted. Not that it looked like that was going to happen any time soon if Colt got his way. With a sudden thwack of his hand against my ass, I jolted in shock, then quickly moaned as he kissed the sting left by his hand. "If you want my knot, you better get to work. This flight is only two hours."

Needing no more motivation, I gripped his cock with one hand and licked the tip as it oozed with pre-cum. Humming to myself at the taste, I flicked the crown of his dick a few more times teasing him just as he'd been teasing me. When I got another smack on the ass, I knew playing this game would mean I lost in the end, so I got down to business. Taking him deep into my mouth, I expected to have an issue when he hit the back of my throat, but it appeared that being an omega meant I didn't have a gag reflex. Normally at this point, I would need to back off, but instead, I went deeper, letting him down my throat until my lips kissed the skin of his lower abdomen.

"Oh fuck yes, little one, that's a good girl," Colt grunted.

Pulling back, I bobbed my head working his whole length, making sure I wasn't moving too fast or too slow. His hands on my hips clenched when I took him all the way once more and swallowed a few times.

"Fuck, fuck, fuck," he muttered, his hips thrusting up into me, trying to get deeper. "Holy fuck."

Lifting my head, I gripped the base where his knot started to swell, and I squeezed as tight as I could while I managed the rest of his cock. Apparently, I'd done enough to earn forgiveness because Colt dove into my pussy like it was his last meal. His tongue swirled around my clit followed by a graze of his teeth. Tossing my head back, I let out a moan as I pressed back, forcing myself on his mouth as his tongue thrust into me. My eyes started to roll back in my head when he inserted two fingers into my pussy and his thumb in my ass and started to thrust.

"Don't stop now, little one. I've just started," Colt informed me before latching his lips around my clit.

"Yes, oh God, yes, just like that. Fill me every way you can," I begged, pumping my hand up and down his shaft before getting back down to the task at hand.

Now I worked him fast as I felt my climax building. The way he moved his fingers in my pussy was hitting all the right spots even though I craved more. I needed the fullness only a knot could provide, but I had to convince Colt I deserved it first. Reaching lower, I grabbed his balls and started to play with them making him grunt and clench his ass cheeks at the touch.

"Little one, if you keep doing that, this is going to be over before you get what you desperately want," Colt said with a growl.

I looked over my shoulder at him with a smirk. "Does that mean I'm forgiven if you're willing to give me your knot?"

Colt's answer was to shove me forward off him, so my face was in the blankets on the bed, ass up in the air. The only warning I got that he was entering me was the fact he ran his cock through my wetness once before he was balls deep. There was no way I could hold back the scream of pleasure as he started to fuck me hard like he still wasn't sure if I'd been punished enough or not. His strong hands were clamped on my hips, pulling me back on him as he thrust forward, shoving his cock as deep as it would go.

"Tell me you're never going to leave me again," Colt ordered as he bent over to pull me up so my back was pressed to his front. Then he wrapped a hand around my throat as he thrust up into me, his lips brushing my ear. "Make me believe that you truly want to be with us and will trust us to take care of you. Tell me that you're mine, ours to keep forever."

The onslaught of pleasure and the hint of pain combined with his words sent me barreling into an orgasm as I cried out my answer. "God, yes, I'm yours. I will always be yours!"

"That's what I thought," Colt said, turning my head so he could kiss me thoroughly as his knot started to swell. "Finley, I don't give a fuck why you left or who might be after you as long as you know who you truly belong to."

"I belong to the alphas and betas of the Knoxville pack along with my elven mate and no one else," I gasped as he sped up to a pace no human could ever achieve.

Pushing us both down on the bed so his body was draped over mine, he railed me until I didn't think I could hold on any longer, shooting me into another climax, but this time, he followed me over the cliff. His knot fully swelled, locking us together as he began his short thrusts making it so I couldn't tell where he ended and I began.

The world was technicolor as my brain was overloaded with sensations while Colt sucked on his mate mark, throwing me directly into another orgasm, making me whimper in a pleasure-filled stupor. Then, finally, he relented and rolled us to our sides, where we both panted, trying to catch our breath and let our bodies come back down to earth.

"Finley, I know we haven't been together long at all, but I'm falling in love with you," Colt whispered, his lips brushing along the back of my neck.

Unsure of how I felt or how I should respond, I wrapped his arms tighter around myself, getting him as close to me as I could. These men were becoming to mean more to me than anyone else in my entire life, but I didn't know what it felt like to be in love. That was one emotion I didn't know I had ever felt for real. I didn't remember my parents, and there was certainly no love in the Organization. Plus, I'd never had a relationship before. All these circumstances left me woefully unprepared for a moment like this.

"What does love feel like?" I asked as I threaded my fingers through one of his hands. "I don't know that I've ever experienced that before."

He pressed another kiss to the skin between my shoulder blades, resting his head in the crook of my shoulder. "Open yourself up to me. I know doing that overwhelms you with my emotions, but there isn't a better way to explain how I feel right now with words."

Trusting him, I slowly started to let down my walls allowing me to access that empathic part of me. Colt had been right. There were no words to describe what I was feeling, and every time I tried, it just seemed like it wasn't enough. Nothing matched the intensity of this emotion that he called love. It was overwhelming, but not in a way it made me want to pull back from it. Instead, all I wanted was to wrap it around myself and never feel anything else. It was so pure, warm, and inviting that it made me sigh and relax into Colt's arms, molding myself to him.

How could he possibly feel something like this for me in such a short time?

"If that is what love feels like, then I know I've never experienced it before," I shared. Now that I was fully exposed to his emotions, I could sense hurt at my rejection and sadness for never having been loved before. Shifting as much as I could while still connected to him, I cupped his cheek. "That isn't to say that I won't someday, Colt. I think if there is ever a chance for me to learn what it means to be loved and feel love, it will be because of you and the others. No one has ever taken the time to show me love or make me understand how amazing love can be. I want to learn, so someday I can love you back," I explained the best I could.

This seemed to settle Colt. "It would be my honor to show you just how amazing love can be between two or seven people, as it were in our case."

"I look forward to it, but until then, know that I care deeply about you and the others. It killed me to leave you, but doing so showed me just how much you all matter to me, and I won't let it happen again."

He let out a growl. "You better not, or I'll really punish you for it, and it won't end up with me knotting you either."

"Understood, alpha," I answered, kissing him deeply.

We curled up to enjoy the time together, just the two of us, as we waited for his knot to subside.

CHAPTER TEN

FINLEY

Colt and I joined the others back out in the main cabin area for the last hour of the flight. None of them commented that Colt just railed me in the back bedroom—loudly. They all seemed to simply be happy I was back.

Seeing the others relaxed, sipping on drinks, I decided that Colt had enough alone time, and I curled up with Elias, feeling the need to be close to him after marking him. He happily wrapped me up in his arms and nuzzled into my hair, pressing a kiss to my head.

"You feel up to telling us what happened, my heart?" Elias asked as he tucked my head under his chin.

This was what I'd expected would happen when I came back out here. It was time to stop holding back secrets. What was happening in my life now affected them just as much as it did myself. "It all started with a note I found in my pocket when we got back from going into town. It told me that the Dark Ring was coming after me and I needed to get away from the pack. They told me I would know the signal alerting me to the best time to leave without being noticed, so when the attack happened, I knew that's what it had to be."

"Wait, you're telling me that all that went down just to give you cover?" Lane asked, his brows knitted together at the idea. "I assumed there had to be a bigger reason. They even had a vampire come looking for you."

"A vampire?" I questioned, thinking back to what happened back in Miami. "That doesn't make any sense if the Organization doesn't mix human and supernatural operatives if they pair people up at all. They had to have been there for another reason. Maybe the attack was the Dark Ring, but when they figured out I was gone, they moved on."

"If the Dark Ring attacked, they would have taken whoever they could to sell them off," Zander pointed out. "It means we have a third player in this game."

My brain was working a mile a minute, trying to look at this from all angles with all that I knew and learned over the last forty-eight hours. They hinted that there was a mole in the Senate. What if that mole wasn't just someone listening and gathering information but another active member? What if a full member of the Dark Ring was in the Senate making matters work for them, avoiding all the trouble, knowing it was coming. From what we heard from the underground, the Senate didn't work well together. The two shifter leaders hated each other, the witches didn't respect anyone, and the vampires were power-hungry, and when the wizards involved themselves with anything, it was never good. The human who held a Senate seat was more of a joke. No one cared what they thought, believing it should have only been supers. It wouldn't surprise me one bit if the humans created the Dark Ring to level the playing field among the races.

"*Nin mel*, I can feel your mind working a million miles an hour. What is it you're dwelling on?" Rath asked, drawing me out of my thoughts.

"Let me explain the rest of this before I share my thoughts. It will help to explain my logic," I countered, shifting so I could sit up straighter on Elias's lap. "After I got out of the tunnels and arrived at the meeting point, a member of the Organization that I knew well was waiting for me with two others I'd never met. I was informed that I was being brought back into the fold and needed to finish the job I started for the Senate, the job where I met Cory and got bit," I explained to the others, unsure if my alphas had filled them in or not.

"The job went south, and I failed to kill my target. My contact told me if I didn't complete this job, I would be killed, no questions asked, which I didn't doubt. You don't fail the Organization, let alone the Senate when they give you an order. So I went with them, and we ended up at a safe house in Florida, where we worked out the plan. My target was another known member of the Dark Ring. I was to kill him before he could sell off more supers for auction. The second part was to find out where he was keeping them and get them the hell out of there."

The guys all turned to Rath, finally seeing where he came into all of this.

"As you might have ascertained, I was a prisoner of the Dark Ring for the past twenty-five years," Rath shared. "The last thing I ever expected was to have my mate walk into the bunker Rupert Sutton was keeping us in. She was attacked by the man they had guarding us, but it was at that moment she also came into her power, allowing her to free herself and all of us. Finley is a powerful Light Elf, the likes our people haven't seen in a long time. I can't remember the last time a female called a Guide to her, let alone six others, before her powers matured. This is going to make everything far more treacherous for us because the other supers she freed know the truth and there is no way for us to keep it quiet for long."

"I'm still not understanding where the connection to the Senate is coming into play," Zander pressed, his full lips turned down.

Feeling restless, I slipped off Elias's lap and started to pace, my magic churning inside me at my agitation. "Once I freed the other supers, I went back up to make sure Sutton was dead. I'd left him somewhat alive in case I needed him for something else. When I got back to his room, I found him dead, but before I could do much else, one of my team turned on me, which led to me gutting him. He told me as he was dying that I wasn't ever supposed to make it out of that job. Instead, I was supposed to be captured and sold off like the rest or end up back with Dalilah, who was under the impression I could make her more omegas to sell. The final thing that he told me as I questioned him about the Senate was that I had to find out for myself how far this whole thing went."

Taking a breath, I combed my hands through my hair, trying to get my emotions under control. "What if the Senate isn't working with the Dark Ring, but they created the damn group? We all know that the humans involved with the Senate hate us supers. I could absolutely see them create a faction that's sole purpose was to use and abuse us, keeping them at the top of the food chain. I mean, they fucking held a Light Elf for twenty-five years! There's no way that could happen unless they had intimate knowledge of all supers' weaknesses. The only text we have left is with the Senate, or at least that's what you told me, Zander."

Noah stood and stepped up to me, cupping my face between his hands. "Breathe, Finley, you need to take a deep breath, or you're going to send yourself into a panic attack." He could see that I wanted to argue, but when he gave me a disapproving look, I gave in. "Follow my lead, deep breath in... now let it out," Noah instructed as he followed along with me. "Good girl, now, take a seat with Mason, and I'm going to get you something to drink and a blanket to snuggle with."

My bottom lip popped out in a pout. I wanted to be upset about the fact that Noah felt the need to manage my emotions, but I listened since what he suggested sounded like exactly what I needed.

"Come here, snuggles," Mason called, reaching out to me with a grin and grabby hands. "Clearly, you haven't noticed it, but your omega side is having a meltdown."

Shocked at his words, I took stock of my emotions and found that my wolf was indeed on the verge of hiding herself in a corner as my magic raged under my skin. It seemed that when I become agitated, it triggered my magic, and the fallout from that also seemed to upset my wolf.

She was whimpering and trying to find a place in my mind where the magic couldn't chase her. I allowed Mason to pull me down, so I was sitting next to him, but that clearly wasn't what he had in mind, so he pressed my head down so it rested on his lap. His strong fingers started to massage my scalp and I couldn't hold back the purr from how good it felt. A soft blanket settled over me, and it smelled like Lane but also had a mix of Colt and myself from having been on the bed in the back.

Noah lifted my legs and sat next to his brother, tucking the blanket around me, then started to rub my feet. An automatic sigh of relief filled my lungs, and when I let the breath out, I felt a little more centered.

"Are both of you her Companions?" Rath asked with curiosity in his eyes, looking at the twins.

"I'm her full-time Companion. I guess you could say Mason is her Hunter, but she said he also feels like her Companion," Noah explained.

Rath nodded, watching me with them as some emotion I couldn't decipher flickered across his face. When I reached out to him, trying to figure it out, I found his shields were up, locking me out of his thoughts and emotions. Knowing how important he felt that connection was, it unsettled me that he was blocking me from reading him.

He seemed to notice and a soft smile graced his face. "Fret not, *nin mel*, I am simply trying not to add to the problem you are dealing with right now. More emotions would be counterproductive at this moment. I'm not trying to hide from you. Although I will say that I feel at a disadvantage since it seems that your omega nature is just as strong as your magic. They are linked, which is why your agitation set off the other. It will make it all that more important for us to get working on training you and your magic."

"My wolf doesn't like my magic at all," I shared. "Just now, she was trying to hide, but my magic wasn't allowing her to avoid it."

"Hmm," Rath hummed, tapping his chin. "I wonder if there is a way to get the two to be combined and work together as one instead of it being two separate entities in your mind. I will need to think that over a bit longer. Maybe I'll do some checking and see if there is a way to find my commune or if anyone is left."

"Do you think her magic is hurting her wolf?" Elias demanded, his face showing how he felt about that idea.

Rath shook his head. "No, I don't think it is harming her. Her magic is something that is a part of her, just as her DNA is. The addition of the wolf is probably setting off some instinctual alert to try and protect her from a foreign entity. As far as I know, never in our history has an elf been bitten by a wolf and lived to tell us. I will say that back before the Elven War, we Light Elves were extremely protective in keeping our kind pure after seeing what happened when we mated with witches and wizards, and they tainted our magic, creating the Dark Elves. If it did happen, I wouldn't have put it past them to kill the 'infected' elf to save them from polluting our blood."

"What about now?" Colt snarled, his hands gripping the armrest so tightly it crumpled. "Do you view it the same way, *elf*? *A*re you going to kill her for being tainted by our kind? Because if that's the case, I'm more than happy to give you a one-way ride out of this plane."

The fight that I'd been worried about them having and thought we'd managed to avoid was now brewing. If Colt and Zander went after Rath, I truly wasn't sure how things would end, but no matter what, someone would be dead.

"You better stuff that growl back down your throat before I do it for you, *wolf*," Rath snapped. "Finley is my mate and perfect in every way. She is more than I ever could have imagined for myself and I plan to treasure her for the rest of my life. On top of that, if anything ever happened to her, we would all die. She could manage to live without us with how strong she is, but none of us would. To kill her is to kill those mated to her. It's one reason our females are so protected. Take out the right female, and you could wipe out all the men with her. Some of our females back in the golden age had upward of fifteen mates. Now it's more like three, so for Finley to have seven of us proves her strength."

The others looked at Rath in stunned silence.

"Say that again," Zander ordered.

Rath gave a frustrated huff rubbing his forehead. "Do you know nothing about elves these days? Anyone who is mated to Finley will die if she is killed. On the other hand, if she loses one of us, she will be able to recover physically, but I wouldn't be able to speak to her mental state."

"How the fuck would we know about elves when there are supposedly none left and all the books about them have been locked away by the Senate?" Mason muttered as he played with my hair.

"They what?" Rath asked. "Why would they hide away that information?"

Now it was Zander's turn to snort, covering up laughter. "How old are you, elf?"

"I was alive when you were born," he answered. "I'm not ignorant to the world as a whole, but when you are living in hiding, it makes it challenging to keep up with all the changes in the world. We keep an eye on the Senate more as a way to avoid them."

"The first Senate that was created decided that all material pertaining to elves would be too dangerous to leave out where the public could access them. So their solution, not wanting to destroy the information, was to lock it away. My mother has been working with a friend who spent time with the elves, but now I'm wondering if it wasn't the elves of old or maybe a commune like yours. Do you know if there are any other groupings, or is where you grew up the last of it?" Zander inquired.

Rath still seemed to be stuck on the fact that the Senate had tried to wipe his race from existence. "There might be others, but they wouldn't have contacted us to ensure they stayed hidden. Creating a larger group is harder to hide."

The speakers above crackled to life, letting us know that we were preparing to land. Glancing at my watch, I saw it was late afternoon at this point, and my stomach started to growl.

"Did you remember to eat at all without me around to nag you?" Mason asked with a chuckle, tucking my hair behind my ear. "Think you can survive until we get back to the house, or do we need to stop along the way?"

A pillow flew out of nowhere, hitting Mason in the face. "How many times do I have to tell you all that she's not eating fast food shit while I'm around. We'll go back to my house and I'll make sure she gets a proper meal like a good mate."

Mason let out a frustrated growl. "Uptight bastard." Glancing down at me, he winked, making me smile, then I snuggled into him as we relaxed for the descent back into Tennessee.

Is this what coming home feels like?

CHAPTER ELEVEN

FINLEY

Stepping back into Zander's home brought me a sense of peace, one I didn't know I'd ever really had before. Having all their scents filtering around the space, knowing I had my personal items here and even a room to call my own, made me realize this was *my* home to me now.

Sitting at the kitchen island, I watched Zander as he pulled food out of the refrigerator to make something to eat. On the way here, my stomach had grumbled again in the car. Both he and Mason were obsessed with me eating enough and making sure I was healthy. It wasn't like I'd spent the last thirty years taking care of myself, but I was learning it was nice to have them taking care of me.

"Is there a place that I might clean up and get a change of clothes?" Rath asked, standing in the kitchen, taking in the house.

Slipping off the chair, I grabbed his hand and looked at the others. "I'm gonna do the same thing so I can take him up. Are any of the rooms on the second floor still open?"

Right before all this went down, we had just decided to have everyone move into this house, but I didn't know if that actually happened.

"The first three have been claimed by us betas, but the other two are open so Rath can take his pick," Noah informed me.

My gaze instinctively went to Zander since it was his house and I didn't want to assume the rest of us had the right to dictate that kind of thing. Meeting my gaze, Zander handed his wooden spoon over to Mason, who took over the cooking and stalked over to me. Gripping my jaw with his fingers, Zander forced me to look up at him. "What did I tell you about this house?"

"That it's my house too," I whispered, my wolf cringing that we had displeased him by not trusting what he told us.

"Correct, and what is Rath to you?" Zander pressed.

My eyes flicked in Rath's direction and I licked my lips before returning to Zander's gray gaze. "He's one of my mates."

"Good girl, now doesn't that make you think he would have a place in your house? He can pick any room he likes as long as it isn't my bed or your nest because that space is for you alone," Zander stated, his tone brokering no argument.

"There aren't enough rooms, though," I murmured. "We are one room short."

"Mason and I can share a room. We've done it most of our lives, so it doesn't bother us," Noah answered, solving the problem. "One of the rooms we picked is larger than the other so we can make it work, but that isn't something you need to worry about. As your mates, your pack, and *nos,* we will always make sure that what's yours is looked after, including your mates."

"You were absolutely born to be her Companion. You come to it naturally and do it well," Rath praised Noah. "Thank you for making me feel welcome in your home and pack. I know it's hard when this is not how relationships normally work for your kind."

Zander met Rath's gaze. "No matter what, Finley's care comes first, however that presents itself." Looking back down at me, he pressed a kiss to my lips and released me. "Now go show him to the rooms he can pick from and get yourself cleaned up. I'll have food ready for you when you come back down."

I gave him a soft smile as I entwined my fingers with Rath's and led him up the stairs, still trying to figure out how the hell I ended up with this life. Everything in the house looked just as I'd left it. I know it was only three days ago, but it felt like so much had happened since then. I paused at the two doors across from each other and closest to my nest.

"All of them have attached bathrooms, so no one has to share. Zander's room is up one more level. I'll grab some clothes since I think he is the one closest to your height. That's where they have me staying, but this room is my nest if you ever can't find me in the house." I shared, pointing to the door at the end of the hall.

Rath pulled me close and kissed my forehead. "Thank you, *nin mel,* now go do as your alpha asked. I'll be fine to figure out the rest on my own. There is no need to worry over me. The others are taking this well and I'm not unable to handle matters myself."

I knew that in my brain, but my heart was already so protective over him, I didn't know what to do. Rath seemed to understand my inner turmoil and picked me up so my legs wrapped around his hips. Then he walked into the room on the right. It was simple with a queen bed, dresser, nightstand, and a comfy chair.

The view out the window was of the forest, but I felt like no matter what window you looked out, it had a great view. The colors of the room were soft tans and creams, making it incredibly calming. Peeking into the bathroom, there was the standard shower, sink, and toilet combo. He continued to carry me into the room across the hall, and this one was a mirror replica of the other, but the colors were soft sage greens that reminded me of a darker version of his eyes.

"I think I will settle in here just fine. It is peaceful, and green is one of my favorite colors," Rath mused to himself, kissing me on the cheek. "Now, shall we go up and shower?"

Blinking at him in surprise, I tilted my head, trying to figure out what he was thinking. "Do you not like the bathrooms down here?"

"They are fine, *nin mel*, but you will not relax unless I'm with you. Elven females are some of the most territorial women out there. Right now, you don't completely trust your other mates to look out for me, so you are being driven to keep an eye on me. I have to admit it's incredibly flattering to have you act this way, even in your own home. So to make matters easier on both of us, I figured we could just clean up together," he explained, smiling at me.

Unsure how I felt about what he was saying, I just nodded my agreement, and we headed up to the space I shared with Zander. Once on the top floor, Rath set me down on my feet, and I led us straight to the bathroom.

"For a man who wasn't planning on sharing his mate, he sure has a big enough bed for group activities," Rath commented with a chuckle.

"It's come in handy. When I first shifted, my heat came quickly after, so at one point, all of us were in that bed... until the betas got kicked out of it," I said, remembering how crazy all of that had been.

I flipped on the shower, turning on all the different heads, so neither of us would be cold as we washed up. It was one reason I'd never been a fan of shower sex. Someone was always left in the cold. Zander had found the solution to it, even if that wasn't the intent when he had it built.

Peeling out of my clothes, I stepped under the steaming water and hummed at the feeling of finally cleaning up after all we'd been through. A body stepped up behind me, settling his hands on my hips as I leaned back into him. He kissed down my neck opposite of Colt's mark while brushing his hands upward until he cupped my breasts, his thumbs caressing my nipples that were begging for the attention. My body didn't care that we'd had sex a few hours ago. It begged to be touched as if I was starved.

"So beautiful," Rath murmured in my ear. "The fates blessed me when they gave me you to treasure, my love."

His lips journeyed from my ear down my neck, licking the water off the hollow of my collarbone. My skin burned where he touched it, leaving me completely aware of everything he was doing. I rubbed my ass against his erection, nestled between my cheeks, begging for attention.

"Trust me, *nin mel* I want nothing more than to pin you against the wall of the shower and show you just how much I yearn to know what your body feels like. But I think it's best if we get you cleaned up first. You're tired, even if you aren't letting yourself feel it yet. You didn't get much sleep the other night. Then there is the massive amount of power you used that would have knocked anyone out for a day at least. Let me treasure you for now. We have all the time in the world to explore each other."

I couldn't help but whimper in my disappointment, hearing he didn't want me. My wolf was disheartened and my magic rebelled at the idea our mate would reject our advances.

Were we not good enough for him?

Did he desire another?

That thought made me growl in anger. Stepping away from him, I let out a whine.

"Maybe you should shower on your own then, since we have *all the time in the world*," I tossed back at him, grabbing the shampoo Zander had bought for me.

Rath sucked in a breath, telling me he figured out I was upset with him. "*Nin mel...*"

I sidestepped him as he reached for me. "No, you made it clear that my advances at the moment aren't welcome."

"That is not what I meant at all. We are new to each other and I didn't want you to feel forced to be intimate with me if you weren't ready. Our bond wants us to finish the process. We've bound our souls together but not our bodies, so it's tricking your body into thinking that's what needs to happen. I don't want what happened when you went into heat to happen between us as well," Rath reasoned.

Glaring at him, I shook my head. "You don't get it. They gave me the option to have them leave or have the betas take care of me because it would be easier for them not to mark me. I wanted them. Deep down in my soul, I knew they were mine, and I was theirs. Was it the most romantic situation or something I expected? No. Do I regret it? Fuck no. They are my mates and so are the others. They trusted me to know what the right call was. Lane was like you, feeling as if he was taking advantage of me, but if you believe that the fates brought us together, then there shouldn't be any doubt from you in regard to me."

Rath opened his mouth to argue, but Zander entered the bathroom, shedding his shirt, and entered the shower to scoop me up and cradle me to his chest. "I tried to leave you two alone to figure it out, but I couldn't ignore your whine any longer. My wolf was going crazy, and I wasn't sure I could hold him back much longer. That and it doesn't seem like things were going in the right direction between you two."

Zander sat down on the tiled bench that ran the whole length of the shower, running a hand over my hip, making me purr at the touch. Zander wanted me. I could smell it pouring out of every pore of his body. Holding me like this, I could also feel his cock harden under my ass.

"How much do you know about omegas?" Zander asked Rath.

"I suppose what most people know about them. They hold the pack together, although they are incredibly submissive, holding the lowest rank in the pack. They are guarded and treasured by their alphas and other pack members, and can only be produced by wolves, typically born wolves. The fact that Finley has become one must have something to do with her being an elf since I've never heard of one being created from a bite before," Rath said as he looked down at me in Zander's arms.

Zander nodded as if that's what he expected to hear. "Most of that is true but does nothing to tell you what an omega truly is. Omegas are the barometer of how well the pack is doing. A happy, healthy omega means a happy, healthy pack. They are treasured, and not simply because they are rare or weak but because they are the living, breathing heart of the pack. Finley is new to ours, and the pack is still getting to know her, which is also true for her. Once the bond grows between a pack and an omega, that's when the magic truly happens. Omegas run on pure emotion, giving from themselves as they receive from others."

"Elves are emotional beings as well but only with their *nos* due to the connection they have being mated," Rath shared. "I'm not sure what that has to do with why Finley is upset with me?"

"Omegas also have the need to please those they bond or mate with along with having a high sex drive. Being intimate with their chosen person or, in our case, people is needed for them to feel confident in their connection to each other. You told her no, and I'm guessing the reason you gave her didn't calm her fears about you finding her appealing in that way. I can also tell that something was stirred up in her other nature because she was pissed at you. I've seen her mad, but the scent I got off her told me it wasn't because she didn't agree with a rule or an order you gave her. It was personal."

As Zander laid out my feelings for Rath, I hid my face in his neck, not wanting to look at whatever expression Rath had on his face now that he knew his words hurt me. Rationally, I knew he had no right to be mad at me, and I was allowed to feel how I was feeling, but being back around the pack brought my omega tendencies out more. The interesting part was that it made my magic more volatile and I didn't know what to do about it. My emotions swung all over the spectrum and it caused chaos in all my natures equally.

"*Nin mel*, will you tell me why you are truly upset with me?" Rath asked, his hand running down my arm.

Peeking at him, I found he was now kneeling in front of Zander, so he was eye level with me. "You rejected me. The only reason you would do that is if you didn't want me or had another you wanted instead."

Saying it out loud made me groan. I sounded like a child whose feelings were hurt. Never in my life had I cared if someone was into me or not. Just when I thought I was getting a hang on these emotions, shit like this kept popping up. I started to pull out of Zander's hold, but he gave me a warning growl and held tighter.

"No, little dove, this is important," Zander scolded. "The only way we will all work together in this is if we deal with our problems and not brush them off. I get that emotion and situations like this are hard for you, not having much experience, but this needs to be fixed."

Letting out a sigh, I turned to face Rath. The matter was in his hands how he wanted to move forward.

"Do you really believe that I don't want you?" Rath asked, his seafoam-colored eyes pinning me where I sat.

"I can't scent any desire from you, and you still have me shut out of your emotions. The only thing I have to judge you on is your words and actions, which both told me you didn't want my advances," I answered bluntly.

"Alright, I can fix one of those problems because I'm not sure how to deal with the scent part of it. Elves don't give off much scent. It's what made it so easy to live in the forest among the animals. They were never afraid of our presence or the scent we gave off. It made us the elite fighters we are," Rath educated me. "As for my emotions, I need to learn how to allow you to feel them without them overwhelming you considering your sensitivity to them, but I won't shut you out anymore."

"I'm also willing to work on finding a way for you to have more access to my emotions as well. If you have that connection to me, it might help us both since that is how us elves are supposed to be as a mated couple," I offered, feeling it wasn't fair to just put the blame on him for this problem.

Zander started to purr as he nuzzled my neck. "Good, little dove, now I think it's time we show you just how important you are to us."

He shifted me so I was now facing Rath with my back resting against his chest before settling his hands on my knees and opening them so they hung over his legs. Deciding I wasn't how he wanted me just yet, he spread his legs open, exposing me to Rath, who was getting a perfect view of my needy pussy.

"See something you like, *elf*?" Zander taunted.

Rath licked his lips as he held my gaze. "Has to be the most delicious thing I've ever seen."

"I would tell you how good it tastes, but I don't want to ruin the surprise," Zander said with a smirk, then started to nibble on my ear and down my throat. "What I will warn you, though, is once you've tasted her, there's no going back. You'll be addicted for life."

My alpha's purr rattled my bones in the best way, vibrating my body to the point of madness if someone didn't do something about it, so I let out a whine. "Please, someone touch me."

"Ah, little dove, you know an alpha can't ignore an omega's whine," Zander whispered in my ear. "Better get to work, don't you think, elf?"

Rath gave me a sultry grin before diving in between my legs.

CHAPTER TWELVE

RATHAL

My mate doubted my feelings for her. I needed to make it blatantly clear how much I wanted her. Yes, I was physically attracted to her, but it was more than that. She was the other half of my soul even if we've just met each other. That was how the fates work, they knew who the perfect person was for each of us, and she was *mine*. Elves didn't have the same hang-ups as the wolves did with sharing. We knew from birth there would be at least one other in our *nos*. Now here was one of my *gwanur,* presenting me with an opportunity to share her between us. Zander didn't have to step in and help me. He could have let me fail and swooped in to save the moment, but he didn't.

I will be forever grateful for it because I now had my face buried in my mate's pussy, devouring her. Her scent was strong and spicy with a hint of sweetness to it that made it addicting. I'd told her elves don't have that much of a scent, but hers was enthralling, probably enhanced by being a werewolf. Finley moaned as I sucked on her clit, teasing her entrance with my finger, not ready to give in to my need to feel her in every way. After how I'd made her feel, I didn't deserve it—yet. When she started to beg me for more, I'd know she wasn't as mad at me anymore.

Zander's hands were on her breasts as he kissed along her neck and shoulders, then claimed her mouth, trapping all her delicious moans, keeping them for himself. That's fine. I'd find a way to get her to pull herself away from him to beg me for more. It was just going to push me to work harder.

Lapping at her weeping core, I saw firsthand how it was that an omega could take an alpha's knot. The slick was more than what a normal human or elf would provide in this situation, but it made it all that much easier to play with her. Pulling my mouth back, I took my finger and swirled it around her clit, through her folds, and down to her tight entrance in the back, gently pressing at it but not allowing my finger to enter. I needed to know she forgave me and wanted me to touch her more. Never would I do something against her will and I felt like Zander's order made us unbalanced. She might be his omega, but to me, a mate was an equal, if not the more dominant partner in the relationship.

"Rath, please don't tease me," Finley whimpered, thrusting her hips up, trying to catch my finger where she wanted it most. "I need something to fill me. I feel so empty."

Her need drove me into action. No mate of mine would be left wanting. "How do you want to be filled?" I asked, hoping she would tell me what she needed.

"Till I can't take anymore, I want both of you to stuff me with your cocks," Finley begged, her eyes going glassy with her need.

My gaze flicked up to Zander, and he just smirked, pleased with her request, no longer having to be a bystander. "Hold her while I get my pants off."

I expected him just to slide her over to me, but instead, he dropped her right on my dick, making her gasp as I was now balls deep in my mate. "Oh God, yes! I need more, though… I need, so much need."

"This is how she gets going two days without sex?" I asked as she wriggled on my cock, swirling her hips, making me hiss with pleasure.

"No, this is her taking two new mates and not sealing the deal. It should be Elias instead of me, but that possessive bastard is gonna want their first time all to himself," Zander muttered as his wet jeans hit the floor outside the shower. "You gonna lie back or stand?"

It took me a moment to comprehend his words, with Finley riding me, unable to keep her hips still. Tucking my arms under her legs so I could hold her securely, I stood turning so Finley's ass was open to him. Zander stepped up to her and immediately started to nudge her with his cock.

"Don't you need to prepare her?" I warned, not liking the idea of him hurting her.

Zander looked at me with a cocked eyebrow. "You really don't know much about omegas, do you? When an omega is in need like Finley is right now, every part of her is prepared. Once you get them turned on and the slick going, that is all the preparation you need to give them what they want. They can even take a knot in their ass just as easily as their cunt."

"Would you please stop talking about filling me and fuck me already!" Finley ordered, her magic spiking within her at being denied what she wanted most right now.

It would seem that her omega nature didn't rule out her elfness, even in the heat of the moment. Hell hath no fury like an elf woman denied and I had already forgotten that once today.

"As you wish, little dove, just remember you asked for this," Zander purred into her ear as he slammed into her to the point I had to take a step back or get knocked over.

Finley let out a scream of pleasure, her eyes rolling back in her head now that she was filled with us both. Together we found a rhythm that worked. It was a much faster pace than I would have chosen but Finley didn't seem at all bothered by it.

"Yes, oh God, why does it feel so good to be so full?" Finley panted, her head falling to my shoulder as she held on.

I could feel her tightening on me as if she was looking for the knot I didn't have to offer her. Little did she know that I, too, had something only I could offer her with my elf magic. I could enhance sensations in other ways that would ensure she wasn't left wanting.

Pulling the water from the shower, I had it wrap around my dick in a spiral, swirling in an endless loop, adding to the friction and texture of my cock. Wanting to tease her, I cooled the water down, hardening it into ice, ridged as it rubbed all the right places.

"Sweet Jesus, what did you do, Rath?" Finley gasped as her core tightened even more, enjoying the ribbed nature of my dick. "I've never felt something so amazing before. The cold is driving me crazy, keeping me on edge."

"Do you mind warming it up in a bit? Cold doesn't do wonders for my cock, thank you very much," Zander grunted as his hips thrust into her more erratically.

His movements became shorter and I guessed he was close to locking himself into her. Warming the water once again, I kept it swirling and pulsing, knowing I could continue to torture her as she was knotted to Zander, unable to get away from me. Knowing this, I slowed my movements, watching her eyes go wide as she caught onto what I was doing moments before Zander started to grunt and moan, his arms wrapping around her waist to hold them together.

"You're going to want to have a wall behind you for what I have planned next," I informed Zander.

The alpha didn't even try to argue with me as I pressed them back into the glass walls of the shower. "After I'm done with you, *nin mel*, you will never doubt me again," I whispered into her ear.

Shock pulsed through her body as Zander's knot hit all the right places for her, but I wasn't going to be overlooked. With a flick of my hand, I pulled more water to me and had it caressing her skin, teasing her nipples and clit while I continued to work myself in her cunt. My dick pressed up against Zander's knot, making her tighter than she was already. Finley started to babble nonsense about how good everything felt and curled her fingers in my hair, keeping me close for fear I wouldn't let her finish.

"Are you ready to come for me, my mate?" I whispered along the skin of her neck, kissing along her jaw until I got to her lips. "Do you want me to end this torture and let you come?"

"Yes, I need to come. My mind is going blank with the need to come. I've been on edge, just let me come," Finley pleaded, her hands clenching, yanking my hair as if she could physically pull me to speed up.

I nuzzled behind her ear, nipping her skin before I said my command, "Then come, my love, let your body take what it desires most."

Finley then screamed out her pleasure as the water on her body fell away, and I pinched her clit. Thrusting into her roughly, I used the water around my cock to press against her the way a knot would. Her body slammed down around my dick. I couldn't help but come, getting pulled into completion, moaning out her name as my seed flooded into her. I cupped her face between my hands and kissed her reverently, pushing every amount of emotion I was feeling into that kiss so she had no misunderstanding of how much I needed and wanted her. "*Nin mate, nin cuil, nin faer, forever bui cín haer.*"

She purred, brushing her nose along mine, her hands not letting me pull away from her as she continued to kiss me in soft brushes of her lips. "What did you say?"

"My mate, my life, my soul, forever by your side," I said, pressing my forehead to hers.

"Your language sounds so beautiful. You should use it more so I can learn."

"Mmm, I would love to teach you," I responded, smiling, loving that she had the interest.

Her body shifted as Zander adjusted behind her. "As much as I hate to cut this moment short, I would love to get out of the shower to wait out the rest of this knot. Whatever magic you did on her has me locked in good and tight."

"So much for food." Finley sighed as she curled an arm around Zander's neck and kissed his lips.

As they sat for a moment, I turned off the water and grabbed towels, drying Finley off and wrapping up her hair so it didn't drip everywhere. Once she was good enough, Zander and I maneuvered her to the bed. It was trickier than I thought with him in her ass and facing away from him, so I carried her legs, the three of us laughing the whole way.

"Knots are great and all, but this is ridiculous," Finley pointed out as she smiled and wiped away a tear from laughing so hard. "We need to plan this better or no knotting in the shower since we'd have to move locations."

"Who thinks that clearly in the heat of the moment? If you're thinking about that, then I'm not doing my job right," Zander muttered against the back of her neck, kissing the mark I assume he gave her there.

Finley swatted him on the hip with her hand. "Don't even start doing that, you know that will just drive me back into a needy mess, and there are other matters we have to deal with today."

"Responsibilities can wait. I like you a needy mess trapped by my knot," he teased, thrusting to prove his point as moans erupted out of Finley's mouth.

I left them to have a moment to themselves and took a quick shower to actually clean myself. "Hey, do you mind if I grab some clothes from you?" I called out as I brushed out my hair.

"Yeah, grab anything you need out of the plastic drawers. They're spares I keep for shifting," Zander answered.

The beautiful thing about magic was that I could use it to remove the water from my hair, speeding up the drying process. As children, we were always instructed never to use our magic for frivolous uses like that, but that was just one rule I didn't listen well on. Magic was a gift and it was meant to be used as the wieldier deemed fit. So if I wanted to enhance sex, make clothes, or dry my hair, then that was what I was going to do. Personally, I believed they told us that to keep us from using magic around humans. Almost no one knew just how powerful we were or what we could do with our magic, but the last time we tried to teach people, the Dark Elves were created.

Wandering into the closet, I found the clothes and pulled on a basic pair of gray sweats and a T-shirt. When I entered the bedroom, I found Finley asleep wrapped in a blanket with Zander holding her close. His eyes were closed, but I knew he was awake. Not wanting to bother him, I headed back down to the others. When I reached the second floor, I almost ran into Mason carrying a plate of food.

"Pardon, I wasn't paying attention to where I was going," I apologized, stepping out of the way.

"All good, man," Mason assured me. "My head was still in a fog from listening to you drive snuggles wild. I don't know what moves you got, but I might need to know so I can keep up with all the knots she's got going on around her."

"If I could teach you my tricks, I would, but unless you have elemental manipulation as a skill, I'm not sure it will be of much help," I answered truthfully.

Mason's eyes grew wide. "Okay, way to make a man feel like he has no chance in impressing our mate."

I grinned at him catching sight of his twin jogging up the steps to join us. "I doubt you and your brother will have any trouble pleasing her. There are many moves non-enhanced penises can do that others cannot. You'll just have to think outside the box."

"Whoa, what did I walk into?" Noah asked, brows raised.

Mason just laughed and shook his head. "Man, it's gonna take some getting used to how proper you talk. Who even calls it a penis anymore?" He slapped me on the back and started up to the third floor. "I'm gonna take this up for her before it gets cold. You coming, twin, or staying for the tips-from-an-elf talk?"

Noah looked between me and his brother like it was actually a hard choice.

"Go, she's far more interesting than anything I have to share," I teased, heading down the hall to my new room.

After the past few days and staying awake last night to watch over Finley, I could use a nap before we got back into the issues at hand.

We hadn't even touched on the fact she healed a vampire.

It was going to be interesting to see their take on that information.

CHAPTER THIRTEEN

FINLEY

"Snuggles, you need to wake up so you can eat," Mason whispered in my ear as he swirled delicious-smelling food under my nose.

Cracking open an eye, I looked at him and then the steaming bowl of some type of creamy chicken and rice meal. When I shifted, I felt that I was still attached to Zander, but for some reason, it wasn't awkward to have Mason and Noah hanging out in the bed with us. Zander grabbed a pillow for me to put under my chest so I could sit up higher and eat easier. The food was amazing and tasted just as good as it smelled, making me hum and curl my toes. After a week of being spoiled by them, to go without their cooking for two days was not something I wanted to make a habit of.

"This is wonderful, thank you, Mason," I praised as I pushed forward, pressing a kiss to his lips. "Who knew you were such a good cook."

Mason beamed at me. "To be fair, most of us are pretty good at making food since we all like to eat. Colt's the only one you have to watch out for. He's only good at making breakfast foods. Anything other than this is dangerous."

"Good to know." I giggled, then froze, looking back up at Mason.

His eyes glowed with happiness, letting me know he didn't miss it. "Now, snuggles, I didn't think you made noises like that? Didn't she say she never giggles, twin?" he asked Noah, who was lounging beside him.

"Once I could see as a mistake, but twice... now that's becoming a pattern," Noah agreed. "Guess we will just have to keep our ears peeled to see if it happens a third time, then there's no way she can say giggles don't come out of her mouth."

"What are you two on about?" Zander asked, his voice muffled since his face was pressed to my shoulder.

"Answer this question first, was that a giggle or a laugh?" Mason inquired, resting his chin on his hands like an excited child.

For as large of a person as he was, beating all the others besides his twin with bulk, he acted completely different than his appearance. No one would guess behind the brawn was a child-like heart and teasing attitude.

"Seriously?" Zander demanded, lifting his head to look at the beta. "I don't even know what the difference between those is. A laugh is a laugh. Why the fuck do you need to put a label on it?"

"Dude, that made you sound so old," Mason teased, rolling his eyes. "Did you need me to grab your cane for you when you get out of bed to make it back downstairs?"

Zander started to growl and raise up on his arms. "You are one lucky son of a bitch that I can't go anywhere right now, but don't think that will save you from me dealing with this later."

As if the other two alphas knew the twins were causing trouble, they entered the room with Elias right behind them. Lane paused and took in the scene before him, brows raised. "Ah, everything good here?"

"Just having a bonding moment, right Zan?" Mason shared, grinning at the trapped alpha.

Clearing my throat, I smoothed a hand over Zander's leg, trying to calm him down as he tried to get up to go after Mason. Thankfully his body realized that he needed not to be stuck in me anymore, and his knot eased enough for him to slip out of me.

"You better run, beta, or I'll show you a whole other bonding moment we can have that I'll enjoy more than you will," Zander warned now on all fours, ready to leap over me.

A shrill whistle pierced through the air, making us all freeze and turn to Elias. "Everyone off the fucking bed if you're going to act like assholes. Finley is in the middle of it trying to eat and you felt like now was the time to piss off an alpha?" he demanded of Mason. "Don't think you're off the hook either, Zander. You know he likes to get under your skin, but how could you let that cloud your judgment? If the two of you really started to fight, Finley would be the one to get hurt. You were still fucking knotted in her, for fuck's sake."

The room fell silent as we watched the moody beta, who, from what I've seen, hardly spoke unless he had to. I don't know if he felt this was necessary or if he was becoming even more protective of me now that I'd marked him.

He stood there like my dark protector as he made sure everyone got off the bed, leaving me in peace to finish my meal now that I could sit up. My nose wrinkled at the feeling of sitting in cum, so I moved to another part of the bed. Taking a real shower was going to be needed, but it could wait while the food was still hot.

"Dude, are you sure you're not some undercover alpha?" Mason asked Elias.

Elias crossed his arms and gave Mason a withering look. "My status as a beta doesn't change the fact that I will protect my mate from any and all dangers that I can. Titles don't change your abilities. It only changes how people perceive you in their own minds. I'd rather they underestimate me. It makes it that much easier to rip out their throat when they're not watching."

Lane's jaw fell open at this announcement. Colt, on the other hand, nodded his approval of Elias's plan. Zander just muttered under his breath and headed off to the bathroom. The sound of the shower soon followed.

"Once you eat and get cleaned up, we can let you rest," Noah assured me as he walked over to the side I was sitting on, kissing my cheek. "I'll also make sure to change the sheets unless you want space in your nest?"

"No, space from you guys is the last thing I want," I answered, scraping the last spoonful out of the bowl. "But I think it's better to wait for Zander to get out of the shower before going back in there."

Noah smiled, his eyes crinkling with suppressed laughter. "Smart plan, babe."

With Zander having no hair to wash, it made his shower rather quick, allowing me to slip in right after him with Elias to block the door, ensuring I could actually wash up. Clean and in soft, snuggly clothes, I crawled back into the massive bed that smelled like fresh sunshine.

I wiggled my fingers at the others, welcoming them into the bed with me. Noah was the first to wrap himself around my back, and Elias took the front, leaving the others to find their own space.

"Does anyone need to be anywhere today, or can we nap without an alarm set?" Noah questioned.

Everyone muttered various responses of no, and we all settled in, allowing the comfort of being together to settle my wolf and remind me that my home was with them. They were what mattered most to me, and I would do anything to protect and defend them. If the Dark Ring or the Senate wanted to test my resolve on that, they were welcome to try, but they wouldn't survive the encounter.

It turned out our nap lasted until the sun started to pour in the following morning. Trapped at the bottom of the snuggle pile of bodies, I tried to squirm my way out, but that was turning out to be more difficult than I'd expected.

Mason was wrapped around my legs like an anaconda, his head right on my bladder. Noah was still at my back, one hand holding my boob, while Elias had his face shoved between them with his arms wrapped around my ribs. This time it was the alphas who were draped over, only getting to touch me with a hand, unlike the many other occasions where that was the betas.

As I looked over the scene around me, I felt like something was missing, and when I reached out for it, I got a response. Rath was awake and downstairs, getting acquainted with the house while we were still sleeping. He also let me know that he was now on his way up to rescue me if I needed it. I couldn't help but smile at this interaction, now understanding why he'd been so thrown off that I kept him locked out of my thoughts. It wasn't like we could talk to each other in words per se, but more with intention and emotion. It was clear that after we had sex, our bond strengthened even more, and I could feel him more clearly. Almost like he had his one direct line into my consciousness that was separate from my empathic abilities. We'd bonded physically, but it seemed we needed the emotional part of it to get everything to flow more smoothly.

When Rath appeared at the foot of the bed, he looked down at us with a smile and a huff of laughter. "I can see why you feel like you're stuck, *nin mel*. They have found every possible way to make sure you weren't going anywhere."

"Yes, and while I find it heartwarming and adorable, I really have to pee," I commented, reaching out a hand to him.

Rath ignored my hand, instead moving his hands as if weaving together something out of nothing but air. Moments later, I felt wind surrounding me, lifting me from their hands and bodies before picking me up and carrying me over to Rath. The wind gave out, and I landed safely in his arms, where I proceeded to nuzzle into his neck, marking him with my scent. My wolf really didn't like that he had almost no scent to him so he would bear ours.

"Thank you, and good morning," I murmured, pressing a soft kiss to his lips.

Rath deepened the kiss a moment before setting me on my feet. "Good morning, *nin mel*, did you sleep well?"

"Yes, I feel back to normal and ready to take on anything."

"Good, but first, I think you need to wake up the others from the healing sleep you put them in unintentionally," Rath suggested.

Spinning on my heels, I took in my mates, observing they hadn't moved a muscle. Elias would have been awake the moment I stirred and definitely wouldn't have let a gust of wind take me away from him. The others also seemed to be in a deep sleep. Only the rise and fall of their chests confirmed they were alive.

"I didn't hurt them, did I?" I asked, panic clawing at my chest. "How did I even do that without knowing it?"

"You're powers are so strong and untrained that you were taking care of them in your sleep. If you had any lingering thoughts about how tired they looked or anything to do with their health, it could have triggered this. No harm has been done to them, quite the opposite, actually. When they wake, they will be rested, healed of any ailments, and restored body and mind," Rath explained, resting his hands on my shoulders to ground me as I tried to understand what he was saying.

"Is this what you did to me?" I questioned, looking up at him.

"On a smaller scale, yes, but you are far more powerful than I am to do this to so many at a time. Now, to bring them out of it, you just need to focus and put intention behind your magic. It wants to help you. Your magic wants to be used. All it needs is direction," he instructed, running his hands up and down my arms. "Close your eyes and picture them how they would be waking up normally. Hold that in your mind and push out with your magic."

Breathing in through my nose slowly, like I did with my meditation, I did as Rath instructed. Once I had the picture in my mind, I slowly let my magic flow out of me and swirl around them, caressing them as if I were trying to wake them. Soon their stirring bodies had me opening my eyes to find them all waking up.

Mason yawned loudly, stretching his arms out, smacking Zander in the face.

"The fuck, man," Zander snarled. "Watch what you're fucking doing."

"Looks like someone woke up on the wrong side of the bed," Mason grumbled, stumbling off the bed. "Not sure how that's even possible when that was the best sleep of my life. Snuggles, you are one addictive person to sleep with, that's for sure. I didn't even wake up once with all these idiots jockeying for space."

The others got up as well, seeming a little disoriented but otherwise no immediate signs of what I had done to them. "That would be because I drugged you to sleep in a sense..."

They all paused in their actions to look at me. "Explain that," Colt ordered but grunted when Lane elbowed him. "Please, little one, could you tell us what you mean by that?"

"You really have to stop ordering her around. She doesn't like it and can't say no to us," Lane pointed out as he got up and walked over to me, giving me a peck on the lips. "Good morning, sweetheart. I have a feeling there is a lot we are going to learn today if this is how things are starting out."

"Coffee first," Elias stated as he kissed me on the cheek and headed downstairs.

Flicking my gaze up to Rath, I shrugged. "They are acting totally normal. I thought they would be all relaxed and peaceful after a healing sleep."

"Clearly, you had an incredibly specific memory of how they woke up and your magic gave you what you asked for," Rath answered with a chuckle. "Let's head downstairs. They'll be along shortly."

CHAPTER FOURTEEN

FINLEY

Elias was shuffling around the kitchen gathering items to make coffee when Rath and I entered. A presence came up behind me, but the scent of warm, fresh, clean laundry told me it was Lane who settled his hands on my hips.

Leaning down, he kissed me on the cheek before murmuring into my ear, "What sounds good for breakfast?"

"I'm really not a picky eater, so if there is something that sounds good to you, I'll happily eat it," I assured him.

He gave me a look like he didn't really believe me but nodded all the same, heading for the refrigerator and pulling out supplies. Soon the aroma of coffee filled the air and there was something about it that made me feel at peace. Here I was in my home with my mates, living life together as if the world wasn't out to get me, settling something in my soul. It was as if they refused to let anything ruin our life together. Something I never thought I'd have was now sitting right in front of me—a family.

The rest of the guys showed up moments later, all dressed in jeans and T-shirts for the day. Mason went right over and started to help Lane with breakfast while the others gathered around the island. A coffee cup was set before me, and it had a swirl of whipped cream on top, making me smile.

"What's this?" I asked Elias.

"It's nothing fancy, just my version of a poor man's mocha," Elias said, heading back to pour himself a cup.

Realization dawned on me that he served me first, but my wolf was more enamored with the fact he remembered we liked sweet treats. Tentatively I took a sip, and the taste of chocolate swirled around my tongue, making me hum with happiness. The contrast of the cool whipped cream and the hot coffee, paired with the creamy chocolate and milk, made for the perfect combination.

"Thank you, Elias, this is amazing," I told him with a wide smile.

Elias's lips twitched in his version of a smile. It seemed his shocking personality changed from yesterday now that he was more settled now that we were mated.

The biggest difference was that I could now catch a glimpse of his true emotions hidden under all his gruffness, and he was extremely pleased that I was enjoying his offering. Even his wolf was puffed up that he had provided something tasty for his mate.

Lane and Mason ended up making a massive batch of cheesy eggs, bacon, and toast, keeping it simple. Everything was brought to the table and Zander made sure to pile a plate full of food before setting it in front of me.

"While I admire the fact you seem to be so willing to serve our mate, I have the feeling there is something I'm missing," Rath interjected.

"It's an omega thing. They either have to be gifted food or go last. We've found it's easier to just provide for Finley first. Then we don't have to worry about making sure there is some left for her," Colt explained. "It also seems to go better when one of us alpha's gift the meal to her as well, instead of one of the others. If we're not here, then they can, but to be honest, it makes our wolves feel like better mates knowing we cared for our mate, so we are happy to do it."

"That makes sense," Rath mused, then turned to look at me. "Have you noticed anything changing now that you've come into your elf nature?"

I nodded with a mouth full of food that I quickly swallowed. "The biggest thing is that my wolf isn't in charge of my emotions and body as much. My magic seems to settle her if she gets upset about something and allows me to push past her hang-ups. Alpha's being around is the biggest trigger to my wolf being stronger. When I was just on my own with you, Rath, I didn't have as much trouble. The moment I'm back around wolves or even just an alpha, it seems to strengthen that part of me too."

"Interesting," Noah mused. "Do you think it's because you still have to obey every order an alpha gives you?"

Pausing a moment to look at all of them, I considered whether this was something I should keep to myself. Then I shook my head, realizing that was my assassin brain talking. These men were not to be feared or second-guessed. Letting them know I could break an order would be wise.

"Actually, it seems that isn't the case anymore," I shared, looking down at my plate.

When nobody spoke, I looked up at them, and it was as if they were waiting for me to continue. They didn't seem bothered by the fact they didn't have power over me or that the order Colt had given me yesterday might not stick.

"I still feel the pressure to give in to your demands, but I also know that if I really wanted to, I could break them," I continued. "While it feels better to submit to you all as mates and alphas, I now have the option to fight back and stand my ground."

Colt flashed me a smile which surprised me. He was the one that I was worried about being the most upset about this knowledge since he wouldn't have the ability to keep me safe the way he wanted to.

"Little one, I can't tell you how relieved I am to hear you've gained back some of your autonomy. I'm sure as we work through situations, there will be even more balance between your wolf and elf natures," Colt assured me before his face shifted into a more somber tone. "Would you be up to telling us more about what happened after you rescued the supers and left the house?"

I set my fork down, knowing I wasn't going to be able to eat as I walked them through this. So much of it I didn't understand myself, and that alone scared me. "Rath got shot during the altercation with Blakley."

"Multiple shots to the chest," Rath added. "I knew I was bleeding out, and if something didn't happen right away, I would have died, but I had a gut feeling that Finley could save me." The others looked confused after Rath shared this information. "I knew she was my mate when we locked eyes, but she hadn't claimed me at this point."

"Are you saying that Finley saved you?" Noah pressed.

"Yes." Rath lifted his shirt to show there wasn't even a mark left. "I'm healed to perfection and even some of my old wounds are as well."

The guys gaped at me, eyes wide with amazement as they took in his meaning.

Clearing my throat, I told them the next part, "Not only can I heal wounds, I changed a vampire back into being a human."

Zander shot to his feet, knocking the chair out from under him, hands planted on the table. "You did what? When the fuck were you attacked by vampires? Is it possibly the same one who came after you here? Why didn't you tell us this sooner!"

"Zander," Lane snapped. "Sit. Down."

Zander flicked his gaze over to Lane and then back to me before taking a moment to right his chair and take a seat.

"I'm sure Finley will tell us what happened if you give her the chance," Noah added, giving me a reassuring smile. "You know he acts like an idiot because he cares, right?"

"Clearly, he was dropped on his head as a child and doesn't know how to deal with his emotions right," Mason muttered, shoving a strip of bacon in his mouth.

"Anyway," Lane interrupted, turning back to me. "As you were saying, sweetheart."

"Once I healed Rath, we needed to get out of there and somewhere safe. Miami just so happened to be one of the places where I stashed particular items I needed. Florida was a state I worked in fairly often, so I knew places to hide out. When we got to the building where there used to be a safe house for the Organization, Rath and I discovered it was overrun by vampires. A coven had set up there, feeding off the homeless and druggies passed out in the streets. They knew I was a wolf, but they couldn't tell what Rath was. They decided they didn't care and attacked. Between us both, we managed to take out all four of them. While I was dealing with the last vampire, I lost my knife and couldn't get a good hold on him. My magic ran wild, and so I used it to defend myself. In doing so, I changed him back to a human. I was in shock about the whole thing, but Rath kept his senses and finished him off," I concluded.

Rath reached out and took my hand, pulling it to his lips. "There was no other option. We needed to make sure your secret is kept hidden. The Dark Ring is after you now because of being an omega and we don't really understand the Senate's involvement either. What I do know is, if the Senate found out you could reverse something like that with your healing powers, they would kill you. Or steal and lock you away to use you as they see fit for their own purposes."

"Have you noticed anything else about your powers?" Zander asked, his voice betraying how he wasn't as calm as he was trying to appear.

"According to what Rath has been telling me, they seem to be far stronger than most elves he's seen. That's why I was able to put you in a healing sleep last night without me even knowing it," I added.

The guys just seemed to sit with that information for a moment, with no one saying anything. I could tell through their emotions that no one knew how to feel about this. A few of them were scared for me, while one or two of them felt unsettled. I didn't know if that was because of me or if they felt uncomfortable with my powers.

Just like any other natural skill, my power was a part of who I am. I had magic that was innate to me. I didn't need a spell or materials to be able to perform whatever magical feats I wanted to, unlike witches. Witches as a whole weren't looked kindly on since they sold their potions and talismans to anyone willing to pay for them, no questions asked. This led to witches having been given the most rules on how they could practice their magic since it could be so easily misused by others.

Could this be why so many elves kept to themselves and didn't talk about what they could do? So many of the simple feats that Rath had already shown he could pull off were amazing. He could manipulate anything to do with nature, or at least that's what it seemed like. Granted, he did say healing wasn't a gifted area for him, but he still understood the process and how the process should work.

"Rath," Lane said, breaking the silence. "Is this a skill that you've ever heard or seen before? In my head, this sounds like a specialized skill. I just need to understand if what I'm assuming is correct or not."

"I've heard stories of great healers who were sought after all across the world, but they never said what it was they did to garner that attention. It could be they were also gifted the way Finley is, but something tells me that this particular gift of hers is unique to her," Rath mused. "Her becoming an omega, I think, influenced her magic, altering it to become *more* than would be natural. Clearly, she called so many of you to herself before she matured into her powers leading me to believe the fates knew she would be strong. It also makes me wonder if they knew that the world was going to need someone so pure of heart to deal with the Dark Ring and what the Senate has been turning into."

This caught me completely off guard. I knew the basics of the Senate's treachery, but Rath made it sound far more in-depth and twisted from what I knew. Letting my gaze land on Zander, I could tell from his face and emotions that something Rath implied hit a little too close to home.

"Zander?" I questioned, feeling anger building within him.

His silver eyes met mine, no longer bothering to hide his disgust at whatever he was thinking.

"Did you know Peggy played a part in helping them get to you here?" he bit out, surprising me with the abrupt change in topic.

"Yes, she was just leaving the meeting point when I arrived," I answered. "How did you guys find out?"

Elias shifted, leaning back in his chair. "I found her out in the woods when I went chasing after the vampire. Something in my gut told me she was up to no good, and when I pressed her about what she was doing, she lied. It wasn't until after finding her that I found out you were missing. Zander was the one who finally broke her and got her to spill what little information she could about what was going on."

"Where is she now?" I asked, my wolf feeling mighty pleased that this woman who'd been so rude to us was being punished.

"She's in a holding cell that we use for people like her or others that are newly shifted, and we can't manage. Surprisingly, what we found out from her was that the Senate has been keeping a close eye on me and the pack as a whole. They hate to let other packs who might grow into a source of power and overthrow them, losing their place in life. Funny how those in power are so afraid of losing, they will destroy a pack before it gets the chance to try," Zander said bitterly.

"You never said anything about that before." Colt growled. "Are you saying that your mother is going to take us out and murder our whole pack? You're her son. Why would she take your pack from you?"

Mason's head snapped in Colt's direction. "I'm sorry, *his* pack? Since when did boy-band here become part of our pack?"

"Really, Mason, you're questioning that choice when he's mated to the same woman the rest of us are? Of course, he is part of our pack and yes, an alpha. What other option is there in a situation like this? If Zander had been interested in helping lead our pack previously to this, I would have considered it with Lane," Colt stated. "Last I checked, when it comes to leading the pack, it's for Lane and me to worry about... *beta.*"

The last thing we needed right now was for them to be arguing among themselves when there were far more important matters to deal with. Mason started to growl and rise from his seat as Colt met his challenge head-on. Lane pushed back from the table like he was getting ready to intervene and Zander was doing nothing but watching the whole thing unravel. This might be how werewolves handled situations in their packs, but they could fucking well do it another time.

Lifting my fingers to my lips, I let out a shrill whistle cutting through the tension at the table. Startled, they all turned on me, their proverbial hackles raised, ready for a fight. My magic pressed at me, telling me it could help, so I let it flow out of me and reach out to them, soothing their emotions. When they'd all relaxed and once more returned to their seats, they watched me with apprehension.

"That's better," I approved with a nod. "Now, returning the topic back to Peggy. Zander, you said she's been a spy for the Senate since she got here, correct?" He nodded after trying to speak but couldn't. "Does that mean her sisters are also involved in this as well?"

I got a head shake telling me no. "I'm glad about that. I really do enjoy Milly and Kaitie. It would be sad to remove them from the pack along with her. From what I gathered from my interactions with the other side, is they needed her to create a situation where they could get me out of the pack unnoticed, but that's where her interaction ended.

Peggy, of course, hates me for some reason and was more than happy to get rid of me."

The wolves of the table growled at this while I could feel anger coming from my connection to Rath.

"Do you believe that the only reason the Senate has been watching this pack so long are the reasons that she shared, Zander?" I asked and pulled my magic back from him, realizing that was what was keeping him silent.

"Little dove, I would appreciate it if you never do that to me again," he warned, words tight with irritation, his eyes flashing with his wolf. His emotions told me he was not at all happy to be dominated by an omega, even if I was their mate.

"Then don't make me do things like that," I defended. "All of us are going to have to learn where I fit into all this now that I'm not wholly omega or wholly elven. My magic is far stronger than my omega nature, and if it feels that I'm in danger or need, it responds in accordance with that emotion."

Noah frowned at this, reaching out toward me. "Did you feel that you needed protection from us just now?"

"No, I thought you were all being idiots, and we had more important issues to deal with than your egos," I grumbled, running a hand through my hair, feeling the need to do something with myself.

That answer seems to relieve Noah. "While I can't argue with you on that point, it is the nature of us werewolves to run a little more hot-tempered, especially when it comes to dominance-type problems. Mason and Zander have always rubbed each other the wrong way since they've met and he also loves to push Colt's buttons to know just how far he can press the matter. It will take everyone time to adjust to this new hierarchy, just as you say about yourself. The difference is that they might actually fight it out to settle the matter."

"Does the fighting need to happen now for things to move more smoothly?" Rath asked, cocking his head to the side as he observed the others, and they looked at him oddly. "I realize that I'm uneducated on how matters run in a pack and I might say or do things that might be offensive. Forgive me, my mistakes, they shall only happen once I assure you."

Zanger cleared his throat and shifted in his chair. "No, it doesn't need to be handled right now but sooner rather than later would be best."

"Very well then, I would like to borrow Finley and do some work with her on controlling her magic so we don't keep having surprises popping up in her sleep," Rath informed the others, rising from his chair, reaching out a hand to me. "Am I safe to assume we are protected here on pack lands to be outside?"

"Yes, as long as you stay around the house, you should be fine. Once we tell the rest of the pack about your place here, then you'll be able to go anywhere that you please. I'm just being cautious after the attack the other day. Our people are still on edge."

"A reasonable response," Rath commented and we headed outside.

CHAPTER FIFTEEN

FINLEY

Rath led me out into the backyard, not bothering to have me put on shoes or a jacket despite the wind blowing through the woods today. I wrapped my arms around myself, hoping spring was on its way and that being here in Tennessee, it would warm up sooner rather than later.

"I want you to feel the earth under your feet, let it ground you as you stand there. The world around us is what gives us our magic as much as our species does," Rath told me as he lifted his face to the sun. "Close your eyes, let the natural energy around you greet you. This is your home. These woods will become part of your family. They'll speak to you, alert you of something happening, or if there's an intruder."

If that was really true, then no matter how silly I thought that all sounded, I was willing to give it a try. Closing my eyes, I lifted my face to the sun like he was, feeling the grass under my feet as I wiggled my toes deeper into its thick turf. My magic was beating against my hold, almost as if it had a life of its own, ready to charge off into the forest. Unsure if I should release the bindings, not really trusting how it would act, it begged to be let out, vibrating through my veins, trying to greet its new surroundings.

Rath walked up to me, his height blocking out the sun for a moment, letting me know he was close. "Let it free, *nin mel,* your magic will do nothing unwelcome in these woods. It has as much of a personality as your wolf does and needs to be handled much the same. Between your wolf and your magic, these woods will be under your complete domain. I have no doubt. Those men in there might be alphas of the pack, but you will be queen of these woods."

That had my eyes snapping open. "Rathal, are you telling me that I'm some kind of ruler to the Light Elves because I'm so powerful?"

"No, I'm saying you absolutely are our queen because of your power. There hasn't been a leader of our people since the previous king and queen died in the war. None have been powerful enough to lead our people. This is why we are so divided and living in hiding," Rath explained. "You might not want the job, but once you are well and truly exposed to the world, then that is, in fact, what will happen. Our people will flock to you because they won't be able to help themselves. Your magic will call to them the stronger you become."

Yanking my magic back to me, I slammed down the door, closing myself off from everything and everyone. "No." Colt

He tried to reach out to me, but I took a step back, shaking my head. "I'm no one's leader. You want to know what I am? A murderer, a killer, the danger that goes bump in the night. No one will want me as a leader once they find that out. If working with my magic is what will draw them to me, then I won't use it unless there is no other option. That way, no one will know that I even exist, and if they hear rumors, then I'll prove them wrong. I can't be what you're telling me, Rath. I can't."

"Oh, my love, if only it were that simple." Rath sighed. "If you don't get a handle on your powers and train, then you will end up hurting someone. Of course, you won't mean to, but when it's been bottled up for so long, it will need an outlet whether you give it one or not. At that moment when it bursts from you, there is no telling what might happen." He wrapped me up in a hug, resting his chin on my head. He just held me for a moment, letting me get a handle on my reaction to the news. "Finley, you are so much more than you give yourself credit for. The fates wouldn't have blessed you if they thought you would fail."

"Fuck the fates," I muttered. "What do they know, anyhow?"

Rath just chuckled. "More than any of us wish them to. Now forget everything I just told you and come let your magic play in its new home. I could feel how excited it was to be able to explore. While you do that, we will work on meditation and helping you find your *celu*, or source. It's where your magic springs from. Now come sit with me."

Slowly, I lowered myself to the ground, crossed my legs and took a long, deep breath. Then I dropped my shields so my magic could once again roam the woods. It shot out of me, making it clear that it was extremely unhappy I called it back so abruptly. Now, as it roamed the area, I could feel the energy that Rath had been talking about as my magic greeted everything growing in the forest around us. I knew what types of trees, flowers, and animals that called this place home.

The strangest part of all this was hearing everything greeting me in return, letting me know they were excited to once again have our people back. They celebrated, knowing my magic would nurture them and in return, they supported and grounded it. It was almost as if I was seeing the real world that lived and breathed within this forest. My magic didn't stop at just the area the pack claimed. It went through the whole national forest.

"Rath, can you feel this?" I asked, keeping my eyes closed, not wanting to give up the tranquility I felt. "You must be pretty powerful yourself for us to be covering so much land."

"No, *nin mel*, that is all you. I haven't let my magic out yet, since we need to know just what you are capable of."

My eye popped open and I stared at him slack-jawed. "That can't be right. How the hell is that even possible?"

"I wasn't lying when I told you that you are powerful. This is the reason it is going to be impossible for you to hide your magic away. It is too much for one person to hold. As you live and learn these woods, they will help store the extra magic that oozes from you. This place will become a power source, and in return, the environment here will thrive unlike any other. It is the symbiotic relationship we have with nature."

Flopping back into the grass, I looked up at the gray-blue sky with clouds blocking out the sun. Everything in my life right now seemed so overwhelming, and all I wanted was to go back to the days when I lived in ignorance. I knew there was no way to go back. It was inevitable that I would come into my magic and I should be grateful that I had Rath here to teach me these new skills. Otherwise, I could be so much worse, and who knew what the Organization would think or how they would try to use my powers.

"How do I control something like this? It feels so wild, as if it doesn't really belong to me," I shared.

A hand wrapped around mine, curling our fingers together. "Every person's magic is different, but I have a feeling that your wolf has something to do with its wildness. Open yourself up to me. Let me feel what you are feeling so that I might understand better what you're talking about."

Frowning, I thought I'd already done that, seeing as we now had a much different connection than the previous day. Yet I trusted him, and this time, instead of focusing on my shield, I reached out to him through our bond. When I felt him, it was almost as if I took his hand and led him back, opening the door for him to enter. Rath gasped as I felt him encounter my magic for the first time.

"Finley..." Rath murmured in awe. "Never did I think I would see the day when our people might have a chance to restore themselves to this world, but you, my love, you give me hope."

While Rath was speaking, I could feel his emotions, the truth of his words, even the hope he was feeling. It was as if I could feel it myself though I knew it was his. Now I understood why he'd been so bothered by the fact we didn't have this connection right away. For him to know that a bond like this existed but not be given the chance to experience it, I would be upset too.

"Is this how it is for all mated elves?" I asked, turning my head to look up at him. "Will I get this same connection with the others even though they aren't elves?"

Rath seemed to contemplate my question a moment before answering, "I would be remiss to think anything for you is impossible. They are your mates just as I am, and even though your wolf had picked some, your elvish nature did too." Releasing my hand, he got up. "Wait here. I think it's time we experiment while the woods draw out your excess magic."

Curious, I watched as he headed back into the house, returning a few moments later with Lane and Elias in tow. What amazed me was that the twins didn't follow them out since they were so nosy about everything.

"Please, would each of you take a seat on either side of her," Rath instructed. Elias sat on my left while Lane, the other, looking as confused as I was about what was going on. "Perfect, now pick one or the other, Finley, and I want you to do the same thing you just did with me. One of these men was picked by your wolf, the other by your elven nature, but you are mated to both. This will tell us if they can all have the same bond that we do."

I moved to sit up, but Rath stopped me. "No, you need to keep your body connected to the earth as much as possible. It will keep you from doing something else to them you might not intend to as you work through this experiment."

"Well, that's reassuring," I muttered, relaxing back into the grass.

Deciding to start with Lane since he was picked by my wolf, I held out my hand to him. "Just relax and trust what your wolf tells you to do. I don't know how my magic will affect you, but I know that I will never do something that will hurt you."

"Sweetheart, I trust you with my life," Lane answered as he kissed the back of my hand. "Just tell me what I need to do and I'll make it happen."

Unsure how to proceed, I looked at Rath for help. "Think of it like you are trying to build a pack connection with Finley, but instead of you being the leader pulling her into it, she'll do that part."

Now I understood why he picked Lane to experiment on instead of one of the others. Colt and Zander would have a much harder time having the patience to let me figure this out without them trying to take over. Closing my eyes, I centered myself, reaching for the mate bond I had with Lane, and much like I did with Rath, I followed it down until I found Lane's energy. He, of course, didn't have magic as Rath did, but in some ways, there was magic in being an alpha and the power they had in that.

When I pushed deeper, I heard a snarl and found myself face to face with Lane's wolf. Startled at his sudden appearance and the bared teeth, I froze. The moment he realized I was the one who was pushing into his space, he settled down, wagging his tail slowly as he watched me with the same gold-flecked brown eyes as Lane. Slowly I reached out a hand to him and he ducked his head so I could pet him easier. My fingers sank into his fur, making him step forward and lean against me, begging for more attention.

"Will you come back with me and meet my wolf?" I asked, feeling in my gut that this was what needed to happen.

Lane's wolf yipped his excitement, prancing in place, ready to go as soon as I was. Grinning at the wolf, I curled a hand into the thick fur on the back of his neck, which wasn't as soft as I would have thought and I pulled us both back into my body, tugging on the thread of pulsing music that was anchored in my body. When I returned, I found it was to a different place than where my magic lived, but when I spotted my wolf sitting there eagerly awaiting us, by the jubilation I got from her, I knew it was right. Lane was chosen by my wolf, so of course, that is where this would lead to.

The two wolves played for a bit, making me smile to see their simple affection, then he started to lick my wolf's face, grooming her. I could feel the love and trust between them and knew this was Lane showing me how much I meant to him. Pulling back from this space, returning to my own mind, I noticed the bond with Lane was much stronger and seemed to hum with all the emotions I was feeling from him. He was excited to have this added connection and thrilled to get a better insight into my own emotions. While I was much better at showing them from when we first met, I still had much to learn.

Grounding myself, feeling the earth and the cool air around me, I opened my eyes once I felt certain I was back to reality. I found Lane lying on my chest in his wolf form, tongue lolling and tail wagging when I opened my eyes. It would seem that doing whatever I had done pulled his wolf to the forefront. My instant reaction was to feel guilty about doing that to him and hope he wasn't upset with me. No one but an alpha should be able to pull out someone's wolf as I'd just done.

Lane growled at me, catching wind of what I was thinking, and immediately sent me reassurance. Moments later, I had a naked Lane lying on top of me, his hands cupping my face.

"Sweetheart, it's fine, you did nothing wrong, and I'm not at all upset with you. Neither of us knew what was going to happen and when you called to my wolf, I went willingly. You told me to trust my wolf and there was nothing he wanted more than to follow your call."

Leaning down, he captured my lips with his own, and through our improved connection, he showed me just how happy he was. Unable to keep my hands to myself, I let them roam over his muscular back down to the round of his ass, but I stopped myself from progressing further. This wasn't what we were here to do, no matter how much my body begged me to continue.

"No one here is going to stop you if you choose to keep going," Lane whispered against my lips.

I chuckled and pressed on his chest. "How about we come back to that idea later when I can take my time exploring you better?"

Lane groaned but rolled off me in acceptance.

CHAPTER SIXTEEN

ELIAS

As I silently watched, Finley did whatever it was she was trying to gain with Lane and the power I felt coming off her as she called his wolf out amazed me. I've met some strong supers in my day but never one that seemed to wield that much magic. Lane's wolf didn't even try to resist her, knowing there was no way he could, so instead, he gave in to the call of his mate. Through my bond with Finley, I could sense there was a change in her bond with Lane, but it was more of an echo when it reached me.

While I wanted nothing more than to support and help my mate with whatever she needed, I was worried about what she might find. My past wasn't one that I wished on anyone and it left scars on me in ways I wasn't sure they would ever heal. Would she still want me after she learned my story?

As Lane jogged back into the house for fresh clothes since he shredded the others when he shifted, Finley turned her attention to me. Ignoring Rath's grumbling, she sat up, turning to face me to where our knees were touching and she rested her hand palm up, asking for mine.

"My heart…" I started, but she just lifted a hand, covering my lips with her fingers.

"No, Elias, you forget, no matter how much you try to hide them, I can still feel your emotions. However this turns out or what happens, nothing will change between us. When I claimed you, it wasn't a mistake or a rushed decision. Trust me enough to show you how much I value you in so many ways and how I'm falling for you," she shared, her face showing all the emotions she wasn't quite ready to say out loud yet.

Nodding, I relaxed, showing her I was willing to follow her lead. She held her hands out to me again, and I took them, giving them a slight squeeze while a smile tugged at my lips. This woman before me was more than I'd ever hoped for in a mate. I wasn't even sure I was going to have one, feeling as if the fates would use that as my punishment for the wrong I'd done.

Finley's cobalt gaze watched me a moment before she closed her eyes and seemed to sink deep within herself.

My worries wouldn't let me be as I glanced over at Rath, who was observing the whole situation with a detached air, trying not to make me feel uncomfortable. I appreciated it, but as I told him before, he felt like pack, part of the family—Finley's family that I was lucky to be included in. When he caught me watching him, he simply nodded in reassurance and motioned for me to close my eyes. Facing Finley once more, I closed them, trusting in my mate.

It was odd when I felt her reach out to me, flooding me with her magic, enveloping me in her sweet, spicy scent. I welcomed her with open arms when I felt her nudging at my mind, but when she pushed further, instinctively, I threw up walls trying to shut her out. The further she went into my mind, I couldn't shield her from the memories that lurked just under the surface.

"Elias, you have to let me in for this to work," Finley whispered, her thumb rubbing on the back of my hand reassuringly. "No matter what you are trying to protect me from, I can handle it. Don't forget who and what I was before I became an omega. I've been and seen death in all its forms, we do what we must to survive, and I will never judge you for it."

"What you are asking me to do is let you see the worst of me," I said, my voice raspy with my emotions.

Everyone always assumed I was not a man who could feel emotions, but in order not to beat myself up for what happened in the past, I had to turn off everything. The pain was too great to live with day in and day out, so feeling nothing at all was the better choice.

"How can I help? What can I do to make this easier for you?" Finley pressed, crawling up into my lap and wrapping her arms around my neck. "I know what I'm asking you to do is painful, but the omega part of me is sure that it will help ease your pain and not create more. The moment I laid eyes on you, I could see the pain you hold. Out of all of my mates, you and I are so much alike, burying all our pain and weakness deep within ourselves. Every day you help me to heal and become a better version of myself. Will you let me do the same for you?"

I could answer her with words, though I had never been one to share how I felt the right way. I had always believed actions spoke the truth better than any words could. So I opened myself up to her, allowing all that I'd had locked away for twenty years to come pouring out of me, sweeping us both away into a memory...

"Elias, my boy, come over here and help me with this, will you," Dad called out for me across the field.

The summer sun was hot as we worked repairing the fences on the property. It might seem odd that werewolves would be cattle ranchers, but the packs in the surrounding area were some of our best customers. Wolves eat a lot, and beef happened to be a favorite, so we were never short of orders.

When I reached him, he was trying to get the post to stand straight in the ground so he could fill it, but it kept falling over.

"What gives, old man? You didn't dig down deep enough. That's why you're having so much trouble." I sassed, yanking the post out, and grabbed the hand auger.

Dad growled at me, not appreciating my tone or nickname. It was an argument we had almost every other day, but the guy was nearly two hundred years old. He was honorary alpha to our pack, which was made up of my fifteen siblings, their mates, and their offspring. I was the youngest and last of his kids now that Mom was gone.

"Well, if you think you can do better, then I'd like to see you drill through the bedrock with only a hand auger. My body might not be as strong as it once was, but my brain works just fine," Dad spat.

The way Dad and I showed we cared was to fight—constantly. Hardly a conversation could be had without one of us blowing up at the other. We both had hot tempers. Guess it ran in the family since my siblings were much the same. As I tamped the auger, I could hear the ting of metal on rock and realized Dad was right. There was no way I would be able to do anything more than he had.

"Looks like you are right, old man. Now hold it steady while I shovel the dirt back into it and see if we can get it to do its job," I muttered, moving out of the way.

Dad grunted as he dropped the post back in and we worked in silence. Once the post was steady, we ran the barbed wire to keep the cows where they were supposed to be.

"They came back this morning looking for you," I commented, knowing I was poking the wolf with this topic.

With a glare, Dad yanked on the tension winch. "Next time you see them, shoot. Maybe then they'll get the hint."

"Why don't you want to merge with their pack? They are larger with more resources and will be able to offer our family more protection than we currently have. The whole state is in flux with the latest change in alphas," I pointed out.

Dad was a stubborn old dog who didn't want to give up his territory even if it was the better option.

"Or would you rather be a slave to the whims of that crazy bastard's son, Stephen, now that he'd taken over? He wants us to give him meat as our tithe to his pack when we aren't even a part of it? We own our land outright and have long before they migrated to our area. You allowed them to be so close to us when another alpha would have chased them halfway across the state."

"Do you understand why I did that?" Dad asked, pausing to hold my gaze, telling me this was a serious question.

"Because you might be an alpha in nature, but you're a pushover when it comes to anyone who isn't your blood. That's why we have a pack made out of family and you refuse to allow anyone who isn't a mate to join. We could be one of those great packs we hear about, a true power to do what's needed in this world, but you hide us away up here in Nebraska like you're afraid," I snapped, lashing out with all my pent up frustration.

He just looked at me with pity and sorrow in his eyes as he shook his head. "Maybe your mother was right. Keeping you all up here away from reality isn't helping. If you believe that a pack is only powerful when it's large proves how naïve you are, son. I might not have a normal pack, but I'm respected in this community, and that is why we are left to our own devices. These new pups want to rule over the whole state taking smaller packs and forcing them to join theirs with promises they never plan to keep. Elias, they will tell you anything you want to hear just to get you to come peacefully, but once they have what they want, those promises will go out the window. Never trust an alpha you don't know to keep his word when there are no actions behind it. If they truly wanted to have us join their pack, they would make an effort to show us what that looks like. Instead, they act like they are buying our land and we come along with it. No, son, I won't let them take from me what we've worked for all this time."

That memory faded and I could feel tears burning in my eyes as I realized that was the last time we would have together. What came next showed how right my dad was about everything, but I never once blamed him for giving us the sheltered life we had all those years. It gave me peace to know they all lived a good life until the very end.

It hadn't even been two days since Dad had passed unexpectedly and the doctors still couldn't tell us what killed him. They were going to do an autopsy because it was suspicious for a shifter to die the way he had. All of us were in shock about the situation, unsure of what to do now. None of us had expected to lose him so soon or in such a sudden way. There hadn't been a plan put in place either. According to the human world, Dad left everything to us kids but put Maverick in charge of the business, being the eldest and had worked alongside Dad the most.

Needing something to do, I went into town and did all the grocery shopping we would need for the funeral. Dad was a respected man in the community and there were lots of people who would come when we announced it. The old truck Dad loved and spent hours working on just to keep it going rattled down the drive, leading out to the main road that would take me into town. I hadn't been driving for more than ten minutes when a hummer pulled out in front of me, slamming on the breaks. Another came up behind me, blocking me in.

Guys climbed out of the Hummers and made a circle around my truck. That's when I saw Tatum Volenty get out of the third Hummer that had pulled up alongside my truck.

His suit was worth what we made in a month, flashing all his wealth so no one would doubt his importance. He might have more money than God but was a weak alpha. He made up for it by employing some nasty betas to do the dirty work for him.

"Elias, I'm so sorry to hear about your father passing the other day. My condolences to you and your family in this time of sorrow and heartache," Tatum said as he stood next to my window.

My wolf's hackles were raised and on guard against anything that might happen, instinct telling me he wasn't here to play nice. "Thank you, Mr. Volenty, it's kind of you to say. I know you and Dad didn't see eye to eye on a lot of matters."

Tatum waved off my thanks like it was the most normal response for him to give, even after my dad refused to let him take one of my sisters as a mate. Kathryn had just graduated high school and was planning on going to college, but Tatum had always had his eye on her. Dad was afraid that if she left to go to school, we'd never see her again. So instead, she stayed local and mated her long-time boyfriend. Since then, Tatum had made it known he took personal offense to that refusal and did what he could to make our lives hell.

"Water under the bridge, my boy. Now which one of your brothers took over as alpha of the pack? Or is that still being decided?" Tatum asked, showing his true intent for stopping me.

While my dad had been an alpha, he wasn't a strong one, but none of us felt the need to change roles in our family dynamic. All of us men stayed as betas, but I knew that out of all my brothers and our sister's mates, that I was the strongest. If I had wanted to ask for a battle, I would have won without breaking a sweat, but I wasn't sure I wanted the role of alpha. In my gut, I knew staying here on the ranch wasn't my calling in life.

"We decided not to share that information until after the funeral out of respect for our father," I answered, trying to avoid giving him the truth.

Maverick was a good man and would be the one we most likely agreed on taking the role, but he wasn't one to stand up to a bully like Tatum.

"Hmm... see, your father and I were in the middle of a deal, so I need to know who to talk to about the matter," Tatum countered.

We both knew there was no deal between the two men. It was just an excuse for him to use. If word got out about some fight or disagreement, then his men would start a rumor we reneged on a deal and deserved the retribution we got for it. Maverick couldn't handle this, so I needed to do it and maybe put the thing to rest before it ever started.

"It's me," I stated. "I'm the one you need to talk to." Not a total lie, but absolutely not the truth, but it would cover the scent, so he couldn't tell.

Tatum grinned, showing his perfect white teeth, his wolf flashing in his eyes. "I had a feeling it would be you. The others are too soft for this world. You've always had the smarts to question and push back. Now I think you and I can come to an agreement where your father wasn't so willing.

Your sister, Kathryn, was promised to me and your father broke the deal. I want what is supposed to be mine."

"Mr. Volenty, Kathryn is already mated and has been for five years," I pointed out, knowing he already knew this.

"Yes, but she hasn't had any pups by him, so clearly, he isn't a fit male for her. The deal was I married your sister and became partners in the business, bringing your pack into mine. Surely you can see how this will benefit all of us in the long run," Tatum explained, slipping his hands into his pockets like it was a done deal.

"The answer is no," I growled out the words. "If you continue to press the issue, I will involve the Senate and see how they feel about the matter."

Tatum's eyes flashed with fury. He'd been in trouble with the Senate before, which is why he came to our humble town as penance for his last crime. "Don't start something you can't finish, boy. You might be the strongest of your family, but you are ignorant to the world I live in. I expect an answer tomorrow once you've had time to think matters over. I'm sure the grief of losing your father has clouded your judgment."

With that said, he got back into his vehicle and drove off, leaving me with the rage that was building at his threat. Whipping out my cell phone, I called the main hotline to report issues to the Senate, knowing Tatum wouldn't leave this matter alone.

I never did get to town that day. Instead, I turned around and went home to talk with my brothers about what had happened. We would need to prepare for the fallout that was about to happen and I wasn't willing to let them be blindsided by the situation.

The memory started to take shape and I could see we were in my bedroom. Something had woken me from a deep sleep. Watching this moment over, I knew what was coming and dreaded every moment of it.

Shifting out of bed, I crept to the stairs and listened, straining my ears to locate what I'd heard.

The house creaked in the wind, the mooing of the cows kept close with the storm moving in, and the even breaths of my family sleeping soundly throughout the house echoed around me all at once.

Just when I thought the coast was clear, crunching gravel in the drive interrupted my concentration. Glancing at the clock on the wall, I knew nothing good happened at two in the morning. Rushing to Maverick's room, I didn't bother knocking. Instead, I burst in.

"Mav, you need to get up. There's trouble," I called out in a harsh whisper, not wanting to alert whoever was outside that we knew they were coming.

Maverick grumbled and rubbed at his eyes before sitting up in bed. "What the hell are you talking about? It's probably just the storm rolling in."

"Last I checked, a storm doesn't roll in on four wheels," I snapped.

Maverick paused and listened, hearing the same thing I had. The color drained out of his skin as he looked up at me. "What did you do?"

I snarled at him, resenting that he was going to blame this all on me. The Senate had a person reach out to us, letting us know they would look into the situation and would handle it. Tatum promised to be back the next day, but it's been a whole week. I figured the Senate had taken care of the problem.

"I didn't do a damn thing. If I hadn't gone to the Senate, Tatum would have ruined us," I said, defending myself.

Maverick muttered as he got up, pulling on pants and a shirt. "Go wake the others. If there's trouble, we're going to need everyone." He turned to his wife, Mercy, who was also getting dressed. "Babe, take the wives and kids down to hide in the cellar. We'll deal with this."

Mercy nodded and kissed him firmly before gathering her sleeping kids nearby. With all of us living in one house, each family had a room in the house they shared. It was cramped for those with more than two kids, but Dad always wanted us to be a unit.

We'd talked about adding more houses on the property now we had the choice to do so.

Between Maverick and me, we got everyone awake and hidden away as the sound of more cars arriving hit our ears. What were they waiting for? I knew they could hear us moving around inside the house. They knew we were aware of them.

As if they could hear me, a booming knock sounded at the door. "Open up by orders of the United Senate!"

Frowning, I looked at my ten brothers, who appeared equally confused. Moving to the front door, I opened it and was greeted with the sight of twenty muscled men dressed in military-style clothing. Their expressions told me this wasn't going to be good news, but I stepped out anyway, not wanting to let them in the house."

"What can we do for you?" I asked, keeping my voice calm.

"We need to speak with Elias Haltern about allegations brought up against Tatum Volenty," the man stated.

My stomach clenched at those words. "Yes, I'm Elias, and I did make that call about Tatum," I answered.

"You made a claim that Mr. Volenty was trying to kill your sister's mate to take her for himself. Is that correct?"

"I never—"

"Is it also true you claimed that he threatened your family if he didn't get your sister?" he continued, cutting off my answer.

"Sir, with all due respect, Tatum claimed that he had an agreement with my late father about the matter. My father would never have done such a thing, so I know he's lying and using that as a way to discredit us," I argued, my temper flaring as they tried to turn this all on me.

The man pulled out a set of papers and handed them over to me. When I folded them open, I saw that it was indeed a marriage agreement between Kathryn and Tatum to be married when she turned twenty-one. Flipping through the pages, I found the one that held the signatures, and clear as day, my father's signature was right there. He had horrible handwriting, and his signature was nothing but a bunch of scribbles. It was incredibly hard to forge.

"Can you confirm that is your father's signature?" the man demanded.

Looking up from the papers, I peered over my shoulder at my brothers and brother-in-laws waiting for my answer. I had two choices, lie and hope he believed me or tell the truth, and my sister would be taken from us and forced to be with Tatum.

"No, I don't know who signed this, but it wasn't my father," I lied through gritted teeth. Even to my own ears, the words sounded false, devastation clear in my voice.

"I'll give you a moment to make sure that is your final answer, but know that lying to the Senate is not a wise choice," he warned.

Either way, this wasn't going to end well, but if I kept up the lie, it would only be on me. I could do whatever it took to protect my sister and keep her with the man she loved. If I had to go to jail or pay a fine, I would happily do that to keep her happy.

"As I stated before, that is not my father's signature," I said once more, meeting the man's hard gaze.

"You've got balls, kid, but that won't help you this time. The Senate will overlook many things, but false claims and lying aren't one of those. Know that you brought this on yourself and all you had to do was tell the truth," the man told me before he motioned to the others.

Frozen in horror, I saw them raise guns to their shoulders and mow down my brothers, not leaving a single one standing. Once they were dead, two men tossed Molotov cocktails in through the windows of the house. Seeing as it was the house Dad built when he settled on the land, it when up in flames faster than I could take in air to scream.

Spinning on my heel, I rushed to get in the house, but I was struck by something on the head, dropping me like a rock.

The screams of my family trapped in that house were something I would never forget no matter how long I lived.

The men from the Senate then brought me to Tatum, who proceeded to torture me for days, taking out all his anger on me until I killed him and his whole pack. I hadn't left anyone alive, including the women or the children. They had done the same thing to my family, so why should I spare theirs?

I wandered for years as a lone wolf, turning more wild and feral by the day until Lane and Colt found me. They saw past the rage to the hurting man underneath. When I had heard Colt's story, I knew he would understand my pain and not judge me for what I'd done. With time, they became the alphas I needed in my life to keep me alive and not give in to the pain and take the easy way out. They saved me in more ways than one.

Now, I had Finley. She would be able to do what no one else had.

Allow me to heal, so I might live again.

CHAPTER SEVENTEEN

FINLEY

Watching these memories while feeling everything from Elias was almost like I had lived it myself. I could feel the guilt riding him hard as we moved from each memory he wanted me to see. Elias was baring his soul to me, and I would do what I said, staying right by his side no matter how awful the images I was seeing were.

Elias had lost himself in that pain, allowing his wolf to rule over him, easing the guilt and shame. Wolves didn't feel those emotions. In their mind, Elias had gotten revenge for his family. Why should he be ashamed of that when it was the only course of action to take?

As I caught glimpses of his time alone, his wolf kept them safe and alive, even if it did make him unpredictable and cut off from the human world.

As the memories began to fade and I felt myself returning to the world around us, tears dripped onto my cheeks. The mournfulness I sensed in those tears told me Elias was finally moving from anger and self-hatred to the point where he could actually grieve his loss. So much had happened to him all at once. It's a wonder he was the man I knew today. Yes, he still had a long way to go in his healing process, but this was a good start.

Reaching up, I took his face in my hands and kissed away the tears. Small steps were taken today, and our bond sang with the deeper connection we had, knowing he was well and truly a part of my soul. I could feel him just like Rath and Lane, even though we got there through different means.

It made me wonder if each bond would be different since they were different people. What if that's the trick? There is no one way to do things with magic.

"Finley, I didn't ever think I could love after what happened to my family, but I know without a shadow of a doubt that I am madly in love with you. It sounds crazy, and fate gave me one hell of a journey to get here with you, but there is no one else I can see by my side. You understand my pain like Colt does, but unlike Colt, you won't judge me for killing that other pack," Elias said, looking deep into my eyes as he spoke. "I see myself as a monster, but when you look at me, all I see is the version of me I want to be."

"You were never a monster. A monster is someone who doesn't know how to feel guilt or shame. While I think you did the right thing, the only thing really, you still let it define you as evil, and that is the farthest thing from the truth," I told him, nuzzling my cheek against his. "Now I can see why the fates chose you to be my Protector. You won't be the white knight riding to my rescue. No, you'll be the darkness that comes from the shadows they never see coming. To win against the darkness, you need to understand your own, and you stare yours down every day."

Elias held me tightly, hiding his face in my hair, pressing his lips to my neck. "If there comes a day when I need to come to your rescue, know that the world around us won't survive. Afterward, we'll have to build a new one from the ground up."

I couldn't help but smile at his words. "You know it's not a bad idea. Just think how we could change the world together. The Senate was a good idea in the beginning, but now it's turned into something that abuses the power it's been given."

"If the Senate is coming after us, then we might get our chance," Elias pointed out. "Kill them all and start over, sounds like a good idea to me."

"One step at a time. Right now, we need to find out what the big picture is, then we can figure out how to save the world," I countered, grinning at how simple he made it all sound.

When the sliding glass door opened, I assumed it was Lane coming back out to join us.

"What the hell, *elf*! Why the fuck is Finley out here with no coat or shoes? Are you trying to kill her?" Colt demanded as he stormed his way over, yanking me out of Elias's arms, cuddling me to him like a baby. "I know you're new to this whole mate thing, but one of our basic responsibilities is to make sure she is warm and safe."

Rath just stood there, letting Colt speak his mind, crossing his arms as he waited. "Anything else you feel the need to lecture me on?" Rath paused for a moment, then waved Colt to silence. "I might not be what you expected and while I can understand sharing her with yet another person who isn't even part of your pack is difficult for you, I'm the only one who can help her with her magic. Our whole being is symbiotic with the nature around us, and she was building up so much extra power. If I didn't help her bleed it off, she would have hurt someone. Now clearly, you assume to know her better than I do. Tell me, do you think it would sit well with her if that happened?"

Colt puffed up his chest and I could tell whatever was going to come out of his mouth wasn't going to help the situation.

"Enough," I snapped. "Put me down, please."

He hesitated for a moment, then set me down before removing his hoodie and pulled it down over my head. I was engulfed in it since he was bigger than I was. His whiskey and leather scent wafted around me, along with the warmth of his body. Wiggling my arms into the sleeves, I pointed at Colt, leveling him with a glare. My wolf was hiding in the background, but my magic was in full support of what I was doing.

"This is the last and final time we are going to have this conversation, Colt. Rathal is my mate. We are bonded at a soul level and that is not going to change no matter what you think or feel. I don't care how you find a way to deal with this issue you have but *figure it out... fast*," I ordered. "All of you are important and special to me in your own way. There isn't a competition for my affection or time. It will take time for us to figure it all out, but I promise you, we will."

Colt looked at me with his amber eyes full of fear and resignation. "Little one..."

"Instead of charging out here and acting like a possessive alpha among his fellow brothers who have every right to spend time with me, try talking," I pushed when he trailed off.

"It's going to take me some time to figure out how to trust the others to take care of you," Colt admitted. "They lost you, and you ended up going on a mission, getting betrayed, attacked by vampires, and mated to an elf you don't even know."

I raised a brow at his last point. "Correct me if I'm wrong, but I don't think I knew you for a full day before you marked and claimed me. How is this different?"

"You were meant to be mine. Ours. Wolves know the moment your scent hits us that you are the other half of us. It was odd that you called all three of us, but it felt right in the moment, even if we didn't know it. That's not what I feel with *him*. He's on the outside looking in. An elf can't be pack."

"Do you realize how you sound right now?" I asked, shocked. "What if I told you that it was you on the outside of our *nos,* not the other way around?" Colt's face scrunched into a scowl. "Elves have another level to their bonds that allows them to be connected on a soul level. It's more than what you and I have. He can access my mind, my thoughts, and my feelings while I can do the same for him. There are no walls between us. Do you think you can handle that kind of bond knowing he would have the same privilege with you?"

Colt blinked a few times, looking between Rath and me. "He would be able to see all those things about me as well as you?"

Rath cleared his throat, stepping into the conversation. "The way it works with *gwanur* is that we have the ability to open that connection to each other but also close it. Finley would be the only one we are unable to do that with. She's added Elias and Lane to the *nos* officially, so if I wanted to reach out to Lane, I would, in a sense, knock on his consciousness, and he would have to let me in before I could talk to him or understand anything else about him. Finley can close herself off to us if she needs to since she has a constant flow from all seven of us, and no one wants that many thoughts in their head. Does that make sense?"

Colt turned to Elias, who was standing there observing, looking relaxed, but I knew he would be ready the second he was needed. I could feel his trust and loyalty to Colt, but I could also tell he felt Colt was being irrational.

"Colt," I said, drawing his attention back to me. "This doesn't need to happen now. I want you to be sure when I bring you into the *nos*. Being as we are now changes nothing and I still expect you to figure out your emotions when it comes to Rath and sharing me with the others. While I understand my leaving rattled you, there is no excuse for treating Rath the way you have."

Reaching out, I took his hand and let him pull me to his chest, where he wrapped me up in his arms and kissed my forehead. "I'll work on it. It won't be a problem anymore."

Nodding, I just let myself enjoy the warmth of his body seeping into mine. "That's all I ask. Now there is another issue we need to deal with, but we'll need Lane and Zander."

"Let's get you warm and comfortable while we talk," Elias encouraged. "I'll make you some hot cocoa."

"You guys do realize that while it's chilly out, I'm perfectly fine, right? Just like you guys, I run hotter than the average human. Not to mention, I'm not even a human," I pointed out. "From what I understand, elves are strong and made to exist in nature in all its elements."

"Yeah, well, tell that to my wolf. He's losing his mind," Colt muttered as he led me back up the steps into the house. "He's a controlling, possessive bastard."

Smirking, I glanced up at him. "Just your wolf?"

Colt looked affronted. "I'm not controlling. That's Zander's department."

"What am I being accused of?" Zander asked, exiting the library with a few books in his hands. "Only fair to tell me so I can defend myself in case it's all bullshit."

"You're a possessive, controlling asshole when it comes to Finley," Elias volunteered.

Zander paused, then grinned. "Now that's the God's honest truth. I won't deny it. I was only willing to give Rath five more minutes before I went out there to get her. It's too cold to be out there lying on the ground with hardly any clothes on."

"You guys make it sound like I'm wearing shorts and a tank top," I grumbled. "I have a sweater and leggings, hardly inappropriate for this weather."

"Hate to break it to you, but no matter what you say, little dove, you're not going to change my mind," Zander pointed out, stepping into my space to brush his fingers along my cheek. "Do you feel that... she's frozen to the bone. I'll get a blanket."

"Fine, then we need to talk. Where are Mason and Noah?" I asked as they directed me to the couch.

"They went to go check on Peggy," Lane answered, joining us and handing me a steaming mug of hot cocoa with marshmallows.

I gaped at him. "How did you know?"

"Elias told me. This whole mental connection thing is going to come in handy," Lane explained.

Seeing how excited he was, had me doubting this was the right move. I didn't count on it being another way they could smother me with their love and overprotective nature.

"We'll come back to that subject," I muttered. "Will the twins be coming back soon or do they have other work to deal with?"

Lane cocked his head as he watched me for a moment. "You don't want to have this conversation without everyone, do you?"

Curling up in the overstuffed cloth armchair, I shook my head. "No, it's better if we all go over matters at once." Lane pulled out his phone, but I motioned for him to wait. "I'd like to go see Peggy. There might be more she knows and just doesn't realize it. She's been working with the Senate for years and none of you knew. Safe to say she can keep her mouth shut."

"Little dove, I'm pretty sure I got everything out of her. She broke once she understood what she did put everyone else in danger," Zander argued.

"While I believe you got out of her what she thinks is important for us to know, the knowledge that could tilt this in our favor seem quite mundane and useless," I explained, knowing from other occasions where I'd had to torture someone for information they didn't know they had.

The three alphas seemed to be speaking to each other silently even though I knew they couldn't, yet after a moment, they all came to an agreement. "We will take you to see Peggy. After that, we will meet at the pack house and talk. We need to agree on sentencing for her anyways," Colt said before pinning me with a look. "No matter what she tells us, she needs to be held accountable for her actions. It could have gotten us all killed."

My brows shot up at his accusatory tone like I was the one who was going to be the problem. "I agree, but why do I get the feeling you didn't think I would?"

"The last time we had an issue with one of our wolves, you wanted us to wait so you could help him. In the end, he tried to hurt you, and Elias killed him," Colt pointed out. "Peggy has done something far worse, giving up our pack's emergency measures, and it might very well lead to her death. I just need to know you aren't going to let your omega's need to soothe the pack cause a bigger problem."

"I can see why you would think something might come up, but I assure you this is completely different. Craig was using the situation to get you to kill him. He'd done nothing that deserved that punishment so far. Ultimately, he made his choice and got what he wanted," I reasoned. "The matter with Peggy is one where she went out of her way to cause trouble with the pack, sharing secrets she'd sworn never to give up. So no, I will not stand in your way or cause any issues."

Elias stood and handed me a pair of shoes. "Now that that's settled, let's get this over with."

CHAPTER EIGHTEEN

FINLEY

Zander decided that it would be better for us to drive over to the main pack area instead of walking, so we piled into the SUV and headed down the gravel road. Rath sat next to me with Lane on my other side. It was going to take some getting used to the fact that I could now catch snippets of their thoughts.

"I wonder how the other pack members will take my presence? How much of what we were taught about werewolves was correct?" Rath mused as he looked out the front of the vehicle.

Lane reached out and took my hand, giving me a wink. *"Peggy better not say anything to upset Finley. Nothing was ever going to happen between us. She has never meant more to me than a pack mate."* Then his thoughts went darker. *"What if we have to kill her? One of the alphas has to do it. That's the right thing to do. Will her sisters hate us for doing it?"* Lane was full of emotions, flickering between worry and anger at the situation.

I leaned my head to the side so it rested on his shoulder as I sent him waves of calming vibes. The situations would work out as they should, and everyone would understand that. Pack always sticks together, and if the sisters decided to leave, then so be it, that was their choice. No one but them should be responsible for their feelings. As Lane accepted my help, I could feel him relaxing and agreeing with what I was feeding him.

The drive only took a few moments and we were out heading to a shed that I'd not noticed before. It was by itself off to the side behind the pack house, so it wasn't surprising most people would miss it, but I wasn't most people.

"Look at it again," Rath whispered. "Only this time, pull some of your magic forward to enhance your perception."

Frowning, I called on my magic and saw the air around the shed ripple as if it were a mirage. "Why is it doing that?"

"There is a spell cast on it, so anyone who looks at it ignores it unless they purposefully look for it," Rath murmured. "I don't want to speak about this too loudly in case other pack members don't know this is here."

I sought out Colt knowing he would be the one to have chosen to do something like this. He glanced at me and shook his head slightly, telling me not to push the matter.

As we passed through the spell, my hair stood on end and goosebumps appeared on my arms. Whatever it was, it was strong. Since none of the others appeared to be affected by it at all, I kept a straight face when the bitter taste hit my tongue.

"Snuggles, what are you doing here?" Mason asked as he stepped out of a cell, locking it behind him. "Is something wrong?"

"No, nothing is wrong. I just need to speak with Peggy," I assured him.

The space was bigger than I thought it would be, with two large cells across from each other. The shine of the metal made me think they were made out of pure silver, one of the only metals that will deter a werewolf. One cell was empty and the other held a woman with rumpled clothes and dirty hair hanging in her face. She appeared unharmed physically, but the hollow look in her eyes told me they'd broken her mind. When her eyes landed on me, some life came back to them but only in the form of terror.

"You can't be here!" she yelled. "They said you'd never come back, and everything would be fine."

Before the guys could stop me, I walked up to the cage staring down at the woman sitting on the concrete floor. "It would seem we were both lied to. They told me I was on a job to stop a group of people attacking the supernaturals in our world but instead, they were going to sell me to those very people."

"Good riddance, you will only ever bring trouble to this pack and our alphas. The Senate wanted to know all about you, and when they changed their focus like that, I knew it was nothing good. Then they told me they wanted to get you out of the pack away from your men. I couldn't turn it down," Peggy shot back, her eyes wild with anger directed toward me. "The Senate will get what they want eventually. They always do."

"What else did the Senate want?" I questioned.

Peggy narrowed her eyes at me. "What do you care? This isn't your pack. Those are your mates. You left them the moment they called you. How can you act like you give a shit about anyone but yourself?"

Reading her, I could tell her mind was shattered, but it wasn't from anything that Zander or Elias had done. No, there was something else at work here. Turning on my heel, I looked at the men before me and noticed Noah had joined us with a bowl in his hands with something hot inside it.

"Who else has been in here?" I demanded. "Someone did something to Peggy that muddled her brain, and I know it wasn't one of you."

"Babe, no one but us know that this is here. The pack knows we have these cells, but they've only been used once, and we purposely keep the knowledge to ourselves," Noah answered. "I thought she was acting strange, but I assumed it was the situation and knowing she might die."

"Did you have a witch come out here and cast the spell, or did they give you a charm that you activated yourself?" I pressed.

The Organization didn't teach us as much as I would have liked on witches and wizards, but enough to know what happened to Peggy. Someone had come and scrambled Peggy's mind until she was no use to us or reliable enough to believe if she told us something of value. We'd never know if we could trust it or not. It's a brilliant plan, really.

"We didn't have it built right away, but after we had a bitten wolf shift and kill two people before we could put him down, we decided it was needed. Zander was a part of our pack and he had a connection with a witch that came out to do the spell for us," Lane shared.

Zander swore under his breath as if he realized what I had done. "Son of a bitch, you don't really think they would waste the energy to do that do you?"

"Clearly, she knew more than they wanted her to, or they just weren't willing to take that chance. Either way, she was nothing to them, so what did it matter if they ruined her for life. I can't tell if the anger toward me is real or if they used that and amplified it more."

Elias grimaced at my words, but I knew that Peggy didn't like me, and if they could use that to cause problems, they would.

"What is their end game, though?" Rath asked. "Why bother doing this when it doesn't truly give them something in return?"

"If their end goal is to cause trouble internally, then this would serve a purpose. None of us have that much experience with witches and I would never have guessed that they would send someone to deal with her," Zander said, rubbing a hand over the top of his head. "The Senate was already watching this pack based on how fast it was growing. Now we have an omega as well. It wouldn't have taken them long to learn Finley returned to us alive and well with another man."

Rath listened to Zander speaking, but his gaze was on Peggy as she took the bowl of food from Noah. She acted like a puppet doing what she needed to but not really having any emotion. The hollow look was back in her eyes, telling me that I was a trigger for her. I stepped closer to the cell, and she noticed the movement, focusing on me. Rage flashed to life in her face confirming my guess had been right.

"You should be the one in this cell, not me, you assassin bitch." Peggy snarled, raising her hand as if she was going to hurl her bowl of food at me. Instead, Noah cut in between us, blocking me from her view. Seconds later, she was back to the despondent way of acting like someone flicked the switch off.

Carefully I made my way to the opposite side of the guys, so I was completely blocked from her. "Whoever did this made me a trigger, that's for sure. If she claims I'm the danger and spills everything she knows, then Peggy could single-handedly cause an internal war. Milly and Kaite would understand their sister is being punished for what she did, but if Peggy starts spouting out that I'm the reason the Senate told her to do it, then it could make this into a much bigger situation."

"Maybe it would be best not to have this conversation around her," Elias suggested. "We don't know how much damage has been done or what other spell they could have put on her."

"Wise suggestion," Rath agreed as he led me out of the shed, keeping me hidden from Peggy.

Once we were all outside, I looked at the building, trying to see if there was any hint that someone else had been there. I could feel the magic, but it didn't feel anything like mine. It felt lifeless and stale. As if the spirit had been removed from it.

"Why does it feel like that?" I asked Rath, sharing with him my thoughts.

"Witches use spells created from nature. They use the life force present since they don't have magic in them like we do. Since they don't have their own, they need to draw from something like wizards. There is always give and take. The plant's life force is given up to create the power and the witch or wizard must also give up something in return. More than likely blood, hair, tears, spit, something that carries *their* essence in it," Rath shared. "Once the spell is cast, all life is gone and used up in the casting. That's why it feels lifeless... because it is."

Zander started to mutter something under his breath, but I didn't quite understand what he was saying. The emotions I got from him were self-hatred, disappointment, and anger, taking on the responsibility of the whole situation.

Having connections to the Senate, I'm sure Zander was the person who found the witch and had them do the spell. Maybe that's why I couldn't find out who'd been here. It was the same person who originally cast the spell. Therefore, they wouldn't leave a signature behind. They'd already have their magic floating around the area, so no one would notice the difference. Pausing before I headed up the stairs to the porch, I reached out to the magic, trying to feel if any of it felt newer than the rest. Sure enough, I could feel more substance to it and something fresh rather than the old, deteriorated magic of the original casting.

"Whoever did that first spell is who came back," I blurted out, amazed that I could figure that out and understand what I'd done.

Rath grinned at me. *"It's all about intention, nin mel. Your magic wants to work with you. Now you see how easy it can be if you just ask."*

Nodding, I gave him a smile in return, proud of what I'd just done just by trusting myself and my magic. I wondered if I didn't put limitations on my magic, what else could I do?

The pack house was comfortable, but it didn't feel like home to me the way that Zander's place did. Maybe because it was in the middle of the pack lands and I didn't like to be around that many people. Either way, I was glad we'd decided to settle at Zander's and had enough space for us all to fit.

As everyone settled onto the large leather sectional, Mason pulled me to sit between him and Noah. Out of all my mates, I hadn't gotten the chance to spend as much time with them. Lane and Colt relied on them heavily, but I hoped that would shift a little with Zander stepping up. I wasn't sure how Rath was going to fit in, but I trusted them all to find a way once we got matters settled.

"Where do we even start with all this?" Noah asked, looking at his alphas. "We are talking about the ruling government trying to sabotage our pack here. This isn't something you can just go around accusing them of and live if we don't prove it or find some other way to get them off our backs."

"Once they learn what Finley and I are, they will be even more pressed to get their hands on us. The only thing that's changed is they won't want to kill Finley, well, until they find out about your healing ability. There isn't a reason they should find out about that as it is, though," Rath pointed out. "The Dark Ring isn't wise to write off either. I know the Senate is in our face, but the Dark Ring, we have to assume they know everything the Senate does. Now they will absolutely try again to take her. She just became even more valuable."

Shaking my head, I dropped it into my hands. "How did I go from a shadow in the night that no one has ever heard of to being on the top of everyone's most-wanted list?"

"It's because the world is finally realizing how badass you are, snuggles," Mason teased, poking me in the side and making me giggle. I tried to pull away from him, but he caught me in his strong arms, holding me still. "No matter what you think, you were never meant to live in the shadows. You were absolutely supposed to do something epic with your life."

I sighed and relaxed into his hold, nuzzling his neck and breathing in his coffee and cinnamon scent. "If you say so, just know that I was perfectly happy in my life before."

"Err," Mason cut in. "Wrong answer, snuggles, because your life before didn't have us in it and that in itself tells you how boring it was. Life is always better with us in it."

"While I don't disagree with any of that, I think we need to get back to the matters at hand," Lane redirected. "So what we know for sure is that the Senate is sniffing around trying to cause our pack and Finley trouble. What do we know about the Dark Ring?"

Rath sat up straighter at this question and I could feel he was trying to ready himself for what he wanted to tell us. "The Dark Ring was created by the humans of our world to prove that they were still a threat to us supernaturals. At first, they took weaker species and made them slaves or sport for their entertainment. I don't know who started the auctions and the act of 'collecting' all the supers like they were *Pokemon*, but that's what it's turned into."

Rath rose and started to pace as if he couldn't bear to stand still while explaining this. "Of course, like most grudges built out of anger and spite, it's become a darker, more cruel version of itself. As the Dark Ring stands now, they want to gain power, but they don't want to rule the supers. They just want to be acknowledged as a force to be reckoned with." Pausing, he sighed rubbing his forehead before looking at all of us. "The way we tell our children stories about them in order to get them to behave is exactly what they want. Fear is being instilled in us that the Dark Ring might appear and steal them away from their homes and families. All they want is power, money, and a taste of what it feels like to be god."

I'd seen firsthand how close they were to becoming just what Rath had described. If Delilah could be as powerful in that circle at such a young age, then what are the senior members like? Sutton had been a bigger member, but I gleaned from Rath that he was more of a broker and auctioneer than a true manipulator. He wanted the money and rush from selling off these powerful supers like they were a painting, while Delilah wanted to abuse them to make her feel powerful.

"Do you mind if we ask how you managed to survive your time with them?" Colt asked, hesitantly as if he wasn't sure he wanted the answer. I could feel the guilt, grief, and failure engulfing him at the knowledge he couldn't save his little brother and being faced with someone who had survived.

Rath looked over at him and held his gaze, contemplating the alpha who'd been less than welcoming to him. Reaching out to Rath, I gave him a glimpse of my story with Cory before he died. What he'd been through and what I'd seen myself in my short time in that mansion. I pulled back just as I had to end Cory's suffering, but Rath knew he could feel it in the pain I still carried.

"Being an elf gave me a high perceived value since many believe we no longer exist at all. The Dark Ring still has access to knowledge about my people and our way of life so they understand how beneficial we can be. Most of the time, I was used as an accessory, to be shown off and brought out on special occasions. People would pay for the pleasure of my company where the only limit was I couldn't be harmed beyond what I could heal from. The bonus part to all this was I attended many balls, gatherings, and meetings with the upper echelon of the Dark Ring," Rath explained. "While they kept the knowledge of who was really in charge and how far up the ladder it went, I knew enough to keep myself safe, that is until I pissed off my last master. He wanted me to use my magic to harm others and that is a line I won't cross unless it's in self-defense."

"So he decided to make a profit off you instead," Lane finished for Rath as flashes of those moments in his life showed up in my head.

"Elves can take a lot of damage before they are wounded beyond repair," Rath commented, his voice hollow. "Iron is one of the only metals our bodies have a hard time recovering from and can slowly drain us of magic to the point we die. It's a slow and painful death, one our people only used for the worst of our kind."

"You had on iron shackles when I found you, didn't you?" I asked, thinking back to that moment before getting knocked out.

Rath looked down at his wrists and rubbed them as if he could still feel the bite of the metal. "Yes, but then you found me and saved me. The fates knew we would need each other. I can give you the names of important people in that world and they can give us the Senate."

CHAPTER NINETEEN

FINLEY

"Whoa there, elf, none of us have decided that we want to go after the Senate," Colt snapped, raising his hands as if to fend off the idea. "I agree that the Dark Ring needs to be taken down, but the Senate is a whole other story. If we do that, then we risk everything, and everyone who calls this their pack or supports us."

Rath scoffed at Colt's words, turning to Zander and Elias. "Tell him, tell him the truth about what is already happening here."

Elias glanced at Zander as if unsure he should be the one to say something or leave it to the alpha whose mother was part of the Senate. Zander clenched his jaw almost as if he was fighting back words and shoved off the couch to pace.

"What is he talking about?" Colt demanded of Elias, having more pull to get an answer out of him.

"We might not have a choice in the matter," Elias stated.

Colt growled, hands balled into fists. "Spell it out for me, guys, because I feel like I'm the only one who doesn't understand what we're up against."

"For fuck's sake! He means we are already in too deep. The Senate has been keeping an eye on this pack and they just made their first move to destroy us. You, Lane, and I, along with your betas, are too big of a risk for them. Now we have an omega which, in their eyes, adds to our power base. I'm mated to her, and so are all of you, forcing me to be a part of this pack no matter what anyone says. We are a three alpha pack that is healthy, self-sustainable, and influential to other smaller packs around us. They come to you when they need help or guidance and the Senate will see that as an insult," Zander raged, laying it all out for the others.

Noah frowned, looking incredibly perplexed. "Zander, you make this sound normal."

"Because it is," Zander answered with a bark of laughter. "It's the dirty secret that no one talks about but never does anything to stop. Why do you think those in power stay there? The way the Senate works is the strongest pack or alpha gets a chair, but what if there isn't anyone stronger... ever? Well, then you get to keep your ass right in that chair."

"You've known this happens and never did anything about it?" Lane asked, disgust clear in his tone. "This is the sort of thing your family does and you told them about Finley? Why don't you just cut off her head and hand it over on a silver platter while you're at it."

Anger, betrayal, and fear filled the air making my head spin as the guys lost control of their emotions. I tried to shut down my shields, but it was hard to push them back with all of them in a heightened emotional state. Sensing my struggle, my magic came to my call as I sent it out into the room, bringing with it forced relaxation. Each of them took a deep breath and relaxed, dropping their shoulders and leaning back on the couch. Zander took a seat in the corner, sprawled out, looking sullen but calm.

"That's better," I muttered.

Extracting myself from the cuddle puddle that was the twins, I took them all in for a moment. So much had been explained, but we still didn't know what to do with it all. Did we deal with the Dark Ring first or the Senate? If we took out the Senate, then the Dark ring would follow, but if they were working closer than we thought, it could turn into a war. Looking at all the options and information we had, I knew what I had to do next.

Facing my mates, I settled my hands on my hips after I let up on the magic. "Zander is right. The Senate is going to be a problem that we have to deal with, but not right now. First, we need to take down the Dark Ring and use that to make the Senate unstable. At the moment, we don't know if it's just the shifters that are doing shit like Zander said or if the whole Senate is corrupt enough to remove and start over."

"Finley, what did I tell you about doing shit like that to me," Zander warned as he glared at me.

I just cocked a brow at him. "I believe my answer to that was... don't make me do it."

"Sweetheart, you can't keep us from fighting things out forever. It's gonna need to happen at some point. Our wolves need it to understand the balance of our world," Lane explained.

"Yes, there will be time for that, just not during this conversation," I countered. "If we are going to strike the Dark Ring first, then I need to make a phone call. We need all the information we can get on this group. Every time I go up against them, I find myself at a disadvantage, and I don't fucking like it."

"Whatever I can help you with, *nin mel,* all you need to do is ask," Rath offered.

I flashed him a smile and cocked my head to the side. "Perfect, then I need you to write down the name of anyone you know in the Dark Ring, important or not. We need to find our in, and sometimes you have to look where you least expect to find the answer."

"I just need pen and paper and I'll get started right away," Rath assured me.

"Now I need a burner phone and pray that my contact will come through for me," I said more to myself than anyone else.

"Who are you calling, snuggles?" Mason asked as he handed me a phone.

"Margaret, my old boss at the Organization," I admitted. "She promised that she would help me if I needed it and I think this is the right time to call in that favor."

"What if she is part of all this?" Lane countered. "If you tell her what's happening, then they will know we are on to them."

Smiling at Lane, I nodded. "Yes, that would be true if anyone but an assassin who is trained to detect lies is the one conducting the conversation."

"Ah, snuggles, I don't mean this to sound like a dick, but they managed to pull one over on you for that last mission. How would this be any better when you're talking to the mother of all spies?" Mason questioned.

"The thing about training someone to be just like you is that you learn their strengths and weaknesses along with their tells. The person they sent was the only woman I might consider a friend and we had worked on a mission together that went so well they wanted us to team up. Neither one of us wanted that, but from time to time, they would put us on the same assignment in different ways, knowing we would mesh well. Having her be the lead on that mission is why I didn't question a thing and did what I was told. Tabitha is by the book and wouldn't deviate from it, so my first thought is that she didn't know it was a setup. Blakely and Vicky were both from the Senate to babysit me, so they could have lied to us both. If that's the case, Margaret will be pissed and more than willing to talk to me about it," I explained.

The guys did not look thrilled with my answer, but I didn't need them to be. I just needed them to trust me. I headed out to the porch, took a seat on the swing, curled up on the cushions, and dialed Margaret's personal number that I'd memorized many years ago. Not one to give out information like that, I knew it meant I was special to her in some way but having hope like that was dangerous, so I crushed those thoughts. Now it was time to see if I'd been right.

The call went to voicemail which I expected since she wouldn't know the number. Now I had to find the right message to leave her that wouldn't give anything away if the phone was compromised but let her know I needed her. "Zero-Zero-Five, there is a fox in the henhouse sent by the eagles. I just wanted to make sure you were aware." With that, I ended the call, knowing it would catch her attention, and it was vague enough that she would have to call me back.

If she was working with the Senate, she would want to know what I know, and if she weren't, she would demand to know who was using her agents. Margaret wasn't one to share her assets without getting something in return. All situations to her were a business deal, which is why the fact she offered to help me was so surprising. Granted, I haven't asked her yet to see if she is going to make me pay something in some way for her help. Depending on what it was and how much she could help, I would be open to barter. If you've got the skills, it's better to use them to your advantage, than get caught in bigger trouble because I didn't.

The phone started to vibrate in my hand and I saw it was a blocked number. "Hello?"

"Is this a secure line?" Margaret asked brusquely.

I grinned, appreciating how, no matter what, she stuck to protocol and procedure. "It is."

"I warned you not to make this call unless it was something life or death because it would only happen once. Are you sure you want to use it now?"

"Margaret, Tabitha came claiming she had a job for me and I almost got shipped off to an auction held by the Dark Ring. Can you think of a better time for me to call in a favor?" I inquired, curious to see what she thought of that bit of information.

The line went silent for a moment, but I could still hear her breathing, so I knew she hadn't hung up on me. "Tell me exactly what happened and what was said."

My brows furrowed at the tone in her voice. She sounded worried. "What's going on?"

"Answer me first, Finley. I need to know exactly what occurred before I share information," Margaret snapped.

I flinched at her tone as it caught me off guard, so I explained down to the smallest detail what happened while leaving out everything to do with the supernatural side of the matter. There was no reason for her to know I was an elf or that I had an elven mate who I found. Margaret was now a person on the outside of my life. I was quickly finding that only those I was mated to were safe for me to share every detail of my life with. Once I was done, Margaret swore, and the sound of an object crashing against a wall was a blatant clue that something was desperately wrong.

"Finley, Tabitha went rogue a year ago, and no matter who I sent after her, we couldn't find her," Margaret confided in me. "I feared that she might have gone to the Senate choosing to be their assassin, but I wasn't sure. She could have been dead for all I knew. After what you told me, it's clear she is either working for the Senate or the Dark Ring themselves. Honestly, I'm not sure what scares me more. Both leave us in a less than ideal situation."

"So you never sent Tabitha to come get me and send me on a mission?" I questioned, needing confirmation that I had well and truly been played because of my blind loyalty to the Organization.

At that moment, I wanted nothing more than to have my old life back and fix my mistake. Clearly, that whole situation was showing me how naïve I'd been to be played so easily. Tabitha was the one person besides Margaret who could get me to do something so stupid, another reason why having friends as an assassin was never a wise choice.

"No, Finley, as far as the Organization is concerned, you died on that last mission, and your body was never found. No one should have come looking for you. I'm one of three people who know you're still alive," Margaret explained.

Three people? Who could possibly be the other two?

"Will you tell me who the other two are? If my life is in danger because of those people, I deserve to know what I'm up against. That was why

I called, to find out what you knew and how the hell shit went so wrong," I admitted.

"The other two people are the leaders of the Organization, and I don't even know their real names, just their code names. To ensure they didn't come after you and the Senate left you alone as well, we came up with that cover story. As an omega, you were protected, but some rules aren't always so black and white when it comes to the Senate."

I let out a huff of laughter at that. "Yes, I believe I've seen firsthand how far they are willing to go to get what they want." I hesitated a moment before speaking, knowing I was going to push the limits of our relationship, but I wasn't going to make the same mistake twice. "I need the code names for the two other people who know about me. I also need the name of whoever requested the first assassination from the Senate. Lastly, I'll need access to our database so I can research what the fuck is going on. I'm one of the best, Margaret, and I have my own connections that aren't tied to the Organization that I can go through, but you gather the best intel known to man. Not to mention this sounds like an *us* problem at the moment. They took and used one of our own to manipulate me. They could do the same to others since you never announced that Tabitha was no longer an asset."

"Can't say I'm not proud of you for realizing you have me by the proverbial balls here. As for this being a problem for both of us, I'll agree to that, but I'm not going to give you code names unless you prove to me that they were involved. If I'm going after two scary motherfuckers, then I damn well want to make sure I'm right to do so. As for the Senate, it was an aid for the Senate as a whole. They voted on the matter and decided it was time to take action against the group. We were the first step, but now I wonder if they had a different plan all along, and I don't think they expected me to send a human. Hell, if

Tabitha is working for them, they might have known you were coming all along," Margaret rambled.

Her agitation was clear as her usually permanent calm and collected exterior started to crack. "I still need a name as to who that aide was, so I have somewhere to start when you get me the other information I asked for."

"Can I reach you on this phone when I decide on a dead drop location for the secure laptop? I'll make sure to have all the information you need loaded onto it as well as clearance to access all of our data that will be useful. If you run into something you can't get into, reach out to me, and I'll decide if you can view it or not. While I understand you are helping yourself as well as us at the same time, you are no longer the Finley I trained. She would bleed for the Organization and choose death before sharing secrets. Even over the phone, I can tell how much you've changed being on your own. Who knows what that means for the future, but I still have others to protect along the way," Margaret mused.

Had I changed that much? Memories of my short time here with the guys flashed through my mind reminding me how much they were drawing me out of my cold exterior.

"Yes, you can reach me here, and I accept those terms," I answered. "Before I agree to the dead drop, though, I have to know what your price is?"

"Smart girl, nothing comes free. Tabitha needs to be dealt with and the best chance we have of that is you. Depending on what you find out along the way, there might be a few more names added to that list, but I have a feeling they'll already be on yours," Margaret said, a hint of humor in her voice. "You were never one to let a slight go unpunished."

That was true, and if I was honest with myself, that trait was only becoming worse the more I cared about the people around me.

CHAPTER TWENTY

FINLEY

Finished with the call, I headed back into the house where the guys were talking amongst themselves, none of them looking all that happy. I paused, watching them as Mason spoke with his whole body, arms moving, face animated, while Noah sat next to him, chin resting on his hand, looking thoughtful. Those two couldn't be more different from each other, but they both had a heart of gold when it came to the people they cared about.

Elias turned his head meeting my gaze, letting me know that I hadn't gone unnoticed by him. Although I had to wonder if it was more so our bond than it was him actually sensing I was here. Along with the long hair, perfect skin, and ever so slightly pointed ears, I noticed my steps were practically silent when I walked. Even more so than just from being a werewolf, the fact that Elias was the only one who'd reacted to me being here made me think they might not know.

"My heart, how did the call go?" Elias asked. He didn't even try to raise his voice to speak over the others, but I heard him clear as day.

Was this a skill of my own, or did it have something to do with the bond, or maybe something else entirely? These days I couldn't keep up with all that was changing about me. Moving forward, I sat myself on his lap and nuzzled his neck.

"The call was not how I expected it to go."

"What happened?" Zander demanded, his alpha energy filling the air.

"In a surprising turn of events, it seems that Tabitha isn't working with the Organization any longer. She's been AWOL for almost a year," I shared.

"How could they not tell their people something like that? Wouldn't it be more dangerous not to know, like what happened with you?" Lane questioned as he removed his baseball hat to run his fingers through his hair. "I get not wanting to air out your dirty laundry, but something like this is rather major."

Since I agreed with him, I didn't comment on the choices of the Organization. As Margaret had said, they weren't my center focus anymore, and how they did things was their choice. "The more interesting part of this is that they sent people to hunt her down to bring her back or kill her if she refused. None of the people they sent after her could find her, so they presumed she was dead or was possibly working for the Senate. Even now, with having talked to her, I can't figure out if it's the Senate or the Dark Ring she is now an asset to. Either situation is not going to be good for us, but I think with a little digging, I can make an educated guess."

"What kind of digging are you talking about?" Noah inquired. "You seem confident that you'll find something helpful and I know we don't have access to anything like that."

"Margaret is going to supply me with a secure laptop with access to the Organization's database seeing as now this has the potential to be bad for both parties. Tabitha knows a lot about the inner workings of the Organization. And in the hands of the enemy, it could be quite lethal. We both decided that letting me solve this problem and bring an end to Tabitha would be a wise choice. Margaret also informed me that no one knew the truth about me still being alive except for her and the two leaders of the Organization. Of course, the Senate also knows about me since Zander's mother is aware of most of the details."

Zander's body tensed at my words, refusing to look at me. "Are you saying my mother could be a part of this?"

Slipping off Elia's lap, I knelt before Zander placing my head on his knee, knowing that he needed me to be his omega right now. I nuzzled my cheek against the jeans he wore, purring softly, trying to get him to relax a little.

"I'm not saying anything but facts right now. There is no way for us to know what your mother is involved in or not, but it's something we can't ignore either. There is no way you could have known how muddled this would all get."

Taking a deep breath of my scent, Zander calmed enough to reach out with a hand and stroke it through my hair. I let him sit there silently, massaging my scalp as he collected himself, giving him all the support I could. Not having any sort of parent to look up to, I didn't know how this was affecting him, but I could feel his pain all the same. My wolf let out a sad howl, upset at the fact our mate was hurting like this, but I was doing all I could at the moment. He'd made it clear he didn't like me using my magic on him, so I wasn't going to alter his emotions even though my magic begged me to.

Eventually, Zander leaned over and hauled me into his lap, wrapping me up in a little ball that he cuddled to his chest. He buried his nose in my hair, letting my scent wash over him, causing him to start purring and finally be at ease.

"Where do we even start if we don't know who's actually after us?" Lane asked as he got up from his seat and walked into the kitchen out of my line of sight. I heard the refrigerator door open and bottles rattle about, so I wasn't surprised when he returned with beers for each of them, even Rath. "I didn't know if you drank or not, but I figured I should still bring one."

"Thank you, I don't often, but then again, it depended on the master or mistress at the time if they would let me drink," Rath said, then took a long draw from the bottle. "As for where to start, I know the right strings to pull for the people in the Dark Ring. There is more than one way to gather information if you are not opposed to getting your hands dirty."

Lane and Noah looked the most uncomfortable with this idea out of all the guys, but the others seemed to agree.

"After all they've done to us supers, it's time they got a taste of their own medicine." Colt snarled. "They took my brother from me. There's not a chance in hell I'm letting them take my mate."

"What if going after them brings down more punishment than we can handle?" Lane cautioned.

"Do we think they will try again to take Finley so soon after what happened in Florida?" Noah questioned, feeding off Lane's trepidation.

Elias stood, drawing everyone's attention. "You guys aren't understanding something. They brought this war to our doorstep, and if we don't stand up and do something about it, they will destroy us one way or another. They don't just move on from a problem because we keep our heads down. The options are to run for the rest of our lives or fight with everything we have protecting those who count on us."

"He's not wrong. I've seen people come after those who were taken and get slaughtered for it because they didn't believe the threat was real. If we do this, we need to be all in and all on the same page about it," Rath pointed out. "The thing they don't know is that Finley is as strong as she is and that she has me to teach her all I can. Not to mention she is a skilled assassin and can manage situations none of us can." Rath turned to me, scootching to the edge of his seat. "If we can prove that the Senate and the Dark Ring are working together and that the Organization might be in danger because of it, will they help us?"

I had to think about that for a moment, not really sure of the answer. Would Margaret be able to convince the leaders of our group to make a stand against the Senate or the Dark Ring?

"If they endangered the Organization, I believe there might be a chance. It would have to be obvious and something I can prove without a shadow of a doubt, but Margaret is practical to a fault," I answered.

"Then I know who our first person should be. But, the only problem is, he is well known to the world. If we move on him first, he will have the most information to tell us, but it will also tip our hand," Rath shared. "I do have others that are a more subtle approach, but they won't have the information we need."

"You leave that problem to me. Subtle is what I do best. If this is the person we will get the most information out of, then what choice do we have?" I countered. "The Dark Ring moves fast. They barely waited a week to come after me. Time is not on our side and I don't want to involve others if I don't have to."

Zander's grip on me tightened as if he could hold me back from making this choice, but we both knew it was the only choice to make. "I agree with the elf. It's better to go for the one target to get the information we need than to go after smaller ones and get caught in the process."

The others nodded or spoke their agreement to the plan so far.

Then all eyes turned on Rath to give us the name.

"Maxime Crevier, the tech mogul who works with the Department of Defense to build jets that can't be tracked. I'm sure he does more than that. It's just the project he won't stop talking about to whoever is near him. He is one of the top members of the Dark Ring and the only other man to have a personal elf as his slave. In fact, he is Mr. Crevier's personal assistant walking around like a normal human. It works in Crevier's favor that he hates to be out in the *normal* public, preferring to stick with people who share his predilections that are common in the Dark Ring," Rath divulged. "If we can get Crevier and his elven companion, Jhaeros, we will have plenty of information to work with."

"Jhaeros doesn't try to escape?" I asked, feeling surprised by that information.

Rath looked at me and I could feel a wave of sadness coming from him. My elven mate was distraught just thinking about Jhaeros, but he didn't reveal why.

"Jhaeros is young, about your age, *nin mel,* just a few years your senior. Crevier has had him since he was fifteen years old, treats him like his son, even going so far as to call him that. Jhaeros doesn't want to leave Crevier's side. He thinks that is where he belongs and sadly remembers nothing about his people or the family he left behind," Rath said, tears shimmering in his eyes as he spoke. "When I was captured, Jhaeros was with me. He'd snuck out and tailed me as I went into the city to do errands. As they captured me, he ran out trying to protect me, but as his big brother, I should have been the one protecting him. Not a day goes by that I don't hate myself for getting him caught. Who knows what Crevier has done to him to make my little brother forget everything about us."

Our bond was flooded with his pain and guilt over the situation. Flashes of memories showed up in my mind's eye, casting a picture of what their relationship had been like before they were captured. Jhaeros looked so much like Rath but instead of seafoam-colored eyes, they were a light crystal blue like the clearest water you've ever seen. From these memories, I could feel the love Rath has for his little brother and how much it tortured him when his little brother didn't remember who he was when they met at parties.

"Look, I don't mean to sound like a dick when I'm the last person to question you on this, but are we going after this guy because he's the best target or to save your brother?" Colt challenged, holding Rath's gaze, the tension humming between them.

Rath dropped his eyes, first not arguing the challenge. "You are right to ask such a question, and I will admit, in this case, it's both. The reason that Crevier got to keep Jhaeros is because of how powerful he is, being at the top of the food chain in the Dark Ring. His position of prowess is what gave him the right to claim such a prize from the batch of us they caught. While I am using this to my advantage to save my brother in the process, I would still give the same answer if he wasn't a factor in this matter."

Colt seemed to think on Rath's words before he nodded and dropped the reservations he had on the matter. "So where do we find this guy? I'm guessing he's not someone we can just drive up to his house and snatch."

"He has a primary residence in Nantucket of all places, seeing as his hatred of being around too many people is well known, it's not surprising," Rath shared. "The only thing is that he has a home in all the major cities as he likes to be present for any and all Dark Ring functions. He refuses to stay in other people's homes, too afraid someone is going to kill him and take all his prized possessions."

Frowning, I cocked my head. "Why would he think that?"

Rath flashed me a bright smile. "Could be on account that I tried to kill him when he stayed at my second master's home. It had only been three years since I was kidnapped and I wasn't smart at playing the game like I am now. If I were presented with the same opportunity, I would be far more subtle about my murderous ambitions."

"Fuck, well, now you have to tell us what you did," Mason requested with a chuckle. "Here I am thinking you're way too prim and proper to go plotting someone's death."

"It's not much of a story, I was sent up with the evening tea and tried to stab him with a cheese knife I'd slipped into my pocket earlier. Due to the fact I was so rare, they didn't kill me, choosing instead to whip and beat me, locking me away for a solid month. It took until I had a different master for them to relax and allow me to be around the public again. After seeing what a full-on assault got me, which was to be locked up. I learned quickly to be far more sly and cunning. To wait for the right moment when the small rebellious act I did would ripple out into fruition later."

Mason looked at Rath with a new kind of respect. "Remind me not to ever piss you off. I know we are mate brothers or whatever word you used, but I still feel like there are ways you could get back at me that I don't want to experience."

"That is a wise choice, my friend. I am far more skilled now than I was back then at getting petty revenge," Rath informed with a wicked glint in his eye.

"So it sounds like we need to find out the social calendar of the Dark Ring to track down where Crevier will be," Noah interjected, bringing us back on track. "Is there a better person for us to go after in that regard?"

Rath tapped his fingers together as he pondered, then I got a zing of excitement when he thought of a person. "I think we can kill two birds with this one stone. Delilah is the hub of knowledge when it comes to parties and other events that anyone who is anyone in the Dark Ring should attend."

"Does that mean you know where she's hiding out?" I asked, this idea catching my full attention. "I figured she would go underground, but the way you make matters sound with the Dark Ring, they don't really do that."

"Oh no, a woman like Delilah would never hole up when someone has come after her. You are not the first, but from the sounds of it, you came the closest, and that will piss her off even more, making her stupid and cocky."

Shifting in Zander's lap, so my back was to his front, I faced Rath leaning into my desire to hear the next bit of information he'd share.

"Delilah would have run to her grandfather, Vincent Slesinger, the supreme court judge who lives right outside of Washington D.C.," Rath announced.

Zander shot to his feet. "Fuck! We might as well give up before we even start, that man is pure evil and it's no wonder his granddaughter turned out to be such a cunt. If that man finds out we are after his own kin, there is nothing he won't do to kill us."

"Why do you sound more afraid of him than the Senate and the Dark Ring combined? Is this someone we should have known about already?" Lane asked, worry written all over his face.

"If there is one person you can count on to do all that's in his power to stop something that will give supers any kind of rights or protection, it's that asshole. Many have gone up against him or even tried to kill him, but somehow, it always fails. Now that I know he's connected to the Dark Ring, it makes a hell of a lot more sense. He had lots of scary fuckers to watch his back, along with brainwashed supers," Zander explained. "If this bitch is hiding out under his protection, then going after her is a suicide mission."

"Not if we can draw her out," I countered. "If we present the right situation, I know we can play off her confidence. All we need to do is get the right bait and I know just the thing to use."

It's about time Delilah got a taste of her own medicine and I was more than happy to give it to her right before I killed her like I planned to do all along.

CHAPTER TWENTY-ONE

FINLEY

A knock came at the door, surprising us all since we hadn't heard anyone approaching the house. Closing my eyes, I called on all my senses, trying to figure out who could be outside. It smelled of wolf, but one I didn't know, yet had a hint of familiarity, almost as if their scent reminded me of something. They weren't alone, which made it even more alarming that we hadn't heard them coming long before they reached the door. Magic was the only thing I could think of, and right now, that meant they could be our enemy, or the witch who ruined Peggy's mind was still around.

Zander swore under his breath and set me aside, rising from the couch. "No matter what happens, I need you to trust me."

Not giving us a chance to say anything, he headed for the door. I stood to follow him, but Elias was at my side, pulling me behind him, the others creating a wall of bodies between me and whoever was at the door.

"Mother, Peter, what the hell are you doing here without giving me a warning that you were going to show up?" Zander asked in a harsh whisper. "If I'd known, I never would have told you to come up the front drive and show up at the alpha's house in the fucking middle of the pack."

"Zander! That is no way to talk to your mother," a deep male voice barked out.

"Don't fucking talk to me, Peter. You might be my mother's not-so-secret lover and bodyguard, but you are on *my* pack lands," Zander snarled. "That is unless you are here on official Senate business, Senator Vaughan?"

A woman let out a sigh. "Zan, why must you always make matters so difficult? Do you really want to have this discussion out here on the porch for anyone to hear?"

"I'm not letting you into our space without knowing if this is personal or professional," Zander countered, his voice clipped.

"Morwyn, let's just go. I told you this was a bad idea," Peter muttered. "Your son has never been one to see reason or trust his own family."

"Really, Peter? I wonder why that is? Could it be because my parents' mating is a sham and was only used to gain power between two packs? That you are Mother's true mate, but you have to keep it hidden from the world, yet you make me seem like I'm the traitor in the family for being what I am?" Zander shot back.

"This is going nowhere, and we can't afford to piss off the Senate no matter if it's his mother or not," I said, reaching out silently to my three soul bonded mates. *"Let me pass so I can go to him and defuse this. I'm an omega, they can't do anything to me without cause, and there are too many witnesses with the pack around us."*

Elias stiffened, and Lane scowled at me, not liking this plan at all, but Rath shifted giving me room to slip by him. Elias's hand shot out and grabbed my wrist, shaking his head. *"My heart, this is not a good idea. If she is here to kill you or take you from us, stopping her will bring the*

Senate's wrath down on us in the blink of an eye. Let Zander deal with his mother. I can't lose you."

I gave Elias a sad smile knowing he was caught in a storm of remembering his past and it clashing with his present. Stepping into him, I kissed him, letting my confidence and reassurance flow into him. No matter what happened, we would have to face this moment eventually, and having it occur here on our pack lands gave us some protection. "All will be well," I assured him.

He let go of me but followed right on my heels as I walked to join Zander at the front door.

"Finley," Colt whispered brusquely. "What do you think you're doing? Get back here right now." Colt tried to add an alpha command to that last statement as he stepped forward.

Feeling his order, I steeled myself and chose to ignore it, knowing he was reacting out of fear, not for what was best in mind for the pack as a whole. I glanced at him over my shoulder and gave a slight shake of my head, and mouthed, *"Trust me."* Colt's eyes flashed in anger, and I knew I was going to be in trouble later with him for doing what I'd just done, but if I could resolve this without anyone getting hurt, it would be worth it.

Zander had left the front door open and was blocking the entrance with his body instead. Peering past him, I found a striking woman with long blond hair neatly styled loosely around her shoulders. Her face showed her age with slight wrinkling around her eyes and mouth, her skin a little more weathered over the years but still beautiful. Her eyes told me where Zander got his silver color from and the proud nose and sharp jawline. Morwyn Vaughan was poised as she stood there on the porch of a stranger's home, facing off with her son, who was a stronger alpha than she was, from what I could sense. She wore a simple tailored dress that fit her body to perfection and heels that made her stand out in this setting but portrayed the woman of power that she was. Everything about her countenance told me she wasn't someone to be fucked with or to underestimate—it made me like her instantly. In many ways, she reminded me of Margaret, and I wondered if all women in powerful roles had the same way they carried themselves.

Placing my hands on Zander's hips, I moved him to the side just enough for me to slip past him. "Finley!" He growled, wrapping an arm around my waist to keep me from getting closer to his mother.

Morwyn looked at me with curiosity and a slight warmth in her gaze. "So this is your mysterious mate, just the woman I was hoping to speak with."

"It's a pleasure to meet you as well, Senator," I greeted, nodding my head. "Forgive Zander for being overprotective. We've had an unusual few days that's set all my mates on edge."

"Mates?" a short, stocky male who was standing next to Morwyn asked.

Morwyn gave him a warning look as she turned to the silent men who were waiting at the bottom of the stairs. "I'll be joining my son and his mate for dinner. Wait here until we are ready to leave. I'll keep Peter with me in case of any trouble."

"Yes, ma'am," they both answered with a nod, turning to face out toward the rest of the pack lands.

Peering up at Zander, I poked his arm. "You need to move so they can get in."

He looked down at me, not at all happy with the turn of events. "I wasn't planning on letting them in."

"Zander," I warned. "This is your mother, and clearly, she is here to meet me and spend some time with you. Wouldn't it be better for us all to have a nice meal and talk? You never know what you might learn if you give a person a chance every once in a while."

I willed him to understand what I was trying to say without giving anything away. Zander wanted to believe that his mother didn't have anything to do with what was going on, and this would be the best time to let her prove that. This would be so much easier if I were soul bonded to all my mates. That was something I wasn't going to wait on much longer. The moment I had time with Zander and Colt, I would fix that, then I needed to claim Mason and Noah as well. They were mine and I was theirs. We just hadn't had our moment yet.

Zander grunted but stepped aside, pulling me with him, waving an exaggerated gesture for his mother and Peter to enter ahead of us. "You, little dove, are in so much trouble," Zander whispered in my ear. "Seems this elf side of you needs to learn when is the right time to be assertive and when to be submissive. Letting Mother into this house is a foolish idea."

"Do you really believe your mother is evil?" I challenged. "If so, I am more than happy to deal with the problem here and now. Two bodyguards, Peter and your mother won't be much of a difficulty to handle since they would never see it coming."

He blinked at me a few times before he shook himself out of the shock my words left him in. "I don't think I'm ever going to get used to the fact that you are more deadly than all of us put together. Come on, let's get this over with since it seems like you have a plan or logical reason for all of this."

"Just trust me," I purred, nuzzling into his neck.

Zander groaned and darted in to give me a searing kiss that left me breathless as he pulled me into the house behind him.

Back in the living room, Morwyn was in one of the armchairs with Peter standing behind her like she was his queen. Looking at how he watched Morwyn, she might be that to him, but it was more. It was an expression I've seen on all my mates' faces at one point or another. He loved her even if he couldn't have her to himself or even claim her as his mate. Even so, he was willing to take what he could get.

The rest of my mates stood behind the couch, looking with uncertainty at me as we joined them. "Noah, would you mind seeing what we have to offer our guests?" I requested, running a hand down his arm as I passed by. "I'm sure, even though the flight from Washington wasn't long, traveling always makes me thirsty." Morwyn watched me with interest as I sat on the couch across from her.

Noah did as I asked and returned with glasses and a large pitcher of iced tea and water. "Do you have a preference, Senator?" Noah asked.

"Please call me Morwyn. We are all family here. No need to stand on formality," Morwyn said with a kind smile. "Ice tea would be lovely, thank you. I find it always tastes better when I'm in the south. Not sure why that is, but I try to never turn it down when offered."

Noah's gaze flicked to mine and I just smiled, letting him know that I wasn't bothered by her comment about us *all* being family. If she knew I was an elf, then having more than one mate wasn't going to be a surprise.

"Feel free to share why you are here, Mother," Zander sassed, flopping onto the couch.

"Son, I really don't understand where this anger is coming from? It was only a few short days ago you were sitting in my office asking for me to help with your new mate. Were the books and other information I gave you not helpful? Did you reach out to the contact I gave you to help when she came into her power?" Morwyn asked, her brows creased in confusion.

Zander started to answer, but I placed a hand on his knee, stilling him. "I believe that the change is due to me. When I mentioned we've had an eventful few days, some information about the Senate has come to light, putting Zander in an awkward position. You are his mother as well as a senator, a role you take extremely seriously, making Zander unsure of how much to trust you with."

"Then it's a good thing I came because I don't believe he would trust what I'm here to tell him if it wasn't in person. I'm not sure what gifts your magic has presented you with Finley, but I know an elf can sense when another is lying to them easier if they are face to face," Morwyn stated, her gaze never leaving mine in our little standoff.

I was stronger than her, but she believed her status would make me submit to her. Unfortunately for her, I didn't give a shit about that. The Senate had already proven to me they were not to be trusted, so she would have to gain my respect first then we could consider working on trust between us.

"Speak whatever truth you have to share then," I challenged, even if I wasn't sure I had that skill or not, but Rath was also in the room, and two elves were better than one.

Seeing that I wasn't going to back down or waver, she broke from my stare first, shifting to look at her son. "I'm leaving your father and cutting ties with the pack. The situation has gotten too out of hand and I can't sit by and let them use me as their shield any longer. Peter and I plan on leaving the states and starting a new life overseas once I finish my term as senator."

The room went still as we all processed what she had just said. Out of all the things I expected to be said, that was not on the list. It was unheard of for a member of the Senate to step down before they were either killed or a stronger person took over their position. They made the world believe that they voted people into their spots, and they had to be re-elected to stay on, but that was all for show. The supers treated it like everything else in our world—the strong get stronger, or they die. For Morwyn to even consider the thought of doing what she said, something truly awful must have happened.

"What happened?" Zander demanded as he sat forward, giving his mother his full attention.

Morwyn smoothed her hands along her lap, trying to remove wrinkles that weren't there. "I'm pregnant. It's Peter's child."

"Seeing as how Dad hasn't touched you since I was conceived, I can't say I'm surprised at this news. Mother, you know that if Father finds out, he'll kill you for putting a blemish on him and his family name. The Vaughan's pride themselves on their reputation and a bastard child would not be something he will let slide. That doesn't even cover what will happen when the Senate finds out that you want to leave," Zander rambled as he got to his feet and started to pace, running his hands over his scalp. "They can't know you're pregnant. If they do, someone will go after it and you. How did this happen after so many years?"

"Do I need to sit you down and explain the birds and the bees to you now that you have a mate of your own?" Peter commented, crossing his arms and glowering at Zander.

Morwyn placed a hand on his arm, shaking her head. "Peter, please, you and Zander need to find a way to be in the same room without going after each other. Our child is going to be his half-brother and I refuse to allow a world where Zander and this baby aren't around each other. I don't know what happened between you two and I've never pressed either of you about it, but that changes now." Morwyn turned to me and I saw a flash of fear lurking in the back of her expression.

I don't think anyone else would have been able to see it, but with my abilities and being an omega, I could sense it deep down in her. Morwyn was terrified and she came here to the only family she trusted to back her up. My mother-in-law didn't know me yet, but if there was one thing I was willing to do, it was to protect that child growing in her belly and ensure its parents had a chance to have a safe home. I'd seen too many children in my life who lost their families and ended up at the Organization. That wouldn't happen to someone who was part of my family.

"Ask me," I ordered, knowing the second reason she was here.

"Finley what..." Lane started to ask, but I held up a hand to silence him.

"You have to say the words, Morwyn, so there is no confusion, and I know you understand what you are asking me to do," I pressed, leaning forward slightly, my magic pushing against its confines. "I will warn you that you are making a request of an elf and once a request is made and accepted, there is no turning back. So if you truly want what I know is in your heart and on the tip of your tongue... say it."

Rath moved to stand behind me, his hands resting on my shoulders, helping to ground my magic as it fought against my hold. It wanted to force Morwyn to tell us what she wanted and bind her to it, so we had the reason we needed to act.

"I want you to kill my current husband and mate, Gareth Vaugh-an, take down the Senate, and give me back my freedom," Morwyn declared, her voice clear and confident, ringing with the truth of her desire.

Standing and walking over to her, I reached out a hand. When she slipped hers into mine, magic surged up her arm straight into her heart. A small symbol appeared on her wrist as well as mine, proof of our agreement and knowledge that should either of us betray the other, it will kill us both.

"*Nin mel,* do you know what you've just done?" Rath asked me, pain in his voice.

Releasing her hand, I turned to my elven mate, the one person who truly understood what I had done. "You know I do, and it's exactly what we needed. There is no turning back now. The Dark Ring and the Senate will be destroyed by my hands. Together, the eight of us will set this world free in the hopes that something more will come from it as we prune away all the darkness. That is the world I've lived in all my life and now that I know there is something more... something better... how can I stand by and do nothing?"

"I should have expected no less from a woman who will one-day rules the elves," Rath acknowledged, resigning himself to what I'd just set in motion.

Out of the corner of my eye, I caught Noah raising his hand. "Ah, for those of us who don't know that the fuck is going on, can one of you explain why I feel like what Finley just did wasn't a good thing? Are we really going after Zander's father and the Senate?"

"Twin, we already decided we were going after the Senate before Mom showed up. Why are you freaking out?" Mason asked, smacking his twin's hand down. "But maybe you could fill us in on the whole magic part of it. That made my hair stand on end and not in a fun way."

"Finley made a binding pact with Morwyn," Rath spoke up. "If Finley doesn't do what she promised, then it will kill her and Morwyn. The same goes for the other party. If they go back on their word or try to stop what they requested from happening, it will do the same thing. Both are tied together until the job is done or they are dead. Nothing can break an elven promise once the seal is placed."

"Well fuck," Mason stated oh so eloquently.

CHAPTER TWENTY-TWO

NOAH

It took everything in me not to get upset over what Finley had just done. Normally I wasn't one to get angry or overbearing about what our mate did, but this time, she'd done something that couldn't be undone. Getting up from my seat, I headed into the kitchen and started pulling food out of the refrigerator and pantry, trying to figure out what I would make for dinner. It didn't look like the senator was leaving any time soon as the others started to badger her and Finley with questions about what had happened.

Even though Finley and I weren't officially mated yet, I could still feel a connection to her, sensing what she needed from me. My wolf was fighting for me to go back and join the others and support her in any way we could, but I needed some time. Oddly I feel like she betrayed us all by making this choice before even talking about it with the rest of us. We were a pack and the pack decided things together to ensure the safety of all. What she just committed herself to was the furthest thing from being safe that I could think of.

Taking my frustration out on the vegetables I was chopping up helped slightly, but it didn't do anything to solve the problem we now faced. How the hell could eight people go up against the Senate, take down the Dark Ring, and kill one of the most prominent alphas and survive?

It would take an army to accomplish even one of those, and while our pack was growing, we didn't have the numbers or the right type of people to wage a war.

Moments ago, we'd been worried they'd come after our pack, and that was scary enough, but to willingly charge into the mouth of the lion seems asinine. A gentle hand ran down my back, pulling me back from my thoughts.

"Noah," Finley murmured as she rested her forehead in the middle of my back. "Please don't be upset with me. The last thing I want is to cause more problems for us."

Taking a deep breath, I set the knife down and turned to face her. She looked up at me, her cobalt eyes beseeching me as she waited for me to speak.

"I don't understand why you didn't talk to us about this before you accepted her request. You told her to ask her question already knowing you would agree to it, so why not give us a chance to agree along with you? By choosing to do this, you've forced us to go along with you into this battle because that's what mates do. They fight for and with each other whenever needed. This wasn't needed, not really. I'm sure we could have found another way that wouldn't put us on a suicide mission," I vented, needing her to know that I was hurt.

Finley took my hand and tugged on it, encouraging me to follow her as she walked out the side door onto the patio. Leading me to the porch swing, she motioned for me to sit, then straddled my legs, leaving us face to face.

"I'm going to ask you a question, and I need you to answer it honestly, not giving me the response you think I want to hear." Frowning at her serious tone, I nodded. "Do you trust me? Or better yet... do you trust me to make a hard choice knowing it will be the best option for all of us?"

As she requested, I took a moment to think about what she had asked me. Some might think it would be crazy for me to say since we'd known each other for such a short amount of time, but that was human reasoning. Wolves, once they found their mate, they viewed life entirely differently. Their mate was the other half of their soul. Of course, that didn't mean there couldn't be bad people who did bad things that mated to good people and dragged them into situations that got them in trouble. Finley wasn't that, though. In her heart, she was caring and selfless, even if she didn't see it. Everything she'd done, even if she didn't understand it, was for the benefit of the protection of others. Hell, she ended up as an omega trying to save Cory from the Dark Ring, changing her life forever.

Reaching up, I cupped her cheek with my hand, watching as her eyes closed, enjoying the contact. We hadn't had much time together since she came back from Florida. Maybe that was part of it. I was feeling off-kilter since we weren't mated, and she'd been spending time with the others while Colt and Lane sent us off to deal with pack matters. Learning how to share when it wasn't in our nature was a little more challenging than I expected for myself, but she shouldn't have to deal with the repercussions of my insecurities. Which I'm pretty sure is what was happening.

"Finley, I absolutely trust you," I answered, caressing her soft skin with my thumb. "It scares me to lose you before I've even had the chance to have you be my mate. All of this is happening so fast that I'm feeling unsettled, and instead of pulling you aside to talk about it, I'm lashing out like a pup who's sulking for not getting his way."

She gave me a sweet smile turning to kiss my palm. "You're right, though. I should have consulted with the rest of you before making that choice for us all. Working as a team isn't my strength and I need a reminder from time to time of how it works. Morwyn might've been asking me to do this task for her, but in doing so, she was drawing all of you into it as well." Leaning forward, she placed a soft kiss on my lips. "Just for the record, I didn't see you acting like a child but a man who cares so deeply about me that he wants to protect me from the choice I just made, knowing it would be dangerous."

Pulling her to me, I nuzzled into her neck, breathing her scent in deeply, allowing it to ground me. She was here in my arms, where I wanted her to be forever, but like she'd asked, I had to trust that she wouldn't make a choice that would intentionally hurt us. Although I felt like I needed to be the one to protect her from herself sometimes, making sure she didn't give more of herself than she should.

"Can we stay out here a little longer?" I murmured into her skin.

She hummed her acknowledgment, wrapping her arms around my neck as mine tightened around her waist. This is what I needed, just a moment to have her to myself, knowing she cared about me just as I did her. However, I guessed that my feelings ran deeper than hers, but I was more than willing to wait for her to reciprocate them in time.

I didn't know how long we just held each other enjoying the moment before my twin made his appearance. "So this is where you two have been hiding."

Pulling back enough to peer over Finley's shoulder, I spotted my twin leaning against the railing, arms crossed, grinning at us. "Don't you two look adorable all snuggled up together? I'm a little jealous."

"What do you say I spend the night with just you two?" Finley asked. "I know things have been crazy since the attack, and our alphas tend to be a little domineering of my time."

Mason scoffed at her comment about the alphas, probably thinking it was an understatement.

"What do you think, twin? You willing to risk the wrath of our alphas to steal her away for the night?" Mason asked me through our twin bond.

I rolled my eyes. *"Right, like you would ever say no to an offer like that. They won't argue if she puts her foot down. They know we all deserve some individual time with her. Speaking of which, thank you for letting me have this. I really needed it."*

"Always, man. I've been with you my whole life. I know when you need some space, and while you getting mad doesn't happen often, I think you two needed to work through this on your own."

"Yeah, I think you're right about that," I agreed.

"Well, snuggles, I think the answer to that idea is... hell yeah, we want you to ourselves tonight. Everyone's gotten some lovin' since you got back and we're feeling a little lonely," Mason responded, walking up to stand right behind her so she was sandwiched between us. "Ever experienced being the center of an Oreo before? Because I'm thinking you need to be double stuffed."

Finley snorted at the innuendo, which made us all laugh. "Sounds like you only want me for my body," she teased.

Leaning forward, I nipped her ear. "If that were the case, we'd have made that happen a long time ago. No one can resist our twin powers when we put them to good use." Feeling lighter and more like myself, I lifted Finley off my lap and handed her over to Mason as I got up.

"Just know that you're in for a night you'll never forget," I whispered into her ear, making her gasp before heading back into the house with a grin on my face.

A few hours later, we all sat around the massive dining room table, ready to eat the impressive meal I managed to whip up with Zander's help. I learned that there was a lot more depth to that alpha than we'd seen over the years. Granted, none of us ever really tried to get to know him well since he preferred to live on the edge of the pack lands, keeping to himself. Watching him interact with his mother was another interesting ball to unravel.

"Zan, have you officially become an alpha to this pack now that you share a mate with the other two?" Morwyn asked, cocking her head, taking in the trio.

All three of them paused in their eating to look at one another. We'd started to have this conversation before Finley shut it down due to my brother wanting to fight it out with Zander and we never got back to it.

"Officially, no..." Zander responded. "We've talked about it, and that is our hope, but it's something we plan to bring to the attention of the rest of the pack before just making that change."

"Keep your mouth shut," I warned Mason. *"Even if she really wants to get out of being a senator, we don't need to air out our pack issues in front of her. This is going to happen and you're going to have to get over it eventually."*

"At least he said that he wants to address the pack before it happens this time," he retorted.

I would settle for that answer, for now, knowing there would be a fight between the two of them eventually. It had been the same way with Colt and Lane as well. Mason didn't always know how to leave matters alone, needing to push and push until they pushed back.

"Can this pack support three alphas?" Peter questioned, his tone betraying his doubt on the subject.

A warning growl slipped out of Zander as he pinned the man with a glare. "You know very well that this pack doesn't need to support me. I've got enough wealth to my name to run this whole pack for the next twenty years. Not to mention that Colt and Lane's business is doing extremely well for itself, adding to the pack's accounts on top of what each member brings to the table."

"Wait, if you're officially an alpha to the pack, do I get a raise?" Mason blurted out, sidetracking the whole conversation.

"What the fuck, twin!" I snapped.

"Pipe down. If he says yes, that means you get one too, and we can spoil Finley like the others," Mason countered as he waited for Zander's answer.

"Seeing as you are Finley's mate, making us... gwa... gawn..." Zander started stumbling over the new term Rath taught us. "Whatever the fuck the elf term is, that makes us family. Which means what's mine is yours. The same reason you're all moving into my house, or I would've moved in here with all of you. We essentially are a pack within a pack, so if you want to consider it, getting a raise, then sure, we can call it that."

"Huh, maybe this guy isn't such an asshole, after all," Mason commented.

I let out a huff of laughter. Leave it to my twin to be swayed by something like this. It's not that we were poor or didn't have everything we needed, but we'd come from a pack that never seemed to get their head above water. Half of what we made, we secretly sent back to take care of our mother since our dad was a bit of a deadbeat and blew most of it gambling. He was a beta, but not a respected one that had a place in the pack as we did. Instead, he went from one dead-end job to the next. If it weren't for us always looking out for our mother, they would have never been able to keep the house we grew up in.

"While that is a nice gesture, that is not how it works in a pack," Morwyn corrected. "The pack needs to support their alphas. It's how they show them respect and allegiance. If they are not beholden to you and your care, then what's to keep them from turning on you? I've also noticed how lenient you are in allowing a beta to speak to you in such a manner with no repercussions."

Lane's brows shot up at this observation. "I'm sorry, I don't understand? Mason was simply asking a question."

"Hmm, it's clear that you're a bitten wolf and never been part of a true pack growing up. The beta is a born werewolf and should have known better than to speak to his alpha in such a way. In our pack, he would have been punished publicly for others to learn from his mistake and ensure that it didn't occur again. An alpha's role is to protect their pack and maintain order, keeping their pack in line. A submissive pack is the mark of a healthy pack," Peter explained as Morwyn nodded in agreement.

Colt slammed his hand down on the table, startling all of us as well as drawing our attention. "I would remind you that you are a guest regardless of the fact that you're a senator. Your opinion on how we run our pack is unwelcome and not wanted if you plan to spew bullshit like that. Need I remind you that you came to ask *our* omega to kill your mate because he will harm you and your unborn child? To me, that gives you absolutely no ground to speak on how packs should be run." Colt took a shaky breath, trying to calm himself, but it didn't look like it was working. "Your pack might be powerful, but I never wish to rule mine by fear and threat of punishment. I grew up in a pack where all members respected each other, growing and becoming prosperous until we were attacked."

"It was having a weak pack that caused it to be destroyed," Peter snarled. "They didn't have the discipline to defend themselves. That's what'll happen to this pack if you don't change."

"Not if we demolish the Senate since they are the ones who are behind packs being attacked," Elias interjected, his voice low and deadly. "You can't deny that it happens. I've seen it with my own eyes. The screams of my family still echo in my ears. Why bother asking us to do this for you if you don't actually want change in the world? Think of that baby growing in your mate. Is that the type of pack you want your child to grow up in? If you believe that only the strong survive, then by that logic, if her mate does kill her, then good riddance. She deserved it. Clearly, you were too weak to protect her and your pup. If it wouldn't harm Finley, I'd kill you right now and save her mate the trouble while protecting that pup from growing up in a toxic world."

My jaw fell open at the venom in Elias's words. Never had I heard him speak to an alpha, or anyone for that matter, in such a way. Ever since Finley appeared in our lives, she's slowly started to change Elias, drawing him out to show us the man behind the wolf. Here he was, staring down an alpha and her bodyguard, who was also an alpha, after having told her he would kill her. The balls on that man astounded me.

Peter shot to his feet, snarling, his eyes flashing as his wolf pressed to be released and protect his mate. This set the others off, and now everyone was poised, ready to attack if there was so much as a hint of movement.

The only two who remained calm through this whole conversation were Morwyn and Finley, but the two women were in their own battle, eyes locked on each other. Soon the tell-tale tingle of Finley's magic rippled over my body, warning me she was going to do something, and we probably weren't going to like it.

CHAPTER TWENTY-THREE

FINLEY

Why must everything result in fighting? Verbal sparring I could handle, but when it got to the point where all the men were ready to attack each other, I just couldn't let it slide. There were many ways to deal with our problems that didn't come down to physical attacks. In all the training I received, it was always the last option, and if it was your first, it meant being impulsive—and impulsiveness led to death.

My eyes were locked onto Morwyn, hoping she would bring this silly argument to an end, but she just sat there watching me. *Wasn't she an alpha, a leader of her pack?* Why in the world would she want her true mate to pick a fight with my men and leaders of this pack?

If we started a fight with each other, then it would make fulfilling her task all that much harder. The Senate would be keeping a careful eye on us more than they already had if we developed problems with a senator. There was another angle to this I wasn't seeing yet, but I was close. Worrying about this fight was pulling my attention away from what was important here.

With a flick of my wrist, I sent my magic out and froze everyone where they stood, silencing them so I could think. Did Morwyn honestly want us to destroy the Senate just to protect her child? Was there a way to tell if she was pregnant, or had I been played? What does she get out of this if I kill her mate and the Senate? Of course, it would leave a power vacuum, and someone or something would need to fill it. Was she hoping to be that person even though she said she wanted to walk away from it all? Could a woman who's been in a place of power actually leave it all behind?

Closing my eyes, I pulled a bit of my power and tossed it toward Morwyn, letting it travel through her veins until it reached her uterus. At that point, I let the power spread taking stock of what I could find, but there was nothing unusual or something that would indicate she was with child.

Morwyn had lied to me.

She wasn't pregnant.

My eyes snapped open, and I used my magic to grip tightly around her throat as I stood and walked around the table. She started to claw at her neck in hopes of removing whatever it was that I'd done, but she wasn't at all powerful enough to fight me. When I reached her seat, I yanked the chair out, looking down into her panic-filled eyes as her skin started to turn purple with the lack of oxygen.

"Don't worry, I won't kill you… yet," I assured her, relaxing my hold on her neck. She gasped for breath, her entire body shaking as a coughing fit hit her, tears streaming down her face. "There is one thing that I hate most in this world and that is to be lied to. Facts and accurate information are how I keep myself alive and when someone lies to me, that puts me in danger which isn't a place I like to be. Danger means possible death. Death means my mates go down with me. You see, it's not just my life that I worry about anymore. Elves play by different rules than wolves do. When we mate, it's on a soul level, but I wouldn't expect you to know this since you aren't an elf or spent much time with them. Now I am giving you one chance to tell me why you lied to me and risked our agreement, killing us both?"

"What?" Zander snarled, his rage breaking my hold on keeping him silent. "Mother, what have you done?"

Morwyn looked at me with a hopelessness in her eyes. "I'm dead no matter what happens. Gareth found out about the baby when my scent changed. I tried to mask it, but we had several functions we needed to attend together, which rarely happens, but it was at one of those occasions where we had to play the happy couple that he caught the scent. He beat me to within an inch of my life and I ended up losing the baby. Even werewolves aren't superhuman enough to protect a fetus from that. Since then, he has kept a trained eye on me. Those guards out there are his, not the Senate or my normal security. He only let me come because I was going to be with Zander and he hates Peter as much as Gareth does. I'm too important for him to kill, but knowing him, he is finding a way that I might accidentally die a tragic death that he can mourn and move on from. Finley, I know it was wrong to lie, but I didn't think you would help me if it were just for me alone. How cowardly it must make me sound to go to such lengths to gain my freedom."

"Swear to me on your own life since it's the only one that matters, that you haven't kept anything else from me," I bit out, wrapping my magic tighter, reminding her that I held her life in my hands.

"No, that is everything I have kept from you." She sobbed, a tear trailing down her cheek. "This life of being unable to trust anyone is the only one I've known. I don't know how to be anything but conniving and believing that everyone will betray me, so I keep things close to my chest. If I ever get the chance to raise another child, I wouldn't want them to grow up like Zander did. Your mate is right.

How we have been doing things in our pack isn't the right way, and we could be so much more, but the Senate won't let that happen."

Sensing that she was finally being honest with herself and me, I released her and all the others from my hold. "If you truly mean that, then get me Delilah. She is hiding out at her grandfather's home and we can't get to her as easily as you can. We hold a promise to each other to make this happen and this is going to be part of it. You won't be standing on the sidelines while we do all the work."

"I can do that, and you're correct, there is no way that you would have been able to get into her grandfather's home. It's one of the most secure places I've ever seen, but it was built that way to harbor Dark Ring members that needed a place to hide," Morwyn shared. "He is one of the members that helped to create it, or at least that is the rumor."

Hearing that actually made sense to me. He was a man of power and it would take a lot to question him and stay alive afterward. It would need to be public and loud. Thankfully I wasn't going to need to do the leg work on that part of our problem, but I did feel it was within my right to ask for a boon. "I want her bodyguard as well. The gorilla. He and I have some unfinished business that I'd like to settle once and for all."

"You and Bakos have history?" Peter asked as he leaned back in his chair, looking impressed. "Must admit that fact alone makes me believe you might be able to pull this off."

I wasn't bothered by Peter's remarks. He was a small-minded man who put too much value in looks, thinking I was too small and female to do any damage. My mates weren't sharing the same feelings as I was about ignoring the remark as their growls filled the air. Rolling my eyes, I turned my attention back to the meal, sad that it had gone cold in all our talking. If things got to the point of a fight again, I wasn't going to stop it. Clearly, me doing so wasn't helping to change their minds on handling the situation peacefully.

"I have a question," Lane interjected, breaking the tension and silencing the snarls. "What happened with Peggy, the woman they used to get Finley out of the pack lands? She was fine earlier and now her mind is broken."

Morwyn's shoulders slumped and she poked at her food with her fork. "It is the Senate's policy that all loose ends are tied up so they can't lead back to what the Senate does in the shadows. Peggy was such a person, and we couldn't risk her breaking and telling you that she was our spy since she arrived."

Pausing, she looked up and met Zander's gaze. "Your father wasn't pleased that you left the pack lands to join a no named pack at the time. He wanted you to follow in his footsteps and hoped this singing career would drop off, but it only grew bigger than any of us imagined. Then you started to speak out about werewolves and our lives, educating people, proving to them we weren't just mindless animals. That's when the Senate decided to keep an eye on you, sending Peggy to be our person hidden in plain sight. Once the pack here started to grow and became another kind of threat, we had her gather information and send it back to us if it was a major change. I guess what I'm trying to say is that Peggy knew far too much and it would hurt the Senate if she talked."

Lane's face started to turn red, his hands balling into fists as he tried to keep himself seated. "You had no right to harm one of my pack members. The Senate is our leadership, but that does not apply to the interworking of the pack as a whole."

Peter snorted at that. "God, you really believe that crap? Let me tell you something, pup, never believe a goddamn word anyone in politics ever says because it's all bullshit."

Lane opened and closed his mouth a few times, failing to be able to say what he really wanted to, then turned his eyes to me. *"Help me understand this, Finley. I just can't wrap my head around a group of people who claim to be there to keep the supernatural people of this world safe, but they do shit like this? They might not have killed Peggy, but she will never be able to live a normal life again."*

How I wanted to tell him we could change the way the world worked, but that wasn't our job. *"What is done is done, but we can make sure it never happens again. We will make certain that Peggy gets the best life she can have now with what has been done to her. Ensuring that we get the right people to lead once we bring it all down is the most important thing for us to do. I know a man of your integrity will be able to help change the world for the future."* Lane nodded, but I could tell he wasn't appeased with my answer. It was the only one I had to give him because I was far too jaded to give him more hope than I already had.

There was a knock at the door snapping us all back to attention. "That will be my signal to leave," Morwyn explained. "At the moment, I'm only allowed to be away for so long, and he doesn't trust me to be someplace sleeping overnight. He fears that I might find myself with child again as if I'm a teenager who can't keep her hands to herself. That monster hasn't touched me in that way since I was pregnant with you, Zander, so it's not like he doesn't know about Peter, and I don't know about his women."

"What changed?" Zander questioned, scowling.

Morwyn quirked a brow at him. "I got pregnant. There is a reason you don't have any siblings. It was part of the understanding. We could each have our needs tended to, but there couldn't be a challenge to the Senate spot from our kids. You, my son, are the perfect pairing of two powerful families that sold their souls to the devil. No one else could unseat you."

"That's fucked up on so many levels," Zander muttered as he stood with his mother.

The rest of us quickly followed, saying our goodbyes and letting Zander have a moment with her as they walked out the front door.

"Anyone need a drink?" Colt asked, walking to the wet bar in the living room. "I think I'm going to need a few after the shit show that just happened."

I started to gather plates from the table, needing something productive to do after all that magic I'd had to hold back. It was pushing me to act fast and strike hard, but I knew that was a foolish plan when Morwyn said she would bring us Delilah. Once we had her, the rest of it would fall into place even more smoothly with the added help of a senator gone rogue. Setting the dishes in the sink, I went back for more, but before I got there, I was swooped up in a strong set of arms.

"You guys enjoy your drink. The twins and I are going to have some quality time with our snuggles. Don't look for us until noon tomorrow. I'm not letting any of you fuck with our alone time," Mason yelled over his shoulder as he carried me out of the house.

Laughing, I swatted his ass. "Put me down. I'm not going to run away or anything."

"Oh, I wasn't worried about that. I just didn't want one of the alphas or the elf to snatch you up. Although having your sexy ass right here in my face is rather enjoyable, so I think I'm gonna keep you here," Mason informed me, returning the smack.

Noah jogged out of the house to catch up with us. "Hey, who's going to do the dishes?"

"Not me or you and that's all that matters," Mason answered with a chuckle. "What do you say we have our sleepover in the treehouse?"

"I love that idea. Maybe we can pretend that it's just the three of us stranded in the woods," Noah suggested. "What is there to do when only one woman is around?"

"So true, twin, we need to repopulate the earth. It's a big job, but I guess that's why they chose us to get it done," Mason said, his voice full of humor. "What do you say, snuggles? Wanna play house with us?"

"You two are crazy," I teased, poking Mason in the side.

Noah appeared behind Mason, pulling me from his twin's grip. "Crazy about you!"

I couldn't help but groan. "This is why the world was destroyed in the first place, wasn't it? Men used lines like that to get laid, so no one was having kids anymore."

"Damn, snuggles. You need some ice for that burn she just gave you, twin?"

Noah shook his head and grinned down at me. "Nah, I'll get her back for that later. Just you wait."

CHAPTER TWENTY-FOUR

FINLEY

When we reached the treehouse, Noah set me down so I could climb up myself. I wasn't sure how he was going to manage the rope ladder and having me over his shoulder. When I made it into the treehouse, I was greeted with the sight of the perfect little nest I'd made the last time I was here. It was just as I'd left it, but I noticed other things were added to the space, such as twinkle lights that Noah switched on once he got up the ladder. They filled the space with soft, warm light making it even more magical than I already thought it was.

"We made sure to stock up on some snacks, water, and anything else we might need if you wanted to spend time here. The only downfall to this place is having to pee in the woods. Otherwise, I think I managed to cover everything else," Noah informed me as he wrapped his arms around my waist, pulling me close. "What do you think? If you don't like it, I can take them down."

Peering up at him, I smiled. "Don't you dare even think about touching the fairy lights. They make this space even more perfect."

"Good, I thought so myself, but this is your space as much as it is ours. Both of us want you to feel as welcome in our safe haven as we do," Mason commented as he came to stand in front of me, tucking a finger under my chin, drawing me to look at him. "We can't offer you the same comforts the way our alphas can, but I don't ever want you to think we can't provide for you and your needs."

My brow crinkled at this. "Have I made you feel that way?"

"No, snuggles, you have been perfect and made us feel equal with the others even though we haven't mated yet. I'll admit it's more of a personal issue when it comes to the divide between us and the others. Noah doesn't feel the same way as I do, but I know deep down we can't help but acknowledge the difference in wealth," Mason admitted, dropping his eyes. "We send most of our money back home to take care of our mother, leaving us with enough to get by since the pack provides lodging and food for us."

I was stunned to hear him admit that. Not ever having had a family to worry about, it never dawned on me to ask about his. They'd told me about growing up in a different pack, then coming here to take a higher position in our pack where they couldn't in the one they grew up in. *Why had I never asked about parents or even other siblings?* "Is it just your mother back home?"

"Our dad too, but we don't really get along with him," Noah admitted. "He's a gambling deadbeat that no one likes to have around."

Now Mason's concerns all made sense—he didn't want to be like his father. Pulling out of Noah's hold, I turned so I could face them both, aware from their emotions they needed to know this information wasn't going to change my feelings.

"I never had a family growing up, and for me, I don't know what I'm missing to feel sad about it," I shared, pausing to look each of them in the eyes for a moment. "That's no longer true, though. I do have a family now with you and the other guys. Knowing you care so much about your family to look after them the way you are, shows me how lucky I am to have such amazing men come into my life. I don't know that this will make matters better, but I want to be honest. I have millions stashed away in offshore accounts, and I will be able to live whatever life I want, never having to work again. I don't need anyone to provide for me financially, but the thing I do need is this." I waved my hands around the space. "Having someone to teach me how to love through actions and learning the needs of those in my family so I can show them how much *I* care. I didn't even think to ask you or any of the others about your families because it was never a thing for me. You two teach me every day how to be a better human... well, omega, I guess, would be more accurate. That is something that no money can buy."

Both of them looked at me like I'd just given them the moon and told them it was no big deal. It would seem that whatever they needed to hear, I was able to give to them as they rushed toward me. Mason scooped me up in his arms, crushing me with a hug as Noah joined us in the hug and covered my back, holding both of us tightly.

"How the hell did we end up with someone as amazing as you, Finley?" Noah whispered into my ear, then started to kiss down my neck. "You are everything to us. Don't ever doubt that."

"All of what my twin said and more, snuggles," Mason said with a grin before he pressed a passionate kiss to my lips, only to pull back. "One question, though... do we get to call you our sugar mama?"

Shocked by the question, I paused, blinking at him before bursting out into laughter. "I guess if you want to, I won't stop you."

"Fuck yes! Don't you worry. We'll make sure to pay you back for the rest of our lives in orgasms. Does that sound fair?" he teased, nipping at my bottom lip, a wicked glint in his eyes.

I started to purr just thinking about what he was offering to me. "Sounds like I should get a down payment on this agreement, don't you think?"

The twins snarled, their wolves pressing against me as their eyes flashed with hunger at my words. Mason dove back in, capturing my mouth with his as his hands drifted down to my ass, kneading it with his large hands. Noah resumed his kisses down my neck as his hands slipped under my sweater, gliding up my ribs to cup my breasts. I was officially in the middle of a twin sandwich and things were only starting to heat up.

My magic seemed to agree with me as it seeped out of my skin to envelop both men, making them both shiver at the touch, grinding into me, setting my own body on fire. A whimper slipped out of my lips as Noah's hand pushed up my bra and tweaked my nipples.

I pulled back from Mason, gasping for air, followed by a deep moan as Mason took advantage of the space, latching onto one of my breasts. "Twin, I think it's time we get our mate naked so we can devour her properly."

"Couldn't agree more," Noah said, ripping my sweater right off me, followed by my bra. "Good thing she can buy lots more clothes for us to tear off her."

Mason chuckled as he slipped his fingers into the waistband of my pants and yanked them down. "Would you look at that? There was no underwear under those leggings this whole time. Who knew you were such a tease, snuggles." He took his time slipping my feet out of them, kissing along my leg, followed by nips that sent chills of desire up my spine.

Now that I was bare to them, they both paused to take me in, staring at me like I was the only woman in the world.

"You see that, twin?" Noah asked.

"Fuck yeah, I do, and the best part is she is all ours for the night," Mason answered, his voice deep with his desire.

Noah reached out to me as Mason started to rip off his clothes and laid me down in the nest of blankets and pillows I had built. Once he had me sprawled out before him, he parted my legs and slowly inched his way up to my pussy. He took his time kissing, licking, and tasting every inch of my body along the way, making me squirm with need.

"Noah, you need to stop playing with me, or I'm going to take care of matters myself," I cried out as my body pulsed with need, and another whine slipped out, making it clear I wasn't kidding.

Mason appeared by my head and caught my hands, pulling them above my head and holding them down. "Now, now, snuggles, that isn't fair. Those alphas and even Rath got to spend all the time they wanted enjoying you and this body that's been taunting us for days. We had to listen to everything that happened with your heat and every other time you've had your needs met. So you'll have to forgive us when we don't want this moment to be over anytime soon."

"The two of us work a little differently than our alphas. We don't have any need to give in to your omega whine the same as they do. Don't get me wrong, my wolf wants to give you what you need, but I can resist it long enough to drive you wild," Noah explained, his breath teasing where I wanted his mouth to be, making my hips buck. "Enjoy what only betas can do for you, babe. We have our own tricks up our sleeves."

Finally, Noah feasted on me like I was his last meal. The wicked things he could do with his tongue I'd never experienced before and it was amazing. Moans were torn from my throat as Mason decided he wasn't going to be left out and caught one of my nipples between his teeth. The way he was hovering over me, shifting so his legs held me down, placed his thick bobbing cock right where I could reach it. My tongue flicked out and a grunt of surprise had him thrusting at me. "Fuck!"

"Two can play this game," I purred before wrapping my lips around his cock.

I couldn't take all of him in with the angle I was at, but Mason was more than happy to help me out with that problem as he thrust, his balls hitting the top of my head. Noah must have decided that he wasn't doing enough if I could be so distracted by his brother, so he thrust two fingers into my pussy, adding to the overwhelming sensation. I was so keyed up that with the addition of his fingers, I came, whimpering around Mason's dick deep in my throat as my body writhed with pleasure.

"Fucking hell, twin, you need to have her mouth on you before this night is done. It's like having your soul sucked out of you in the best way possible. I could die a happy man," Mason mumbled as he pulled back, letting me gasp for air. Lifting my head, I tried to gulp him back down, but he shifted back further. "Snuggles, when I come, I don't plan on doing it in your mouth the first time. No, I want to be deep inside you while my twin fills the other hole making sure your body never forgets us."

Hearing what he wanted to do to me while his brother was still drawing out every last ounce of my orgasm sent me right into another one. My back arched off the blankets and I let out a scream. "Oh, my God, yes! Please don't stop. I want everything you are saying and more."

As my body calmed and I lay twitching, Noah lifted his face, the lower half glistening with my slick. "More... did I hear that right? You want more?"

"I will take whatever you want to do to me. I trust you," I whispered, holding his gaze. The heat in his eyes abated enough for me to see what I might call love shine through.

"Then plan on being carried all day tomorrow because your legs aren't gonna work after this," Mason interjected with a chuckle. "Sit up for me and climb up on Noah. I've always been more of an ass man while he's a traditionalist."

Noah frowned at Mason's words, shaking his head. "Why do you have to make it sound so lame?"

"Because you like to keep things safe. Other than sharing a woman with me, you keep it vanilla," Mason pointed out.

I placed a hand on Mason's chest, stopping him from saying anything more. "Vanilla is something you can always build off, a good foundation for so many other situations. I believe we will find all kinds of ways to make vanilla into something more exotic."

That seemed to shut the man up long enough for me to crawl over to Noah and playfully push him back. "Before we get too adventurous, I think I should sample the goods first."

Before either of them could argue, I swallowed Noah down, curling my hands around his thigh muscles. I relaxed my throat and went to work, only lifting off when I needed air. Watching Noah's eyes roll into the back of his head was more empowering than killing a man.

It was easy to take a life, but making someone lose their mind with pleasure was a whole other challenge I was happy to accept.

"Babe, hold up. Stop. If you keep going, I'm going to lose it," Noah begged, his hand fisting my hair like he wasn't sure if he wanted to stop me or help me.

Slowly I backed off him, letting the head pop out of my mouth with an audible sound. "Before the night is over, I will finish each of you with my mouth. A woman can only be told no so many times before she might think she isn't all that good at it."

Noah gaped at me like I'd grown a second head, then both of them burst out laughing. "Babe, that is absolutely something you don't need to worry about. You can suck my cock any time your heart desires, but right now, my wolf is clawing at me to claim you in a more traditional sense. Once we get that bit out of the way, you can do what you want. My body is your playground."

"Deal," I squeaked as I gripped his shoulders and pulled myself over the length of his dick until it caught on my opening. "Now, I believe I was told you belong in here."

Tilting my hips, he slid into me as I sank down until he was fully seated inside. I moaned at the feeling of being filled, one of the sensations I could never get enough of since becoming an omega. It was like an addiction, and as far as addictions go, I didn't think I minded this one so much. Noah's hands wrapped around me, hips holding me still as he growled, wanting to take control of the moment. I could feel Mason coming up behind me, placing his hand in the middle of my back and pressing forward so I was skin to skin with Noah, leaving my ass perfectly exposed for him.

Taking two fingers, he scooped up some of my slick and used it to work his fingers into my ass, warming me up even though I was more than ready to take him. His fingers left me wanting more and I didn't have to wait long before the blunt head of his cock pressed at my entrance.

Relaxing, I shifted back slightly, encouraging him to enter me. Mason took his time working in shallow thrusts until he believed I was good and ready for the main event.

"Goddammit, snuggles, this is better than I imagined, and we haven't even started to fuck you," Mason said, his voice breathy with his need.

The feeling of both of them filling me to the brim was all my wolf wanted and I couldn't help but purr my enjoyment as they started to find a rhythm. They alternated as they got used to the action, then sped up faster and deeper. The only reason I wasn't shooting out from between them was their bodies held me in place.

I screamed out my enjoyment as the next wave started to build. Their movements were so fast I was amazed, knowing that no human could withstand this, making me so glad I was the farthest thing from being normal. Mason faltered as he slipped out of my ass, and in his efforts to get back to where he was, there was a misjudgment on which hole he was entering. The next thing I knew, I was stuffed with two dicks in one hole.

"Holy fucking shit," I gasped, my fingers digging into Noah's shoulders. "Fuck, that is so much all at once. It's like taking a knot the whole way through."

Both men froze, unsure of what to do at this point.

"Mason, why is your dick in my hole?"

I couldn't help but snort a laugh at that question, causing me to tighten up around them.

"Ah fuck," Mason muttered, his head dropping to my back. "Look, I'm already here, so let's just leave it be. We did tell her she needed to be double stuffed."

"I didn't know you meant literally," Noah argued, shifting us all, making everyone moan, betraying how good we all felt in this situation. "Fine, but you better not tell anyone about this."

"Chill the fuck out, twin. Just because our dicks are sharing space doesn't mean anything weird unless you make it that way. Just focus on blowing our girl's mind since that's what really matters," Mason countered, thrusting in for good measure.

The moment Mason started to move again, I latched onto Noah's pec muscle with my teeth, muffling the obscene noises coming out of my mouth. Noah snarled, his grip on me tighter as he held firm, then slowly started to find his own place. Having both of them in there didn't give them much room for speed, but they made up for that in many other ways.

"Too bad you can't see things from my angle, twin. Our good little omega is stretching to take us both," he taunted his brother. "Bet you're not missing your knot, now are you, snuggles?" Mason challenged, his lips brushing the shell of my ear. "You like taking us both at the same time in one hole?"

"Yeesss," I moaned, drawing out the word. "I've never experienced anything like this before and it's amazing. My body feels like it's going to melt with all this stimulation flooding through me. Fuck! You're both so thick I can't believe you both fit."

"Lucky for us, omegas are full of surprises," Noah added, fisting my hair and pulling me into a kiss, his tongue fucking my mouth as much as his dick was.

When my climax hit me, it was as if I got slammed into by a Mac truck as pleasure burst through my body. A cry tore through my throat moments before I passed out, unable to handle the second wave as they came with me, filling me with their seed.

CHAPTER TWENTY-FIVE

MASON

Feeling Finley go limp in my arms as I rutted into her, letting her squeeze every last bit of cum out of me, wasn't the ending I expected for this epic moment. Gingerly I pulled out of her, allowing more room so Noah could lift her off his chest and lay on her back.

"What the fuck just happened?" Noah demanded, panic written on his face.

Reaching out, I clasped his shoulder. "Easy, twin, she just had her mind blown, and it couldn't keep up. Let's just say she is having a system reboot."

"Are you saying we gave her an orgasm so powerful she passed out?"

"Yeah, that's exactly what I'm saying. Congratulations, man, you've accomplished something not just any man can do," I teased, slapping him on the back.

While he watched our mate intently, I grabbed a basket of towels he thought to keep up here for moments like this. Taking the time to clean her up as well as myself, I noticed something different. It wasn't anything physical, so to speak, but now that my heart rate was calming and the fog in my brain was clearing, I felt a tugging sensation toward

Finley. There were other connections as well that I could feel, but they weren't as strong, more distant, but still clearly there if I needed them.

As I was examining this new feeling, I felt pressure coming from one of the connections, almost as if something was trying to gain access. Having a similar connection to Noah made me guess what might have happened. I let down my mental shield and allowed the person knocking to have access to my mind.

"Welcome to the nos, Mason, Noah. It's good to have you finally bonded to Finley," Rath greeted, speaking to both of us at the same time. *"You two already know how this works with each other, having a twin bond. Well, for an elf, a mate bond is similar in many ways, only you won't be able to shut her out completely if she wants in. The others wanted me to ask if you were planning to spend the night out in the treehouse, or should we free up the master bedroom at Zander's for you?"*

I glanced at Noah, stunned to be talking to the elf so calmly in this manner like he hadn't just popped in to check on us through mental communication. *"Ah... can everyone do this now?"*

"Lane, Elias, you two, and myself for now. While Colt and Zander are bonded to Finley as a mate, it's more so with her wolf. So we need her to pull them into this connection. Since you two mated with her as elves would, you were brought right in. Your wolves might still wish to mark her to satisfy their needs, but you're officially a mate now," Rath explained.

"Fuck yea! As for your question, we are keeping her all to ourselves tonight up here in the treehouse. I don't trust the others not to wiggle their way back in for some action," I shared, feeling overly possessive about my time with Finley right now.

"Enjoy your night and we will see you for breakfast. I think that's the longest I can hold them off," Rath commented before pulling back and leaving me alone in my head once again.

Noah laid down next to Finley and pulled her to his chest, curling around her as the big spoon. I took the other side, leaving a little space so I could watch her sleeping face while I ran my fingers through her hair. After some time, I looked over her head at my twin and found him already staring at me.

"We can't let them take her from us," he stated, his voice hard. "I don't care what it takes, but I won't let anyone harm her or use her for their own purpose. Fuck the Senate and all we believed about them. I will light the match myself to blow them off this fucking earth if they think they can come after her. Same goes for the Dark Ring. They want to claim to be the top of the food chain, well I'll gladly prove them wrong."

I just nodded in understanding, not sure what to even say to his rant. Never in my life had I ever heard my twin talk like that. I understood where he was coming from and agreed with him, but I was worried that in this moment, my levelheaded twin was going to do something stupid. At least if he did, there was more than just me to bail him out of trouble if needed.

Dropping my gaze back down to Finley, I reached out to the bond between us, checking to make sure she was all right. Then I felt her stir at my prodding, so I stopped, not wanting to wake her if she really needed rest.

Lazily her eyes opened and she pinned me with her vibrant blue eyes as she grinned. "I thought you were going to make sure I couldn't walk tomorrow. Is one round all you have in you?"

"I don't know. You were the one that blacked out, figured it would be best to let you wake up first. I'm not the type to ravage an unconscious woman. Besides, I selfishly want to make sure you remember everything," I explained, running my thumb along her cheek, then over her lips. "If you're feeling feisty, I think I remember you saying something about this mouth doing some wicked things to me and my twin."

Finley nipped at my thumb before she sucked it into her mouth, purring. "I think it's my turn to run the show."

"Alright, snuggles, tell us what you want," I said, motioning for her to go ahead.

Finley sat back on her heels and looked at both of us as if considering what her next orders were going to be. I'd already decided that no matter what it was, I would do it short of letting anything more happen between Noah and me. Sharing our mate more intimately was one thing, but I'm not looking to go into the taboo realm.

"Stand please, side by side," Finley instructed.

Noah and I got to our feet and did what she asked, allowing her to adjust us into the right spot. I wasn't confident in what her plan was, but the moment she grabbed my dick with her hand and gulped down my twin, I figured it out. This woman was going to double down on us. A grin tugged at my lips, more than happy for this moment since it meant I got to be the next to dive between her legs.

Finley made sure to get my brother good and sloppy before turning to me, pumping Noah with her hand. Unable to have her touching me without touching her, I slid my fingers into her hair, guiding her movements—not that she needed any help. Finley was on a mission, and when she put her mind to something, it was fucking epic. I was quick to discover that she was edging us, using her mouth until she felt us start to stiffen, then pulled back to languidly use her hand while she switched cocks.

"Babe, you are playing a dangerous game here," Noah cautioned. "We only have so much control before our wolves take over."

Finley looked up at him through her lashes while her head bobbed up and down on him. The little vixen was taunting him almost as if she wanted him to lose control. I didn't have the heart to tell her Noah was the master at controlling his feelings and actions. There was only room for one wild child and that was me. A glint showed in her eyes as her free hand that had been holding on to his hip slipped down to cup his balls, rolling them in time with her other movements.

Noah grunted and thrust deeper into her mouth. "I'm making this clear to you now, Finley. If you keep pushing, I will push back."

"I am fully aware of what I'm doing and more than happy to deal with the consequences," Finley shared with us both.

Oddly it was the most natural thing in the world to hear her talk to us like that. As if she was always supposed to be in our heads. Now she was, I felt more complete, settled, if you will. Caught up in my thoughts, I didn't see what she did, but it pulled a snarl from my brother, who proceeded to grab both sides of her head, keeping her steady as he fucked the ever-loving shit out of her mouth.

"Is this what you wanted, Finley, to get me to break my hold on my control? To let my wolf take over and claim what's his?" Noah taunted, his voice gruff with his wolf so close to the surface. "You get upset when we want to fight matters out between us, but you like to be controlled in the bedroom, don't you?"

My brows shot up at the words coming out of my twin's mouth. In an odd way, I was proud, he always deferred to the others doing what was asked of him and Finley must have somehow sensed he needed some control. It seemed she planned to let him control a portion of his time with her and Noah was going for it.

Pulling her off him, he turned her head back to me. "I want your pretty little mouth on him while I fuck you from behind. I didn't get to have your pussy all to myself and I think now's the right time to make that happen. I want you to give it everything you have and let my brother's cum shoot down your throat as you take him down to the balls. Can you do that? Can you be a good girl and do as I ask?"

"When the fuck did you get so good at dirty talk? That was always my move," I commented as Finley fixed her hands on my hips, settling herself before me. *"I don't know what she did to you, but all I have to say is about fucking time you took what you wanted for once."*

"Be careful and don't screw this up for me. If you do, I might change my mind about letting her allow you to finish," Noah warned, catching my eye as he knelt behind her, stroking his cock.

Grinning back at him, I shook my head. *"Look who has a sleeping alpha side. I knew it couldn't just be me. Enjoy your moment. I won't interfere. I'm getting everything I want."*

"Any second thoughts, Finley, before we rule over your body?" Noah asked, unable to take total control without consent.

"None at all. I am yours to do with as you wish," Finley answered, giving Noah the last confirmation he needed before he slammed into her pussy.

She let out a yelp, then it was quickly followed by a moan of pleasure as Noah started to thrust deeply and powerfully into her. As she used me to keep from getting knocked over, my dick slapped her cheek as I fought against my twin's movements. The fucker was strong, but this wasn't the first time we'd played these roles, only I was the one who was typically in his spot. Having him running the show was new, but I couldn't say he didn't have good ideas. A growl was pulled from me the moment Finley's hot mouth wrapped around me once more. This time though, I had her full attention, and she made it clear I wasn't going to be able to last as long as I would like.

The treehouse was filled with the sounds of flesh slapping, moaning, sucking, and grunts of pleasure as we lost ourselves to this moment. My wolf howled in joy as we relished this time with our mate and having shared the experience with Noah, the one person who has and always would have my back. The pleasure of knowing we shared Finley and there was no fear of a woman tearing us apart made it all the more perfect.

My body started to tense, and after being edged for so long already, I wasn't sure I could hold back any longer. I was going to explode and there was nothing I could do to stop it. Wrapping my hands around her head, I pulled her close and fucked deep into her mouth, feeling my cock sliding down her throat until I couldn't control my own movements. With one last powerful rut, I came, shooting into her mouth and down her throat. She swallowed everything like the fucking goddess she was.

Now that my wolf had marked her sufficiently with his seed, he wanted to leave one more mark on her. Pulling her from my cock I kissed the fuck out of her, palming her breasts, not giving two shits that I could taste myself on her tongue. I shifted so I was kissing down her neck—the opposite side of where Colt had marked her—and I bit down, the taste of her blood seeping into my mouth, letting me know I'd bitten deep enough. Now the world would know that she was mine and I was hers forever.

"Fucking fuck," Noah swore as he came in her, his hips bucking wildly. He moved to bite just under my mark in the crook of her neck, side by side as we've always been.

The three of us fell to our sides, a jumble of legs and arms intertwined. We stayed like this as we fell asleep for a short while, regaining our strength before coming up with new ways the three of us could be together—round after round of mind-blowing passion followed by quick naps to recover.

Finally worn out, we drifted off to sleep, the air filled with sex, love, and a satisfied omega.

CHAPTER TWENTY-SIX

FINLEY

The shrill ringing of a cell phone startled me awake out of a deep, dreamless sleep. The sun drifted into the treehouse through the windows, giving me light to maneuver from between the two men wrapped around me. I tried to do my best not to step on, a knee, or elbow anything too important or sensitive, but the grunt Mason made told me I wasn't successful.

"Snuggles, where are you going?" he whispered, his voice rough with sleep.

"The burner phone is ringing and it could be Margaret calling me back," I replied as I got to the phone just as the call ended.

Scooping it up out of the pile of clothes we all left behind, I saw it showed a missed call from a blocked number. Now I had to hope that she would call me back. It was our protocol that if we couldn't answer, we would let it go to voicemail, and they would leave a coded message or try to call back. My gut told me she wouldn't leave a message—too risky with a phone neither one of us bought or set up. As I was holding it, the phone started to vibrate in my hand before it began its song, only this time Lane's name appeared.

"Good morning," I answered.

"Oh, ah... good morning, sweetheart. I wasn't expecting you to answer so quickly or at all the first time," Lane admitted with a chuckle. "How are you? Did they let you get any sleep?"

I could hear the others in the background arguing about something as Lane waited for my answer. It seemed everyone was awake back at the house. "Yes, I did get a little sleep, but I'm thinking a nap later would be a good idea."

"Sounds like a wise choice. Can we expect you for breakfast in the near future?" Lane questioned.

Glancing over my shoulder, I found the twins sitting up, watching me with blurry eyes awaiting my answer. "Yeah, everyone is up, and I think Margaret tried to call me, so I think it's best for us to be awake. I'll have to shift and run over since someone had the bright idea to literally tear my clothes off me."

Mason grinned at that, giving me a thumbs up. "Best choice I ever made."

Returning his grin, I looked out the window to find the sky was clear and the sun bright. "It's a nice spring day. Who knows, I could just go for a walk in the nude. I hear from people it's incredibly liberating."

Snarls from the room and on the other end of the line told me everyone was listening.

"Little dove, I would advise against that if you want to be able to sit for breakfast," Zander called from the background.

"Sounds like shifting is the best plan," Lane suggested, humor in his tone. "We'll see you in a bit."

After I hung up, I looked at the twins sitting before me, appearing as exhausted as I felt. Coffee would do us all wonders, but if Margaret called back, we would need to head out to meet her.

"What are the chances the others will let me meet with the contact without all of you coming with?" I asked, cocking my head slightly, taking in the sight of them standing to get dressed.

My wolf stood up and took notice of her sexy mates, and my scent filled the space, revealing my thoughts. *How was it that I could possibly still crave them so much when we indulged in each other so freely last night?* Something told me I would always want them, just like my other mates. Yes, omegas tended to be more hyper-sexual to encourage breeding, but I don't think that was what this was. My feelings for them were far deeper than needing to reproduce. No, it was the feeling like I was no longer complete without them.

"Babe, you need to stop looking at us like that or we are never going to get to breakfast. My willpower is only so strong," Noah warned with a smirk on his full lips.

"As for your question, snuggles... no. I don't think there is a snowball's chance in hell that you can meet up on your own." Mason raised a hand to stop me from speaking. "What you might be able to do is get them to stay in the car while one of us goes with you."

I mulled that over a moment and nodded. "That is something I could work with. I'm just worried that having all of you around will make it hard to keep this exchange from going unnoticed. Zander can't go anywhere without someone recognizing him."

"That's a good point, and I'm sure as an assassin, that type of person around you makes things challenging," Noah commented as he pulled on his pants.

"I would never ask Zander to change his life, but it does mean I will need him to sit things out on occasion," I agreed.

Once they were dressed, I dropped down out of the treehouse and shifted. My wolf was pleased to be going on a run after so many days trapped in my human body. Stretching, I shook out my fur and lifted my nose to scent the area around us, taking in a deep breath. My magic seeped out of me and into the ground, greeting the trees and plant life. Leaves rustled in the light breeze as if they were waving back at me. A sense of tranquility floated around me as the forest reached out, telling me what was happening in the woods around us. I got images of a hiker lost in the foothills of the mountain that was wandering in our direction but was still a day's walk away. Sending my thanks, the forest released me and settled back into its normal routine, leaving me to deal with the problem.

"The forest just told me a hiker got lost in the foothills, heading our direction. You might want to let the scouts know to the northeast to keep an eye out," I relayed to Mason and Noah. They both looked at me with raised brows.

"Damn, this new connection is going to be so nice now that we can talk while in wolf form," Noah muttered as he shoved his hand in his pockets and headed off in the direction of Zander's house.

"I'm going to run ahead so I can shower and change," I informed them before I darted off into the woods.

Mason's deep laughter filled the air. *"Afraid if we join you that you won't get clean?"*

"That's exactly what would happen," I shot back.

Even though that was a real outcome, the other part was that my wolf was begging to stretch her legs. I also knew I could get in a run burning off some of the energy I had stored from being a human for so long. Now that the trees and other plants of the forest were watching out for me, I wasn't worried about getting caught off guard while on my home turf. My muscles sang as I pushed my body to go faster, digging my claws into the soft earth, propelling me forward. The joy I felt couldn't be contained, and I let out a howl, scaring a flock of sparrows up in a tree, causing them to burst out into the sky. While being a werewolf wasn't something I had planned on happening in my life, now that I'd embraced it, I wouldn't change it for the world.

When I finally arrived at the house, the patio door was open and I darted inside but didn't account for the fact Zander had all hardwood floors and came sliding into the kitchen. Trying to stop the sound of my nails on the wood drew my other mates' attention, but Colt, who was right in my path, didn't turn around fast enough to see me coming right for him. Crashing into his legs, he toppled over onto me, and we both landed on the floor in a heap.

"Finley?" Colt blurted, surprised to see it was me. "First time on wood floors?" he asked with a chuckle.

I snorted at him, picking myself up off the floor, shaking my head, frustrated at how foolish I'd just appeared.

Lane came and squatted down in front of me, reaching out a hand, scratching behind my ear. "Don't take it too hard, sweetheart, all of us have made that mistake at least once or twice in our lives. There's no instinct for knowing how to deal with slippery flooring. Go on head up, shower, get dressed, and we'll pretend this never happened."

Glancing at the others, they nodded with smirks on their faces, making me second guess if they would really let the matter drop. Either way, I wanted to get ready for the day and clearly needed to do that on two legs. Letting out a huff, I flicked my tail at them and carefully made my way to the stairs that were thankfully carpeted, so I could bolt up to Zander's room without further incident.

⁂

Ready for the rest of the day, I came back down to the kitchen and found the counter filled with almost empty platters of food. They'd gone all out and made eggs benedict in different ways, but I was more excited about the two chocolate chip pancakes left. There was even a canister of whipped cream to add to the experience that made me smile. The guys were already seated, even the twins, with plates full of food which explained the lack of food left. I checked for a plate, but I couldn't find one sitting out, so I went to the cabinet.

"Little dove, what are you looking for?" Zander called from his seat.

Glancing over my shoulder, I showed him the plate I'd grabbed. "Need something to put the food on."

"Am I to believe that you think we wouldn't have made you a plate before we dove in?" Zander demanded, his brow creased.

Pausing, I looked over the table and found a plate with a cover over it to keep it warm in the spot I normally sat in. "Oh."

"Come sit, *nin mel*. He's just being testy because you weren't in the house last night and he missed you," Rath shared, reaching out a hand to me.

Zander glared at Rath but didn't correct the statement, making my heart melt a little, knowing he missed me that much. Taking my seat,

I started in on my food, my stomach growling its delight at being fed. After the pace the twins put me through, I shouldn't be surprised I was starving.

"Didn't they have snacks or something for you in the treehouse?" Zander asked, concerned.

Between him and Mason, I'd never had people care about how much or how often I ate. "Ah well, I can't say that was something we were worried about..."

"Honestly, Zander, let the woman eat her meal in peace," Colt grumbled, waving a fork at him. "None of us got much sleep last night, so we're all acting like assholes, but she doesn't deserve that from us. At some point, we're all going to want alone time with her, and that means we can't make her feel bad for doing it."

"While I wholly agree with you, Colt, I'm more surprised you're the one who came to that conclusion first," Lane commented, smirking at Colt from behind his coffee cup. Colt just huffed and shoved more bacon into his mouth, effectively ending the conversation.

The table fell into a comfortable silence as we ate only for it to be broken by a cellphone ringing. Mason pulled the phone out of his pocket and looked at it before tossing it to me. "Looks like it's for you."

"Hello?" I answered the moment I caught it.

"Knoxville zoo, two hours. Reptile building, look for the maintenance man by the poisonous lizards," a voice on the other end of the call said, then hung up.

The guys watched me expectantly as I set the phone aside. "Who wants to go to the zoo?"

"The zoo..." Colt repeated. "Why the zoo?"

"It's a place with plenty of people and it gives you a clear reason to be somewhere. What could be more normal than a woman and her boyfriends enjoying a date at the zoo?" I asked, resting my chin on my hands as I looked at them. "I think I've been to almost every zoo in America at this point. Although this will be a first time at Knoxville's, not much demand for assassination in Tennessee, if I'm being honest."

"Why do I feel like we should be offended?" Mason asked. "What makes Tennessee less worthy?"

"While I'm sure that is something we all need to mull over, shouldn't we be getting ready to leave?" Lane pointed out, looking at his watch. "It will take us a half hour to get there or more depending on traffic. Then we need to park, get tickets, and I feel like we should spend a little time there before heading to the meeting, so it's not suspicious if the Senate has someone keeping an eye on us."

"God, could you sound any more like a dad?" Mason teased, shaking his head. "Zander can't come, though."

This had the man in question snapping his head in Mason's direction. "Why the fuck not?"

"Ah, because you're an international superstar who has people following after him, watching his every move. Come on, man, think about it. We are going on a stealth mission and you are like a neon beacon to the world around you."

Zander looked like he was going to argue but then took a moment to think about what Mason was saying. "Fine, I need to meet with my manager at the office downtown anyways. You can drop me off, so it gives a reasonable excuse for why I'm not with you guys. If the Senate or Dark Ring is watching, they will notice I didn't come with you."

Getting up from my seat, I walked over to Zander and let him pull me onto his lap. "Thank you, I know it's not what you wanted to do, but it will be the most helpful thing you can do for me. When we get back, I think a group nap is in order, don't you?"

Zander started to purr, running his nose along my neck as he nodded his agreement. "That sounds like a perfect plan, little dove." He pressed a kiss to my neck right where my pulse was just under the surface before lifting me off his lap to stand next to his chair. "If I let you sit there much longer, I won't be able to leave you when we get into town."

Bending over, I grabbed his face and pulled him into a deep kiss reminding him what he had to look forward to. "Just to get you by until later."

"Hmm, little dove, being a tease is a dangerous game to play with me right now," Zander warned.

I pulled back, grinning at him as I headed off to find shoes and a jacket, getting a slap on my ass as I walked away.

CHAPTER TWENTY-SEVEN

FINLEY

In the back of the SUV with Elias, I snuggled into his side as he ran his hand up and down my back, lulling me into a nap. I didn't think I was all that tired but feeling safe, cuddled, and my wolf soaking up the attention, I couldn't help but drift in and out. The hum of conversation as the guys talked along with the soft music on the radio made it all but impossible to stay awake, but I didn't feel it was wise to sleep and lose focus on what we were about to do.

"My heart, just let go. The rest of us are here to deal with whatever might come up and I doubt anything will happen to us on the drive. It would involve too many people and situations they can't control," Elias whispered, pressing a kiss to my forehead. "You are tired and we are going into an unknown situation. The nap might help."

He had a point and this wasn't anything more than retrieving the promised laptop for me to start working on gathering data. I wasn't going after a target. I didn't need to be physically ready to take someone down. If that did end up being the case, then I had six men to be able to come to my defense. I wasn't doing this on my own anymore. I was part of a team and that's the way I wanted to think of it. The work of retraining my brain to accept working with others was going to be challenging, but I could do it. Taking the first step in trusting others would be to simply take a nap right here and now.

"Wake me when we get into the city. I want to make sure I say goodbye when we drop Zander off," I requested as I got more comfortable.

"Of course, I'm pretty sure he would wake you regardless to make sure that happened," Elias answered with a huff.

I let myself drift off to sleep with a smile on my face, enjoying the fact that all my men were starting to look out for each other in a deeper way than just being pack.

***

"Little dove," Zander called, a finger tracing the outline of my jaw. "We've arrived at the studio."

My eyes slowly opened and I had to blink a few times to clear the fogginess to see Zander clearly. I smiled at him, catching his hand and pulling it from my face to kiss the palm. "I'm sorry you can't come with us."

"It's alright, little dove. There will be other things we can do together on a real date," Zander said, brushing off my worry. "Try to have a little fun while you're there, so the trip isn't wasted."

I nodded and sat up so I could throw my arms around his neck and hug him tightly. "I love you," I whispered in his ear, keeping it low enough that he should be the only one who heard it.

When I sat back, the grin on his face made taking the risk of saying it so early worth it. "And I, you," he responded, keeping our moment just for us. "I'll call you guys when I'm done here and maybe if you're done with the exchange, I can join you."

"Go be amazing," I said, encouraging him to step out of the vehicle when I sensed he wasn't going to do it on his own. With a groan, he hopped out and waved to us as we pulled back out onto the road and headed for the zoo.

Lane had managed to buy tickets online, so it was simple and easy for us to walk right up to the gate and into the zoo itself. We had about forty-five minutes until the meet, so we looked over the map to see what side of the zoo the reptile building was located on. The most interesting part of all of this was the guys' reactions. My mates were so excited to spend time here looking at all the information plaques and talking about the different shifters species they knew.

"Remember that tiger shifter we guarded who refused to do anything in the afternoon because that's when he scheduled his naps?" Mason asked Noah. "Man, that was the best and worst bodyguard job ever."

"All bodyguard jobs are strange in their own way, especially since Zander was always the one recommending us to his famous friends," Noah added.

Mason nodded as we wandered down the path, taking in the red panda enclosure. The small red creature was climbing around in the bamboo trees, keeping a careful eye on us as we approached. I'd noticed that many of the animals in the zoo seemed far more aware of us than I'd ever seen previous times I'd been to a zoo.

"Do they know we're shifters?" I asked, leaning on the railing and looking up at the panda.

Lane leaned his back against the fencing next to me, keeping an eye on the people around us more than the animal. "There isn't any real proof, but I think they know we're different than normal humans. We carry the scent of a predator, and it can set off instincts in other animals, even in our human bodies. The worst are other dogs or wolves since we scent more like them, which confuses them on how they should interact with us. It would be interesting to see what happens with you being an omega since Colt and me being alphas typically upset them."

"It's time," Elias interjected, running a hand down my back in reassurance for himself or me, I wasn't sure.

When I tried to check in on him, I could tell he was keeping his thoughts to himself and wasn't giving me much to work with. I'd thought having this connection to him would give me a deeper insight into who he was, but it seems that it had become his default over the years of avoiding emotion. Helping me do this wasn't something they supported, but they understood what we would get from it outweighed the possible risk. I'd done these kinds of drops many times over the years and not once had there been any issues. There was no reason to suspect there would be this time.

I reached out and took Elias's hand as we walked to the reptile building, trying to reassure him. He glanced at me out of the corner of his eye while giving my hand a squeeze before letting it go.

"You might not be worried about this, Finley, but as your Sentinel, I can't help but be ready for the worst-case situation," he explained to help soften the rejection as he picked up the pace to be a few steps ahead of me.

Rath was right at my elbow, offering me support while the others fell into an easy formation around me without drawing attention to the fact they were ignoring everything else but the people around them. Lane opened the door only after Elias went in first and sounded the all-clear through our connection. Thankfully, those I had one with were keeping the lines open between all parties, leaving Colt to be the only one on the outside. That didn't matter since he took up the rear, making sure no one could sneak up on us.

A blast of humid air hit me in the face as we entered the building, along with a scent that seemed to be the same no matter what reptile exhibit you went to. The instructions were to look for a maintenance person at the poisonous lizards section. Per our code, I would have no idea what this person looked like, but they would be able to pick me out. This made it easier for us assets to act normally, knowing we could get called out or approached and not have to scan the space for someone.

Spotting the plaque pointing to the area we were looking for, I drifted that way, pausing to take in a few other snakes or spiders as I went. The room wasn't all that big when I turned into the right area, and sure enough, there was a man working on a railing that had fallen down. Ignoring him, I started on the end furthest from him and headed in that direction. When I made it through the whole exhibit, I was going to leave when Rath grabbed my elbow, his face confused as he flicked his eyes at the man.

Smiling, I leaned in to kiss him on the cheek. "Trust me," I whispered.

"Ma'am!" someone called after me as I left the room.

Glancing over my shoulder, I saw the maintenance man holding out a cloth bag to me. "Yes?"

"Didn't want you to leave your purse behind. You women always carry important items in them." He chuckled.

Stepping back toward the man, I took the purse and slipped it over my shoulder. "Thank you. I can't believe I almost left it. Hun, why didn't you say anything?" I asked, turning on Rath with a scowl.

"I'm sorry, dear. It's so dark in this area, I didn't see you set it down," Rath answered, playing along, holding out a hand to me and nodded to the man. "Thank you, sir. I would have never heard the end of it if she left it here."

"Happy to help. Enjoy the rest of your day." The man waved and went back to fixing the railing.

Clutching the bag tight to my side, I felt the shape of a laptop in it along with a few other items, but my guess was they would be props. They wouldn't risk this laptop ending up in anyone else's hands. It would risk revealing far too many secrets to the world.

None of us spoke as we finished looking at all the other reptiles in the building before exiting back out into the zoo. There was a café a little ways down, giving us the perfect excuse to rest for a moment and take stock of what else might be in this bag.

"Can we stop for a snack?" I asked, pointing, and as if on cue, my stomach rumbled.

Mason's head whipped to look at me with a frown. He hated it when I didn't eat enough throughout the day to keep up with my new shifter metabolism. "Snuggles, what are we going to do with you? Do I need to start carrying food with us wherever we go?"

"That's a tad bit drastic since there are plenty of places for us to eat around here. Let's just grab a bite and rest for a bit before we head to the other side of the zoo?" I suggest, trying not to roll my eyes at my mate.

He sighed and the others merely grinned at our interaction as we headed over to the café. I took a seat at one of the outside tables knowing Mason would order one of everything off the menu for me to eat or share with the others. Rath, Elias, and Colt stayed with me as the other three went to manage the meal they were about to bring back.

I placed the canvas bag on the table but didn't open it right away. Instead, I took stock of what was happening around me, feeling like I was being watched. It was possible Margaret could have sent another person to make sure things went according to plan, but something in my gut told me that wasn't right. Part of me felt like this happened too fast. How had she gotten the leaders on board with this? Or had she gone behind their back to do it?

"What's wrong, *nin mel*? I can feel your anxiety rising. Did something go wrong at the exchange?" Rath asked, leaning in the brush hair out of my face and tucking it behind my ear.

I leaned into his touch as I opened up my mental communication with all the others. "*I think we are being watched.*"

"*Any clue who you think it might be?*" Elias asked.

With a slight shake of my head, I shifted closer to Colt and placed my hand on his. "This isn't how I wanted to do this, but I need you to be able to hear the rest of us. Close your eyes, take a deep breath, and trust me when you feel the pressure of my magic. I'm sorry I don't have the time to explain all the details right now, but I'm going to pull you into my elven bond."

Colt searched my face for a moment, then did as I requested, letting his shoulder relax as he let a deep breath out. Feeling much more confident in this process, I let my magic travel from me into Colt until I found his wolf, who let out a yip of surprise. Colt flinched but didn't resist me as I soothed his wolf, running a hand over his head and scratching behind his ears. "*It's alright,*" I murmured. "*We might be in some danger and I need your help to make sure that we keep each other safe. Can you come with me?*"

He growled, looking around for the danger, but when he couldn't see or hear anything, he sneezed, shaking his head in frustration before butting against my hip. When I didn't move right away, he did it again harder, followed by a nip as if I was a pup.

"None of that," I chided, smacking his muzzle. "As I lead you back, I need to hold onto you as we connect your magic to mine. I'm going to do my best to get us through this without you shifting, but that might happen. If we had another option, I would, but it's too risky to have only you out of the connection."

His amber eyes regarded me carefully, not really understanding what I was saying, but he nodded and sidled up to me so I could rest my hand on his back. Reaching out, I wove my fingers deep into his thick fur and started forward, guiding him back the way I'd come until he reached my magic source. My wolf came bolting out of nowhere and skidded to a halt right in front of him with her tail wagging and licked his face trying to get his attention. To his credit, Colt's wolf didn't move a muscle until I removed my hand, freeing him from the magic I'd used to get us here.

"Say your greeting, but I need to send him back right away. This isn't a time for us to be frolicking about," I warned as Colt's wolf started to snuffle my wolf's neck, nipping playfully at her.

The two of them stopped immediately and turned to face me, both on alert. My wolf clung to Colt's, taking all the courage she could from him, not at all liking the fact we might be in danger. I called my magic to me and wrapped it around Colt's wolf, coating him in it so he would take some of it with him when he returned. Satisfied that it should work, I opened the doorway for him, and instead of shoving him back into Colt, I let him run back on his own, following the trail of his magic back home.

The moment Colt's wolf returned, I yanked myself out of my source and back to what was happening around me. Colt gasped beside me, his hand clenching mine to the point I thought it might break, but I could feel my magic settling inside him. Once it found a comfortable place to rest alongside his wolf magic, his breathing evened, and he opened his eyes which still glowed from having his wolf so close to the surface.

"What did you just do?" he asked, sounding slightly breathless.

"*This is what it means to mate with an elf and be accepted into the* nos. *Now you can speak to any of the others, mind to mind, except Zander, but that will happen the moment I can,*" I explained.

I could feel the others adjusting to Colt's arrival, tethering to their connections with me as well. "*Welcome to the party. Now you can't yell at Noah and me for talking like this,*" Mason called out.

"*Sweetheart, what did you mean you think you're being watched?*" Lane questioned. "*I can't sense anything, but with all the animal smells around, it's hard to say what should be here and what shouldn't.*"

"*It's like I can feel the weight of someone's eyes on me. At first, I thought I was just being paranoid getting to the exchange, but if they were observing to make sure it went down right, they would have left,*" I shared, trying to explain. "*My wolf can't pick out any trouble either, but my magic is another story. Let me reach out to the trees and see if they will tell me anything.*"

"Have you checked the bag yet?" Elias asked as he reached out for it.

I grabbed his wrist, stopping him. *"Let me. I'll know if something shouldn't be there."*

Elias gave a curt nod but stood and came to stand behind me, resting his hands on my shoulders as I slid the laptop out. I lifted the lid to ensure there wasn't anything that got stuck in there and found a photograph. Plucking it off the keyboard, there was a grainy black and white security photo of a man I didn't recognize at all, leading me up the steps of some building. The date stamp on the bottom of it was from twenty-five years ago. Flipping the photo over, I found a note written in bold print: *"It's time you knew your father is still alive. His name is Ellisor Beinorin. Look him up in the database."*

CHAPTER TWENTY-EIGHT

FINLEY

My hand started to shake as my brain registered the information I had just been given.

My father was *alive*!

Not only was he alive, but he knew about me. Could he have been the man who came to collect me at the orphanage all those years ago and brought me to the Organization? Was he the person watching us right now, or was it totally unrelated? I knew Margaret had sent it to me. She was the only one who would have risked everything to tell me. Now I had to figure out what it meant. She said to look this person up.

"We need to get home *now*," I said, keeping my voice calm but urgent.

"What about whoever is watching?" Elias asked in a low voice. "We can't just leave now. It would be too suspicious."

At his comment, I looked up and found Mason and the others returning with the food they'd ordered. Elias was right. We needed to play this smart, even though I wanted to dive into this. I needed to be somewhere safe.

Lane set down a tray of food and watched me with a questioning gaze. "Everything alright?"

Tucking the photo into my coat pocket, I closed the laptop and slid it back into the bag, ignoring everything else inside, not up for any more surprises. "Fine, just found out a bit of news that I wasn't expecting, is all."

"I see..." Lane commented, not at all convinced.

"One of you text Zander and get an ETA. Seems we need to come back another day to see the rest of the zoo," Rath mentioned offhandedly.

Colt pulled out his phone and started to text Zander. *"Little one, what did the photo say."*

"It was a picture of a man leading me into a building. The date would put me at five years old. The note on the back suggests that this man is my father and he is still alive," I explained to them all. *"Margaret made sure that I could learn what I needed to with this laptop which is why we must get home."*

They tensed at my words but tried to play it off as Noah handed out cheese fries, pretzels, and hot dogs. The table also had a bunch of water bottles. I grabbed one and chugged the whole thing down, trying to keep my mind from racing. I needed the universe to stop throwing me curve balls every chance it got. I was running out of the ability to roll with the punches.

"Zander said he can cut his meeting short whenever we need to leave," Colt said, drawing my attention.

Dipping my head in acknowledgment, I grabbed a pretzel and tore a chunk off. The saltiness of it tasted good and my hunger won out over the chaos running through my brain. Before I knew it, the whole pretzel was gone, and I felt slightly better. Mason gave me a knowing look and placed a hotdog in my hand, signaling with a jerk of his chin that I better eat it. "A hungry shifter is more likely to make mistakes, snuggles. Feed your wolf and she will be able to help you with everything else."

It didn't take us long to demolish the rest of the food and clean up our spot. Mason was right as usual when it came to me meeting the needs of my wolf when I continually forgot. As we headed back to the car, I could still feel someone watching us, but I couldn't quite get a location on them. It was almost as if there was something hiding them from me.

"Rath, can our magic cloak us from others?" I inquired.

He stopped so fast that I ran into the back of him, letting out a yelp. Spinning on his heel, he grabbed my shoulders to steady me as I pitched forward. "*Nin mel,* why are you asking?"

"There is someone following us, but every time I reach out with my wolf senses or even my magic, it's like it catches wind of something, then it's simply gone. Like there is something out there telling me that it really isn't there at all," I said.

Opening my mind to him, I tried to show him what I was experiencing, and instead of being worried about it, a huge smile bloomed on his face. "You are exactly right on your assumption and who's magic could be behind it. Seems it hasn't taken long for them to seek you out."

"Why won't they come out of hiding?" I asked, looking around the parking lot.

"What would you do if you were seeking out the source of some incredibly strong super and found it guarded by five strong werewolves and an unknown elf?" Rath countered. "They will make their presence known if we meet them on neutral ground."

I couldn't argue when he put it like that. It would be stupid to expose yourself when you don't know if you can trust anyone. "Where is neutral ground?"

"Is there a forest or nature preserve owned by the state nearby?" Rath asked, turning to the others.

The guys paused to think for a moment, but Noah came up with the solution after looking at something on his phone. "Looks like there is a botanical garden near here we can meet at. Otherwise, the next closest would be heading into our territory. North of here is a colony of felines that we are on good terms with, but it wouldn't be neutral."

"The botanical garden will work perfectly," Rath murmured as he wandered away from us toward the park.

Lane cocked his head to the side as he watched the elf wander off. "What is he going to do?"

"I assume talk to the elf in their native tongue, so they know where to meet us," I guessed.

As we watched, Rath paused by a group of trees and I could hear him talking in that musical language I hoped to one day learn myself. Whatever he said must have worked because soon, I felt the single presence that had been watching us leave.

"Seems that it worked," Noah commented as he pulled open the car's door. "Now, someone text Zander to meet us there. I don't want to do this without him"

"Adding more people might not be the right move," I mused. "How would you take it if you agreed to meet someplace and they showed up with reinforcements."

Mason slung an arm around my shoulders and hugged me tight, kissing me on the lips. "Sorry, snuggles, but you're not gonna win on this one. We are going to meet an unknown elf that can cloak themselves. I want all the backup we can have."

"All right, everyone into the car. Seems we have a meeting with an elf to make," Colt ordered as Rath jogged up to us.

The garden wasn't far from the zoo, so we made good time, but we waited for Zander to join us before heading into the garden. Thankfully it didn't take him long as a town car pulled up and dropped him off.

"I leave you guys for a few hours and now we are meeting up with a stalker?" he demanded, arms crossed. "Just so we are clear, I'm not getting left behind ever again, no matter how much attention I draw. What if something happened to any of you or Finley and I wasn't there to help?"

Knowing he needed some reassurance, I wrapped my arms around his waist and rested my head on his chest so I could listen to his heartbeat. "You're right. We do this together as a team from here on out."

"Did someone record that?" Mason asked. "Snuggles, can you repeat that so we can remind you when you try to argue with us later?"

I glared at him over my shoulder, then pulled away from Zander. "Now we're all here, I think we should get going."

"Yeah, let's hurry up and meet the stalker elf. Sounds like a lot of fun," Colt grumbled. "How is it that no one argued against this?"

"Because Rath warned us that they would be seeking her out," Lane pointed out. "Besides, they haven't done anything but observe."

Colt just huffed at that statement and led the way into the garden grounds. It wasn't a large area, but you could tell that the people who ran it took amazing care of it. There were beautiful stone buildings you could wander around with crawling ivy and well-marked gravel paths. One path took you into a garden that made me think it was straight out of a book. A sign noted it was called the 'Secret Garden,' which I felt was appropriate for the space.

"This will be the perfect place to meet," Rath shared as we took in the space. "I explained to him that we are your *nos,* and yes, you are a hybrid elf who was bit by a wolf."

I mulled that over in my brain. "It's funny that I see it the other way around, but I guess I've always been an elf even when I thought I was human. It is sometimes hard to remember that I was never once human."

Rath reached out and brushed his fingers along my cheek, sympathy in his eyes at my words. "No matter what you are or how you see yourself, I'm glad you found me. Together we will all find our way through this journey and discover many realizations about ourselves along the way."

"*Sidh n- with cin,* cousin," a soft voice called out.

My mates snapped to attention, hiding me behind them as they circled me, making it so I couldn't even see what was going on.

"*Sidh n- with cin,*" Rath responded. "I would ask if you can speak English, that you do for this meeting. My *gwanur* and mate don't know our language."

"She called you cousin, but you act like you don't know her," Colt muttered.

A tinkling laugh filled the air. "It seems they know nothing of our customs either. My dear wolf, all elves are born from the same goddess, therefore making us all family. We call each other cousin in honor of the ties we share whether we are blood-related or not."

"Can one of you please move," I asked with a sigh. "We did ask her here to talk and that's what I would like to do."

Colt and Elias both growled at my request, but Lane stepped aside, allowing me to exit the circle of protection. There stood a woman about my height, a slightly muscular body with hair that was such a dark blue it was almost black until the sun shone on it. Her pointed ears peeked out, accented with dangling gems that made them look dainty. She wore tight jeans and a T-shirt with an oversized sweater falling off one shoulder. Her face was delicate, almost like a China doll with striking aqua eyes that were slightly larger than normal for humans and slanted. On her forehead and chin was scrawling line work in a beautiful pattern that only added to her beauty. If this is what most elven women looked like, it made me question if I was really one myself.

"Hello, young cousin, it's nice to meet you. I'm Ayla Dorgella," she said with a slight bow, her hand over her heart. "When I caught onto your power signature, I couldn't stop myself from coming to see who could possibly be holding that much magic within them. Then I learn that you're not only powerful but also a shifter... Pray, how did that happen?"

While I didn't think that Ayla wanted to do me harm, I wasn't sure I wanted to be trading that kind of information here and now. "As I'm sure you know, life is full of surprises, and that story will have to be told another time."

Ayla flashed me a bright smile that was all teeth and followed by a soft laugh. "Wise and powerful, young cousin, this is most intriguing." She paused and took in the men around me, twirling a strand of hair around her finger. "You called all these men to you as well so soon after you came into your power. Something like that hasn't happened since before the battle with the Dark Elves. Can I ask who your lineage is?"

"Can I ask yours?" I countered. "You seem to be asking all the questions, but I have some of my own. How about a trade. Question for question?"

Ayla approached, her movements fluid and silent as she came to a halt right in front of me and held out her hand. "I can agree to those terms."

"One rule, if the question could endanger my mates or me, I can refuse to answer," I added, meeting her gaze unmoving.

"Oh, dear cousin, I think you and I will be such good friends," Ayla cooed. "I agree to your terms and ask that I get the same right to refuse."

Nodding, I grasped her hand, and we shook on the agreement.

"Now for my first question, what is your name?" Ayla inquired.

"Finley."

"That's it? No surname?"

I dropped my gaze as I thought over if this was something I should answer. "I don't know who my parents are, and they never told me my last name or where I was raised. It wasn't needed."

"So mysterious, positively delightful! Now I've asked two, so you may do the same," Ayla pointed out as she bounced on her toes, waiting for my question.

Not wanting to waste any questions, I thought about what I really wanted to know. "How long were you following us? I caught onto the sense someone was following us at the zoo, but I'm curious if you'd been watching longer."

"Well, I caught onto your magic signal when you claimed the woods around your pack and into the mountain. I didn't lay eyes on you until you got to the zoo, so you caught wind of me right away. That, dear Finley, is rather remarkable because I am the best at cloaking magic in my clan. For you to notice me at all is telling how powerful you are, but I don't think that's all it is," Ayla mused.

"I still have one more question before you get your turn again," I reminded and she motioned for me to continue.

"You mentioned your clan," I raised a hand to stop her from speaking. "I'm not going to ask where it is. All I want to know is if they have noticed me as well, or are you yourself, someone who is rather strong?"

Ayla clapped her hands and gave me a wink. "You, my lovely, are fascinating and incredibly quick to draw conclusions from hardly any real information. My clan is aware of you, but only because I told them about sensing you. In my clan, there are only two others stronger than me, and they are our elders, but I have no wish to be an elder. I choose to be a warrior like yourself."

That statement caught me by surprise. I suppose as an assassin, I would be considered a warrior but not in the pure sense of the meaning. I didn't go out and fight battles for my leaders. I hid in the shadows and removed obstacles for the real warriors to do their work.

"I just have one more question for you. We elves keep our ears open for anything of note that might affect our way of life or ability to hide, so don't be surprised when I ask you this." Ayla leaned in so we were almost touching noses. "Can I join you in your fight to take down the Dark Ring and, in the process, the Senate?"

My jaw dropped at her question and she kindly brought her hand up to shut it again for me. "I told you not to be surprised," she teased as she booped me on the nose. "Now, I suppose I should tell you my skills so you know I'll be an asset. While I am a skilled fighter, I'm also a spy, skilled in gathering information anywhere at any time with my magic. I already know how hard this is going to be and have a list of key players in the Dark Ring that would be smart to go after that will cripple it."

"Why? Why do you even want to do this?" I challenged. "This is a suicide mission that we have a small hope of being able to win. I don't have an option to back out of this. I have a sworn agreement with someone forcing me onto this path. Why would you willingly choose to go after the two most powerful groups in our world right now?"

Ayla took a step back and turned away from me, wrapping her arms around herself. "They took everything from me, my clan, my entire family, my home, my freedom, and a male that I'd hoped to mate with when we got the approval of our clan. It's all gone and I can't stand back and watch them do it to anyone else when I have the chance to step up and do something about it."

"You mentioned your freedom..." Rath interjected but drifted off before asking what he really wanted to know.

She looked over her shoulder at him, giving him a sad smile showing a small shadow of the pain that was hidden behind her playful mask. "I was their toy for fifteen years before I was able to escape and I've been hunting them down ever since."

Taking a deep breath, I spoke the truth I knew in my heart. "I know you said you have a clan you're living with now, and I hope to one day meet them, but I would gladly welcome you into my pack if you so choose. Beyond the fact that you would be an asset to our fight, I think if we survive this, we could be family. All of these men understand what it means to survive at any cost and have been victims of the Senate or the Dark Ring at some point in their lives. I know the idea of creating a combined werewolf and elf pack sounds crazy, but it's what I feel is the future for our people. One day I hope all the elves can come out of hiding and live amongst the world again with the help and protection of a pack. I think it can happen."

Ayla spun around and flung her arms out wide, wrapping me up in a tight hug. "It would be my honor to join the queen's pack and assist her in any way that I can, whether it be as your soldier or as your friend. You have a loyal servant in me."

I patted her on the back awkwardly, finding it completely different to receive affection from someone other than my mates. "I'm not your queen, Ayla, not even close. I'm an assassin who got bit by an omega and found out weeks ago I was never human but really an elf. All I want is to make the world safe for the people I love and taking down the Senate and the Dark Ring is the only way to do it."

She pulled back and gave me a knowing look, quickly followed by a smirk. "That is exactly why you're going to be the best queen the elves have ever seen, but first, we need to cause some chaos and turn this world as we know it on its rear. It's gonna be a sight to see and they will have no idea what's coming next."

"We don't even know what's coming next," I said with a huff.

Ayla twisted me around so I was facing the guys and she whispered in my ear, "Look at them. What do you think they see when they look at you?"

"Their mate," I answered, not following where she was going with this.

"Err, wrong," Ayla countered. "Who wants to tell her?"

To my surprise, Zander was the one who spoke up. "You, little dove, are the shadow they never saw coming. The omega who is going to change everything."

To be concluded in Perfect Nature

About Author

Elizabeth is an International Best Seller, originally from Illinois but now living in sunny Phoenix, AZ. Elizabeth has been writing for nine years and started out in YA Fiction but recently found herself loving the Reverse Harem genre. Like her favorite books, Elizabeth loves to write about strong women of all varieties. Not all strength is flashy or apparent at first glance—some lies just under the surface.

Don't Miss Out!

Be the first to know what is coming next by following Elizabeth's social media! You never know when or what will be coming next!

Website: ElizabethKnightBooks.com

Facebook: Elizabeth Knight's Unicorn Queens

Instagram: elizabethknightauthor

TikTok: elizabethknightauthor

Newsletter: sign up here

ALSO BY

<u>Hidden Empire Series – Complete series</u>

Book 1 - Two Tricks

Book 2 - Three Tricks

Book 3 - Four Tricks

Book 4 - More Tricks

Book 5 - Our Tricks

<u>Hidden Empire Novel</u>

Harper's Renegades

<u>Omega Assassin - Complete series</u>

Book 1 - Dual Nature

Book 2 - Hidden Nature

Book 3 - Perfect Nature

www.ingramcontent.com/pod-product-compliance
Lightning Source LLC
Chambersburg PA
CBHW071413300726
48976CB00006B/2080